CAUGHT BETWEEN MONSTERS

AN EDGE OF HUMANITY NOVEL

STEFON MEARS

Also by Stefon Mears

Cavan Oltblood Series
Half a Wizard
The Ice Dagger
Spells of Undeath

Spells for Hire
Devil's Shoestring
Zombie Powder
Spirit Trap
Dragon's Blood (coming December 2019)

The Rise of Magic
Magician's Choice
Sleight of Mind
Lunar Alchemy
Three Fae Monte
The Sphinx Principle

The Telepath Trilogy
Surviving Telepathy
Immoral Telepathy
Targeting Telepathy

Edge of Humanity
Caught Between Monsters
Hunting Monsters

Power City Tales
Not Quite Bulletproof
No Money in Heroism

Devil's Night
Portal-Land, Oregon
Stealing from Pirates
Fade to Gold
With a Broken Sword
Twice Against the Dragon
The House on Cedar Street
Sudden Death
On the Edge of Faerie
Confronting Legends (Spells & Swords Vol. 1)
Uncle Stone Teeth and Other Macabre Poems
The Patreon Collection, Vol. 1-4 (Vol. 5, coming soon)

Published by Thousand Faces Publishing, Portland, Oregon

http://1kfaces.com

ISBN: 978-1-948490-11-5

CAUGHT BETWEEN MONSTERS

An Edge of Humanity novel

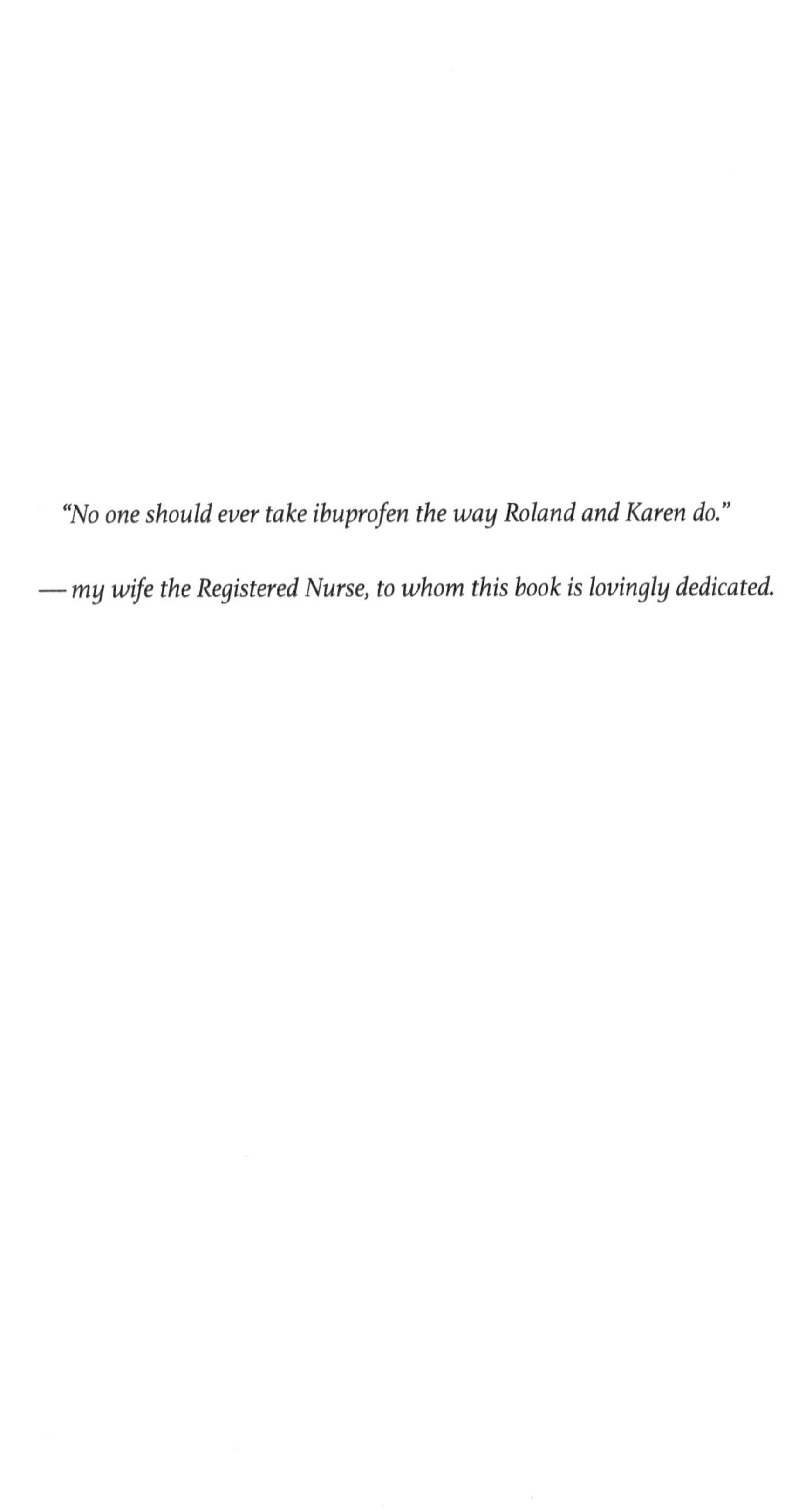

"No one should ever take ibuprofen the way Roland and Karen do."

— my wife the Registered Nurse, to whom this book is lovingly dedicated.

ACKNOWLEDGMENTS

Many thanks to my amazing beta readers: Bill, Lori, Rob, Wendy.

And to Professor John Lindow, who taught me about the Norse contest of wisdom.

1
______

Sometimes being human sucks.

That was all I could think as I lay there among the dirt and garbage, my head spinning from its sharp crack against the side of the old, abandoned Safeway. At least I missed the edge of the dumpster. That was some small mercy. I rubbed my aching head as my sore ribs expanded, letting air back in along with the stench of decay. Painful, getting the wind knocked out of you, and that blow to the head was going to need a lot of ibuprofen later. Why was I here again?

"Roland! Little help here?"

I looked up and saw my partner, Nelson, squaring off against that thing. The scene should have been comical. Nelson had too much pudge and too little hair. You might have mistaken him for an accountant, especially in his short-sleeved shirt and tie. Well, you'd have been half right. He used to be an accountant. But Nelson had the soul of an MMA champion – you could see it in his stance, his bearing, the way he held his billy club. You could almost believe he was a hero. Of course, it helped that the thing he faced had let its human guise slip. While we shadowed it, the thing looked like Jed Brunner, track star and poster boy for the Aryan Nation. A few nasty blows later, its hair grew long and coarse, its fingers into claws the color of bruises, and its teeth into fangs stained yellow-brown from their diet of human flesh.

It took us five days to find this ghul. Had to be the right kind, too, none of those Western European cemetery haunters. No, the Rajah insisted on...

"Roland!"

The ghul lunged and Nelson rolled to one side, swinging his club at its knees as he went. He missed. I shoved myself back to my feet and almost lurched onto my face. My head pounded a rapid dance beat. No, wait. That was from Hy Brasil, the dance club on the corner and the only thing in this half-empty shopping center still pulling in a crowd. All my head did was throb.

No sign of my knife or billy club. The pockets of my khakis only contained keys and my wallet, and my windbreaker only held the sample bottle. Nelson and the ghul circled each other again. Both had taken enough lumps to hesitate, now each wanted an opening before attacking.

I sighed. I had no weapon. My options narrowed to something stupid, but let's be honest here. Everything about my life these days was stupid.

I roared and charged. Nelson feinted with his billy club to hold the ghul's focus and I drove my skinny, six-foot frame into its side in an open-field tackle that would have made my high school football coach proud. I caught it from behind, just below the rib cage, and we went down in a heap.

Nelson was right there. His club whistled past my head and slammed into the ghul's skull, the blow magnified by the asphalt. I grabbed the ghul's elbows and pinned its arms to its sides. Two, three, four, five more blows and the ghul stopped struggling. Nelson gave it one more for good measure, but this thing was out, and when it woke later it would have a worse headache than I would.

That made me feel a little better.

"Took you long enough." He showed me teeth marks on his billy club. "The thing damn near bit me."

"Sorry," I said with a shudder. "Got my bell rung pretty bad."

"Well you're buying the beer."

"Wait, I get beat half unconscious and I buy the beer?"

He shoved his billy club in my face. The fang scars looked worse up close, but Nelson would have suffered more than lacerations if those teeth had struck true. "All right, the first round is on me."

"I—"

"The first round, take it or leave it."

"Cheap bastard."

"My paycheck's no bigger than yours."

Speaking of paychecks ... I pulled out the sample bottle with its rubber top and shoved it against what I hoped were the ghul's incisors. Its teeth were all so sharp I couldn't be sure. Rubbing from the back of the jaw, I massaged a biting motion and listened for the spraying sound of venom jetting into the bottle. A minute later the bottle was full and I sealed it with its special cap. I slipped the bottle into the pocket of my windbreaker.

While I was busy Nelson found my club and knife for me.

"Think we should kill it?" Nelson toyed with the handle of his knife, an army surplus Ka-Bar like mine. "It's going to be pissed."

"Ghuls are too practical for vengeance." I shrugged. "All it will remember is that we beat it and left it alive when we could have killed it. It'll probably go out of its way to avoid us."

"It eats people."

"What if we have to get more venom? Do you want to track down another ghul?"

Nelson grimaced, but then looked up with a smile. "But we have the venom. And now, beer!"

"And now the Rajah. Beer after."

Nelson sighed.

We left the ghul where it was, among the garbage.

The Rajah's mansion perched high in Los Altos Hills, on six

acres of hilltop that, even undeveloped, would cost more money than a guy like me would see in three lifetimes. Add in the ten thousand plus square feet of opulence, and the Rajah's place must have cost more than the GNP of several small Central American countries.

"You'd think this guy could afford to pay us better," I said as Nelson and I stood on the doorstep. Mind you, that doorstep included a covered porch twenty feet wide and ten feet deep, made from some sort of milky-white stonework with veins of purple and gold running through it. Three steps of the same material led up to it, and I could not see a single chip or smudge anywhere on that gleaming, polished surface.

And that was for people to stand on. People who might never make it past the ornately crafted red front door. I could only imagine what the Rajah spent on his bedroom. Probably enough to feed and clothe the Bay Area's homeless for a decade.

But it wasn't just the money. This sort of extravagance carried an arrogance along with it. For example, behind us I would have sworn the fancy sheet rock driveway — private road really — resented the presence of my beat up, used Camry.

I took the whole scene in with a wave of my hand. "You know he's getting top dollar for what we bring him."

"Every time, you say that." Nelson shook his head. "At least come up with a new complaint."

The door opened and there stood the butler. I could never tell exactly how old the butler was. Somewhere between sixty and ninety. His perfect posture accented his slim build the way the neat trim of his ghost white hair accented the red tint of his pale skin. As always, he wore a full, formal uniform, without a wrinkle or a mote of dust showing anywhere. Immaculate, from the trim of his eyebrows to the perfection of his shave to the shine of his shoes.

"How are you tonight, Jeeves?"

I didn't know what his name was. The butler never spoke in our presence. But I had to call him something, and Alfred would have implied that the Rajah had some kind of cool, Batman vibe.

Jeeves ushered us into our usual small waiting room. Two huge comfortable chairs for us, high backs and wide arms, both sunset blue. Between the chairs sat a carved teak tripod table holding a spotless silver ashtray. The chairs faced a leather recliner that sat taller than our seats. Above it on the wall was a painting of a tiger, shadowed in its den. The whole room was done in dark woods, with a throw rug on the floor in a red and orange pattern that looked Eastern to me.

"Something to drink, Jeeves?"

Jeeves favored me with a patronizing smile and left.

"When has he ever brought us drinks?" asked Nelson.

"Never hurts to try, right?"

"You always have to push."

"Look, hospitality implies certain etiquette."

"Are you trying to get us killed?"

"Anytime you're finished, gentlemen."

Nelson and I stared slack-jawed at the chair facing us. The door never opened. No special effects. Just, suddenly, the Rajah was seated, a short, thin Indian man with black hair and eyes, wearing a cerulean shirt and pants and a blood red smoking jacket. He wore slippers that matched the jacket, and a gold ring with an emerald the size of a dime on the middle finger of his right hand. He also had gold stud earrings, one in each lobe.

Some people might mistake the Rajah for human. Which would make sense, since most people don't know that ghuls and things like the Rajah – whatever he was – were running around the San Francisco Bay Area, preying on human beings. There was a time when I didn't know that either. I wish I still didn't. I'd love to go back to that blissful ignorance, but it's way too late for me.

Of course, even then, I would have recognized that there was something wrong about the Rajah. Heck, I did recognize it, the sense of menace, of threat that he carried. I still felt it — his wrongness — but I'd been around him enough that I only noticed it as a flutter in my stomach.

Still, when the Rajah looked at you, you felt like a rabbit facing a wolf; you wanted to freeze or run, but it didn't matter which because it was already too late. You were dead. You just didn't know it yet.

"Good evening, Rajah." I forced the words out because I knew Nelson could not have. He had been working for the Rajah longer than I had, and had lost the ability to speak in the boss' presence without a direct order. Poor Nelson was sweating more right now than he did in our fight with the ghul.

"Are you here because you have milked a ghul for me or because you have failed and are ready to be eaten?"

"We have the venom!" I almost fumbled the bottle in my haste to toss it to him. "Here."

"There is still empty space in the bottle."

"There's a fill line. On the back. I passed it."

The Rajah held the bottle up to the light. "So you did." He opened the lid and held the bottle up to his nose. His nostrils flared. "Pure ghul. Three shapes tonight, including primal. I would guess ..." he took a deep sniff "... older than one hundred, but not older than one hundred fifty." He replaced the cap. "Very high quality. Well done. Not only will I not eat you tonight, you will each receive a bonus. Return tomorrow for your next assignment."

"So soon? We both got pretty ... badly ..." My words trailed off. Nothing in the Rajah's posture or expression changed, but I suddenly felt as though he were reconsidering eating us. As though I needed to shut the hell up and live to see the morning.

"Tomorrow then," said the Rajah as he stood. We stood by reflex, and suddenly Jeeves was there, guiding us back out through the front door.

"Always have to push," said Nelson.

I DID BUY NELSON HIS BEER AT OUR USUAL PLACE, THE RED CAPET Lounge. Sounds fancy, right? Wrong. The Red Carpet Lounge was a dive, the sort of place you didn't admit you'd ever gone into. It was a bar in a shopping center, and it didn't even have a real sign, just a neon image of a martini glass.

Nelson and I didn't care about any of that. They sold us Angry Stoat Lager in bottles (probably the only drinks they didn't water down) and at fair prices. More important, the Red Carpet Lounge was downright mundane. Nothing supernatural ever came in, and as far as we could tell, nothing supernatural ever came near it.

It was the perfect place for guys like Nelson and me to drink after a hard evening's work.

Three beers later, I was home. Home was the front unit of a four-plex, the part that looks like a house from the front, but has an apartment behind it and two more upstairs. My place was tucked into a row of similar apartment buildings, with four or six apartments each, and parking spaces in the alley out back because street parking was a nightmare. Across the street from us was one of those giant apartment complexes, the kind with tennis courts, a gym, and at least one swimming pool.

That's life in the Silicon Valley. You get your choice of apartments because most of us could never afford to buy a house here. I felt blessed because my apartment came with two parking spaces instead of just one, which meant that both Karen and I always had places to put our cars.

Well, almost. All too often some jerk treated that second space as public parking. I got sick of going door-to-door to find the culprit and asking politely for something that I paid for as part of my rent. Finally I had to post a warning sign about towing, because no joke. I'd have towed them and smiled as I did it. After all those warnings and requests, it would have served them right for stealing my spot.

Anyway, Karen's spot was empty when I pulled up, so her shift at the diner must have run till midnight. She waited tables at a tiny place with great food. And I do mean tiny. They didn't have more than ten tables total, including booths. But they had a great location, right off of 280 near a community college, they were open twenty-four-seven, and they could out-cook any chain restaurant any day of the week.

As jobs go it wasn't much, but better than what she was doing when we met. I wish I could say as much for myself.

I unlocked the door, flipped on the lights, entered, and double-locked the door behind me. Our place was decorated in Early Crap: hand-me-down couches and thrift store tables and dishware. You could probably have bought all our furnishings for the cost of one paycheck, assuming you made minimum wage. Well, that's not strictly true. Our bed was pretty nice, which I guess said something about our priorities.

I stopped over by the flat screen television – which said some-thing else about our priorities – and checked on Lancelot, my gecko. Lancelot sunned himself under his heat lamp on the left side of his tank, showing off his bright, Peacock Day colors.

"Have a good day, Lance? I bet you're hungry." His tank sat on a hexagonal end table. No drawers, but two doors that swung wide open and gave me a place to keep Lancelot's supplies, including his supper: a small cage of live crickets. I fished out a few and dropped them in the tank with Lance. No reaction. "Not yet, huh? Well, they'll be there when you want them."

Three bedrooms and two baths might have sounded like a lot except that the plumbing sucked and the walls were thin. How thin, you ask? They were so thin that we had lived in the place only a single night when we found out we could hear every detail of the very verbal lovemaking of our closest neighbors. They said things I could not imagine anyone finding sexy, but when I mentioned that to Karen, she said only that she had heard worse.

Still, their sex was more amusing than their fighting. I think it was their first big blowup about money that really cemented my night-time habit of listening to radio talk shows for hours on end.

On the plumbing side of things, our pipes must have mastered the art of Zen meditation. They certainly never felt any pressure from water. A single good burrito could back up our toilets, and we had learned quickly that if one of us was in the shower, the other could not so much as wash his hands.

Oh, and we lived inside the San Jose border, so drinking the tap water was not an option. Stick some metal in the glass to use as poles and San Jose water will serve as good enough battery acid to produce a measurable voltage. A friend of mine proved it while we were in high school.

So I dug a handful of ibuprofen out of a bottle in the bathroom, but poured myself a glass of water from a filtered jug in the buzzing refrigerator. The appliances came with the apartment, but they fit in with our stuff perfectly – ancient and almost ready for collapse.

Probably the placebo effect, but swallowing the pills seemed to ease my headache. Or maybe it was just the water after the beer. I dug around in the fridge and found some leftover lasagna in a sandwich bag with a sticky note on it: "Thought you might forget dinner. There's more in the freezer if you're still hungry. Love -K."

I threw the lasagna in the microwave and re-read the note while it heated. I liked reading Karen's notes. She had that clear, loopy style of printing that I always thought of as girl handwriting. My own scrawl came out as fast as I could get the letters formed. Illegible according to my old teachers, but it looked fine to me.

I tossed the note and started the coffee pot, filling the grinder with a fancy Argentinian blend that Karen favored.

The microwave dinged, announcing that my instant dinner was ready.

While I ate I did my nightly homework: reading obscure occult texts. It's not that I wanted to start casting spells. Only idiots believed they could get something for nothing, and when you played with magic the price was usually higher than it looked like before you started. No, ever since I took a job that had me doing things like milking ghuls for their venom and stealing secrets from ghosts I started trying to arm myself with knowledge. There were ways to read between the lines of the old texts that made them cough up real information, solid data accumulated by other innocent humans stuck dealing with monsters.

All right, so maybe calling me innocent took a stretch, but I was still just a human being. No claws, no fangs, no magic worth a damn. Guys like Nelson and me had nothing to go on but our wits and gumption. Which meant, of course, we would've run screaming from any and all contact with the supernatural, if we weren't in debt to the Rajah.

The screen door creaked and I heard keys in the deadbolt. Hoping it was Karen, I poured us each a cup of coffee, real cream and fake sugar for her, black for me. I poured the first taste from my cup into the sink, then turned as the door opened.

"That lock still sticks." Karen stood an inch shy of five and half feet tall, just slender enough to give her peach-blah uniform curves that doubled her tips compared to the other waitresses. She always complained that her face was plain and her hair was mousy. I thought she was the most beautiful thing I'd ever seen.

"Want me to oil it again?"

"I want you to call the landlord. And remind him about our dishwasher when you do."

"What about the dishwasher?"

"It doesn't."

The smell of her coffee put a smile on her face and she dropped her purse to take the cup in both hands. "God I love you."

"Damn right you do."

We kissed. I reached past her to double-lock the door, then started to turn away, but she stopped me with a drill instructor tone.

"Hold it." She reached up and prodded my cheek, sending fire through the left side of my face. When did ... oh, yeah. Ghul punch. "You've got to quit that job."

"Not really an option."

"You didn't get in fights like this when you managed that motel."

"Wasn't exactly a good job though. Only bright spot to that whole time was you." I smiled. "Remember when we..."

"Don't change the subject." Her words were soft now, her face serious, like she was looking at me in the hospital instead of me with a bruised cheek. "Even the early shift at that club is too rough. You need to quit and find something else."

Karen was guessing. She didn't know I worked for the Rajah, much less what I did. I never lied to her, exactly, I just never told her.

"I can't quit. Not until I work off the debt."

Her mouth narrowed to a line, her finely plucked eyebrows lowered as she looked up at me. I knew that look. We were both in a bad way when we met. She got out, but she could tell I still had one foot in that old world.

"We can move," she said, just above a whisper. "One bag each, ditch the car somewhere in Mexico."

"Not far enough."

"Canada then. East coast. Europe maybe. Anywhere."

So this was why she insisted on us keeping our passports renewed and handy. Unfortunately...

"This guy will find me anywhere I go. I just need a little more time."

Karen trailed her fingers across my cheeks, then laid a gentle kiss on my bruise, followed by another on my lips. She laid her head on my shoulder, wrapped her arms tight around me, waitress reflexes keeping her coffee cup level.

"All right. A little longer. But Roland, it has to be soon." Her next words were barely whispered, more for herself than for me. "I want you safe."

2

I woke up by the crack of noon, tangled in the sheets alone with my face under my pillow. My head felt as though I'd put myself to sleep by pounding my skull with a shovel – hitting my face once for good measure – until blissful unconsciousness found me. I shoved the pillow onto the floor. The only sound I heard was the pounding of my head.

If Karen wasn't home, she must have been off playing chess, because she never got the early shift the day after a night shift.

I dragged myself out of bed, wondering how I managed to land a girl with a chess ranking, and let the bedspread and sheets trail to the floor behind me. My back and shoulders were stiff and sore, but next to my head they felt almost pleasant.

Our bathroom always smelled like spring rain. I didn't know what brand of air freshener Karen kept plugged in beside the sink, but she had started buying the industrial strength versions back when she first realized how bad our plumbing was. She would swear she could smell our water. I never could, but if the air fresheners made her happy, they were fine with me.

Our industrial size bottle of ibuprofen sat prominently in the middle of the shelf in front of the mirror, next to the plastic Spiderman cup that I'd had since I was six. It said a lot about Karen that she never asked me to get rid of that cup, had even started using it herself. I shook out six or eight pills into my hand, splashed water into the cup, and grimaced as I choked down the pills with a side of metallic tang.

Then I saw myself in the mirror and my whole head throbbed in sympathy: from temple to jaw and from nose to ear, the left half of my face was one big bruise. I decided against shaving.

If I were a religious man, right then I would have been thanking some God that I didn't appear to have a concussion. But if there was a God, I sure hadn't seen any signs of His Love in my life.

Well, apart from Karen, anyway.

The hot shower was a mixed blessing. It felt like heaven on my back and shoulders, but hell on my head and face. Either way I survived it, and had enough blood flowing through my system now to towel dry, comb out my hair, get dressed and make the bed.

By the time I reached the kitchen clad in khakis and a long-sleeved shirt, I was ready to sit again. I felt like I was seventy-two instead of twenty-four. Karen was right. I had to get out of this business before it killed me.

Of course, if I tried to quit, the Rajah would kill me. And eat me. It sounded weird to say, but both Nelson and I had looked into the Rajah's eyes, and neither of us doubted that the Rajah was serious about eating us. These jobs we did for him helped, but on some level we both felt as though the Rajah were a cat, playing with us until we stopped moving or he got bored of the game and moved on to the eating.

I probably would have sat at the table, lamenting the sad state of my life, but Karen, bless her, left the coffee on. The smell of that alone was enough to revive me. Fine Argentinian beans roasted with loving care, ground to a fine blend, and brewed to perfection with filtered water.

I poured a cup and smiled at the empty saucer in the sink as I poured out the first sip. Karen had brought the saucer in off the window sill for me. She never asked why I left a saucer of milk on the window sill every night. Probably assumed I was feeding some local stray. That wasn't too far from the truth, but in this case the stray wasn't a cat.

I toasted four slices of whole wheat bread, then slathered them with store-brand peanut butter and grape jelly. I sat down to feast on my breakfast of champions when someone started pounding on the door.

The sun was up. That eliminated about half of the possible threats. Or rather, half of the possible *fatal* threats. Sunlight alone was not deterrent enough to banish all the beasties and nasties who might want a piece of me. Or worse, a favor.

"Who is it?" I called, picking up my billy club from the umbrella stand beside the door.

"Who the hell do you think? We're going to be late if you don't get moving."

Sounded like Nelson. Probably Nelson.

"Say your name."

"Nelson, you idiot."

Idiot was a believable insult from Nelson. But the word was common. Anyone might have used it. I needed more before I would open the door. Something distinctly Nelson to confirm his identity.

"What was the last thing you said to me last night?"

"I reminded you that my debt is almost paid, and that if you get me killed I'll haunt you and your kids for the next five generations."

I opened the door. Nelson saw the club and his eyes grew wide. He stepped across the threshold and into my home without formal invitation, just to prove he could do it.

Definitely Nelson.

"You're getting paranoid, Roland."

I shook my head and sat back down at the pressboard kitchen table. I set my billy club next to the empty napkin holder and held up my plate of toast to offer Nelson some, but he declined, pushing his palm at me in a halting gesture.

I took a bite and said, "You're not paranoid enough. You've seen as much as I have. More even. But you don't study. You don't check."

"Nope. I sure don't." He grabbed a cup from the cabinet beside the fridge and poured himself some coffee, adding plenty of cream and sugar. He pointed the cup at me. "And neither should you."

"That's stupid, man. You've got kids."

I shouldn't have used the "k" word. Nelson roared at me like a lion protecting his cubs. "That's right I have kids! You think I want them stumbling onto the kind of books you read? Finding out what daddy really does for money? Leaving out saucers of milk for the faeries?"

"Good folk. You don't want to call them—"

"Fuck all of that! Another year of this, tops, and I'm square with the Rajah. I walk away. And when I do I want to forget about all the shit we've seen. The things we've done." He looked away, out the window above the sink. "I want a life."

I wanted to let it go, to let him have his dream. But there was a flaw in his plan. "You can forget them but they won't forget you."

"They will if we move away. I'm thinking Boston." Nelson looked back at me, hope in his eyes now. "Tish has family in Andover, and Boston should be big enough for us to find work while being near family but not too near, you know?"

"And the first time you see signs? What if the Boston harbor has selkies? Or the Massachusetts mines have kobolds?" I dropped the piece of toast I'd been ignoring. "Or worse you catch wind of a *bean sidhe* or a black dog? Then what?"

"I ignore it." He looked out the window again. "I lived forty-five years without knowing these things were out there. I bet I could live forty-five more pretending they aren't. Especially when no one's paying me to go look for them."

"It's too late though. You know. You've rung the astral bell, and they've all heard you."

"I don't even know what that means." He shoved his cup at me in an aggressive point, splashing coffee onto the floor. "And don't you tell me. You're a damn fool for reading those books. Humans were never meant to play with magic. Just learning what you know is bad enough."

"Knowledge is our only weapon."

"But ignorance is our best defense! And I plan on staying ignorant." Nelson downed his coffee, then grabbed a napkin from the holder on the table and wiped up his mess with jerky movements. "Now come on. You can finish your breakfast in the car."

I slugged down the rest of my coffee and picked up my toast in a napkin.

<hr>

THE RAJA WATCHED US, EYES HALF-LIDDED. HE LOUNGED IN PURPLE pajamas under a royal blue robe, with matching slippers. I fidgeted, less comfortable in the overstuffed chair than I had been last night. Nelson merely sat, his eyes downcast, waiting.

"We need a few days to heal," I said. "You know how old that ghul was. We barely took it down."

"Take them then." The Rajah gave a slight shrug. "If your rest causes you to fail your next assignment, you know the penalty."

"We'll serve you better healthy."

"You will *serve* adequately either way."

"Give us our task, sir. We'll complete it on time."

I blinked in amazement. I had never in my six months of service heard Nelson speak in front of the Rajah.

"Rajah will suffice," said the Rajah. "And that is why you may yet live to pay off your debt, Nelson Milner, though you, Roland McCreedy, may not."

The Rajah did not move as he spoke, not even the little movements you would normally expect: blinking, turning to directly address individuals, gesturing as he spoke, and so on. I had to look hard just to see him breathe.

"This is your task. The Djinn's Tear has surfaced." He smiled then, and I wished he went back to not moving. The Rajah's smile spoke of pride in private sins, of pleasure in the memory of others' pain. "A delightful little toy. When soaked in the fresh heart's blood of a dying virgin, it grants any wish but absolution."

The smile broadened, and I imagined the expression of a jungle cat as its prey hobbles underneath its perch. "The owner wishes to sell the Tear for that absolution. He has promised proof of the product by this weekend, but I need no proof. So very like a human to believe he might reap the benefits of foul deeds and evade their consequences."

The Rajah closed his eyes for a moment and drew a deep breath in through his nose. Unable to resist, I sniffed the air. Cumin? The Rajah held that breath for a moment, savored it, then exhaled in the largest movement I had seen from him since Jeeves let us in. I considered a half-dozen questions, but the Rajah spoke first. "Obviously your task is to acquire it and bring it to me."

Nelson stood to leave.

"Wait," I said, imploring a pause with one raised hand. "You want use to 'acquire' something that powerful? This is crazy. Every major player in the Bay Area is going to try to get their hands on that thing, and most of the minor ones. How the hell are we supposed to get there first?"

"If you knew anything at all, you would know that the Djinn's Tear cannot be found nor hidden by supernatural means."

"What does it look like? Where did it come from? Who—"

"Do not mistake me for your history professor. I have told you all you that you require. I have even granted a critical detail, one that should provide you with an advantage. Use it."

The Rajah met my eye and I saw nothing human I could talk to. No sense of emotion, good, bad or indifferent. Fear knotted my gut, but my lips kept moving before the terror could reach them.

"This is no stolen secret or ghul venom, Rajah." Nelson turned to me, jaw slack and sweat breaking out on his forehead. I continued, "This is a big deal. If we pull this off, we're square. All of us. Nelson and me, we do this and we clear our debts."

The Rajah smiled again, and I felt like a mouse lecturing a hungry cat. "No, Roland McCreedy. If you complete this task, you are each one step closer to your freedom." The Rajah raised a lazy hand, let it half dangle in the air. "And because you dare try to dictate terms to me, if you fail, I shall not only devour you both, I shall then undo the tasks that initially placed you in my debt."

"Shut the fuck up, Roland!" Nelson looked ready to pull my teeth out through my stomach lining.

"You once chose between the lady and the tiger, Roland McCreedy. You chose the tiger. That has consequences, but as things stand the lady is safe. Would you return her to her jeopardy?"

"That's not fair!"

"Fair?" The Rajah leaned forward, his expression as patient as the tiger in the painting above him. "Do you mistake me for your Satan? Some devil bound by the letter of a contract?"

The Rajah shook his head, so slight a movement that I only saw it because my entire life was focused in watching him. "Perhaps you need to remember the details of our little arrangement."

I remembered.

A pimp named Mighty Joe Devereux ran about twenty prostitutes out of the EZ Sleep Motel on El Camino Real in Sunnyvale, down near where it crossed into Santa Clara.

Mighty Joe maintained a good working relationship with the three small-time drug dealers who also worked the place. And they all got along with me and gave me a taste, which meant everyone was happy, because I was the night manager of the EZ Sleep Motel. Not exactly the lofty gig I aspired to when I majored in Hotel Management, but the sideline work made the pay good, and sometimes the girls would throw me a freebee.

The first time I saw Karen she wore a green sleeveless scoop neck blouse with a denim skirt so short she could never have risked picking her big tan handbag up off the ground, or checking her fishnets for tears or her black pumps for scuffs. Those things didn't matter though. She already had what she was picking up: a John, a married, middle-aged, middle-management type. I pushed a room key to her across the beat up counter with its peeling Formica and she winked a promise at me.

As I watched Karen lead her John to the stairs I hoped that wink meant the new girl planned a thank-you for me. I think Mighty Joe encouraged his new girls to do that, since work out of my motel was easy and safe. Doubly so because I helped keep the cops in the dark as much as possible and warned everyone when I couldn't.

And in the case of this particular new girl, I was smitten.

Her working name was Catalyst, but on our third time together she told me her real name was Karen. She didn't charge me that night, and the next day we started dating.

Real dating, I mean. Not just having sex. Serious dates like fancy dinners where I wore ties and shirts I'd actually ironed myself, and she wore dresses that would have suited a Hollywood movie premiere.

We went on silly dates too, like our spontaneous urge for midnight bowling, despite the fact that neither of us had ever been bowling before and had only a vague idea of what we were doing.

We must have hit more gutters than pins that night, but we were laughing so hard we never noticed.

I was over-the-moon happy with Karen, but I had trouble with her work. She had trouble with my trouble. It all came to a head one night when we had taken a drive up Skyline to a rest stop that gave us a view of the whole peninsula, gloriously lit up under the midnight sky.

I meant to tell her I loved her. We'd been together for a year and some change and neither one of us had said it. But I was ready. I knew what I felt, and it was time to let her know.

I stroked her cheek, met her smile with one of my own, opened my mouth, and said, "I want you to stop hooking."

"Not this again," she said with a sigh.

"I've never said—"

"Not in words, but do you think I haven't noticed? The little glares you've started giving my Johns. That you grit your teeth when it's time for me to go to work? The little way you try to schedule time away for us that just happens to coincide with the special parties you hear Joe talk about setting up?"

"It can't be good for you."

The words I hadn't said made my voice tremble. Karen pounced on that momentary weakness.

"What's the matter with it? I always use a condom and a diaphragm, and I'm on the pill. I'm safe. And Joe keeps me safe. And you keep me safe. The work is easy and the pay is good. I'm off the coke now, so I'm socking money away even faster than you are. Why should I stop?"

I thought about other points. Legal troubles and jail time. The chance that one of these Johns would hurt her before Joe or I could get to her. The health risks that I felt sure were there despite her precautions.

But those arguments jumbled together in my head and what came out of my mouth was, "Because I love you and this isn't right."

Karen pulled her head back. Her eyes narrowed in suspicion. The first time I told her I loved her and it must have sounded like manipulation. She set her jaw and put her hands on her hips.

"Big talk from the guy who paves the way for all the hookers and druggies. Okay, Mister Lofty Goals, you say you love me? You want me to quit? You quit too."

"Let's do it." Words flying out of my mouth, with thoughts a beat behind, even though I meant every syllable. "We'll get straight jobs together. Start a real life."

Karen still looked at me as though she expected a trick. But she was listening now. Her head tilted slightly, considering.

"It's just that easy."

"Why not?"

"Joe might have something to say about it."

I'd gone this far, I wasn't going to stop now. "I'll handle Joe."

"You're serious."

"Yes!" I clapped my hands once, loud, as a way out for us occurred to me. The sound echoed from our high spot above the peninsula. "If I can't do it, I've got an idea about someone who can. There's this big time guy who plays in the Room 23 Friday night poker game."

"The Rajah? You want to get mixed up with the Rajah?"

"It'll work." I was smiling now in my naïve exuberance. "Everyone's afraid of him, but no one says why."

"Isn't that your first clue about why you should stay away from him? When the bad people are scared, that's a flashing neon sign telling you to back off."

"But it means that he's a bigger bad guy than Joe. He and I will work something out."

"I don't like the sound of this. That guy is creepy as hell."

"I don't like the idea of you hooking. There's gotta be a better life for you. For us. I'll talk to the Rajah."

"Remember," said the Rajah, perfectly at ease in his huge recliner. "You came to me. You begged me to save your precious Karen Falk from her wicked life. You said you would do anything for her. Did you lie?"

I shook my head.

"No, you did not." The Rajah sucked in a breath through pursed lips as though sampling the flavor of the air. "I can always taste a lie on the breath of a human. And for all your bluster, you are going to bring me the Djinn's Tear aren't you? To keep Karen Falk safe, if not to save yourself."

All I could do was nod.

I couldn't even taunt Jeeves as he escorted us out with his

usual brisk businesslike movements. The sun shone down from high overhead in a clear autumn sky. The air tasted fresh and clean.

And none of it helped cheer me up. Even the multitude of bird songs sounded like nothing more than territorial demands from those who stood ready to fight to the death for the right to dig up their worms on the Rajah's estate.

I cleared my throat, but Nelson silenced me with a quick head shake.

We crossed the slate driveway/private road to Nelson's fifteen-year-old once-green Taurus and got in. His car was bigger and more comfortable than mine, though I'll never know how he justified his fuel costs. But gasoline was the last thing on my mind when he fired it up.

"Wait."

"Not until we're off the Rajah's property. Then I'll pull over."

At two miles per hour under the speed limit, Nelson got us past the gate and halfway down the hill before he parallel parked along a stretch of curb. On our side of the road were a few feet of well-mown grass between us and a high stone wall.

On the opposite side a grove of redwoods looked as though it had a path leading through it, perhaps a small walking park. Tough to say though. There might have been a house hiding back there.

Nelson turned off the engine, and looked at me with more patience than I might have had in his shoes. Maybe he knew what question was coming.

"Six months we've been working together," I said, "and we've never talked about how we got ourselves into this mess. Well now you know my story. I'm a scumbag with an ex-whore for a girlfriend. Who the hell are you?"

Nelson glanced around, as though afraid someone were watching. Probably the Rajah, not that he would deign to follow us.

"I'm not exactly a saint myself. I used to cook the books for one of those card places you see around San Jose. Don't ask me which one. Part of the Rajah's deal was that I never go back or point people to it."

He sighed and it was like he deflated. As though shame had made him shrink six inches.

"Anyway, they had about five loan sharks on staff, plus assistants, but they can't officially be on staff, so I had to hide and disguise a bunch of details, falsify records, the usual."

Nelson rubbed his forehead, pressed his fingers against his eyes. "Did it for years without thinking twice about it. Not until Gina was born. Then, suddenly, I knew I had to get out."

Nelson laughed, a bitter tone, and rubbed sweat from his expansive forehead. The movement made me realize that his whole car smelled of sweat. It didn't usually. Usually Nelson's car smelled like old cigarette smoke that's been trying to hide behind one of those tree deodorants. That, and feet. I never knew why, but Nelson's car always smelled just a little bit like feet.

"I never worried about Peter," he continued, "but the moment I first held my little girl, right there in the hospital, everything changed. I couldn't stand the thought of her finding out what her daddy was really like, how he made his money. I couldn't stand myself, making money that way." He shook his head. "But these are the kind of guys who don't just let you quit. The Rajah got them to let me go, even got me a severance package and a promise of no retaliation, so long as I kept my mouth shut."

He reached out to me. I thought he was going to put his hand on my shoulder, but he grabbed my collar in a fist and pulled me close before turning to look at me, dangerous desperation in his eyes.

"And now you've fucked me, Roland. You fucked me, and Tish, and Peter, and Gina. You fucked yourself and Karen too, but you fucked my whole family because you can't keep your damn fool mouth shut. You bet everything on our finding some trinket out of the Arabian Nights when half the loonies and weirdos in the Bay Area are competing with us.

"That's on you, Roland. If we fail this time my family will be at the mercy of the cruel bastards I used to work for. And you will have made that happen."

He leaned closer and I smelled Karen's coffee on his breath. "The

Rajah says I have to work with you. But if we get out of this in one piece, I'm going to kill you myself before you can pull a stunt like this again."

Nelson started his car and pulled back onto the road. I couldn't even bring myself to ask where we were going. Nelson wanted to kill me. The worst part was, I couldn't fault him for doing it.

3

———————

BY THE TIME WE WERE HUNTING FOR A PARKING SPACE ON CASTRO Street in Mountain View, I knew where we were going. I didn't confirm this until after Nelson gave up on street parking and found a spot in the public lot behind one of my favorite new and used book stores, Dead Tree Society. Well, the lot was also behind a Qi Gung school, a Polynesian restaurant, a huge bead shop, and one of those Hollywood religion places with the tests.

That assortment was downtown Mountain View in a nutshell. Offbeat, kitschy little places that should not quite work side by side, yet somehow, there, they did. Not as far out there as Berkeley or anything, but enough to give Mountain View a cool vibe.

Nelson turned off the engine, and while it ticked I said, "You want to talk to the naga?"

"Don't call her that. Her name is Snigdha."

"You like her."

"I trust her more than I trust you right now."

"Have you read—"

"No, and don't tell me."

Nelson got out of the car and slammed the door behind him. I had no choice but to follow. He could deny what she was all he wanted, but we had seen Snigdha's serpent form once, a twenty-foot python with a beautiful face the color of caramel, and long black hair that shimmered like her scales. Her green eyes matched the highlights in those scales.

The street smelled like fried banana and autumn. Autumn in the South Bay smelled like dried plant life and falling leaves. Early October. Chances were we wouldn't see much rain before late November.

The street was busy for a Tuesday afternoon, but I mean busy for a place like Mountain View. In other words, we had to wait all of ninety seconds to cross the street at the crosswalk in the middle, and we didn't need a traffic light to do it. Diners enjoying their meals at a café we passed reminded me I was hungry, even more than the smell of the fried bananas did.

I wondered if Nelson was too angry to have lunch with me, but decided to let that question wait until after we talked with the naga.

Excuse me. Snigdha.

Snigdha's place was a big fancy new age bookstore called New Dawn Books. She catered to a broad base of clientele, which meant that her store carried fancy Celtic knot work bracelets and necklaces, statuary for every flavor of religion you could name and a few you probably couldn't, scarfs and purses, and fancy boxes that cost more than some of the statues people would put in them.

She had two classrooms in the back where local "experts" could teach seekers how to change their chi and rotate their chakras. And then there were the books, videos, and audiobooks about meditation, ascension, gurus, philosophy and all that kind of crap.

The store had exactly one bookshelf devoted to actual occultism, and if a useful book ever made its way into the three feet or so available to it, I never saw. I guess even the wannabe occultists took their trade elsewhere.

But what hit me as soon as we opened the front door was the smell: Nag Champa. The favored scent of potheads and new agers everywhere. Probably a few religious types too. All these trends got their start in something sincere, no matter how diluted they became as the money poured in.

Speaking of potheads, Therese was behind the counter. When I first met her, I was fooled by her ghost-white complexion, her nose, lip, tongue and ear piercings, and her tight blond dreadlocks. I admit. I thought she was just another burnout.

But one time Nelson and I had to wait for Snigdha, and Therese and I ended up talking. Turned out she was working on her master's degree in civil engineering. She had no idea that Snigdha was anything other than human, and I didn't tell her. Therese only worked here for the employee discount, which extended to medicinal marijuana, a trade Snigdha did not advertise.

You'd think that, in my line of work, I'd know better than to trust appearances. I guess we all rely on mental shorthand sometimes.

I waved hello to Therese while Nelson asked, "Is she in?"

"She said to send you on back when you showed up." Therese looked over the huge bruise on my face. "What happened to you?"

"You know those express aisle signs that say fifteen items or less?"

Therese nodded.

"I tried to come through with sixteen. Some clerks take those limits seriously." I smiled. "Has she been waiting long?"

"Since we opened, at least."

Great. The naga knew we were coming before we did. That had happened three times before. None of them were good memories.

If that detail troubled Nelson, he didn't let it show. He strode straight back through the store, past the classrooms, and knocked on the office door. I trailed along like an afterthought.

"Come in, boys," Snigdha called. Her high, sibilant voice held a lazy tone. She sounded sated. I tried not to wonder what she had just eaten.

Nelson opened the door, and there was Snigdha, curled up in her bean bag chair, laptop on her lap. She dressed in form-fitting denim slacks and a scoop-neck purple top, with matching sandals. Snigdha had the kind of sleek sexy look that made male shoppers drop far more money than they intended to when they came in. Not because she asked them to, but because they hoped to impress her. Me, I found it hard to see her as anything other than a giant snake. She made the skin of my neck itch.

The room was empty apart from four tall filing cabinets, a blinking wireless router, and a half dozen bean bag chairs. The Nag Champa scent invaded even here, but underneath it was something dry that struck me as menacing. I never understood how Nelson could feel so comfortable around her.

Snigdha smiled and waved us to join her in beanbag chairs of our own. Even that small gesture was hypnotic in its grace. An urge to run fluttered through my stomach, but that might have been paranoia. Snigdha had never done anything to threaten or harm Nelson or me, and she often helped us out with information. Still, I had read the Mahabharata, and knew that the naga reputation was hardly gentle.

Her eyes took in my bruised face, the stiffness of my movements. "So, boys, I presume the Rajah has you chasing teardrops?"

"You know about the Djinn's Tear?" asked Nelson.

"Of course. I remember the man who first brought it from the West." She smiled, and I think only my bias made her look patronizing. To Nelson she probably looked enigmatic. "And I remember the last time it surfaced. Caused quite a ruckus. This was some eight hundred years ago."

"And here you don't look a day over three hundred." Nelson glared at me for that, but I couldn't stop it from slipping out. Snigdha only smiled.

"The Mongols and the Tartars were quite keen to acquire it. I think they spent more than two centuries invading and warring before the question was resolved as all such things are: one man stole it."

She frowned. "At least, the story goes that it was a man. The thief could just as easily have been a woman, of course. Perhaps more easily, given the presumptions about women at that time and place. I guess we'll find out once it's sold."

She shrugged with only the barest movement of her shoulders.

"Anyway, each side accused the other of stealing the Djinn's Tear, and they fought for another fifty years or so before they realized that no one involved in the war had the prize."

"Do you know who has it now?" That was Nelson. Straight to the point.

"A thief." Snigdha shrugged again, and I found it disconcerting because I could not get past the fact that she didn't always have shoulders. How did she shrug in her snake form? "A foolish thief," she continued, "if he or she thinks to sell the Djinn's Tear. Items of such power can only be stolen or taken by force."

"Why is that?" I asked.

"Buying and selling might lend legitimacy to ownership, and a toy like the Djinn's Tear has nothing to do with legitimacy. It is fell power, and fell power can only be taken or stolen, not exchanged."

"Are we going to be competing with you for it?" More direct than I wanted to be, but I had to know, and Nelson could stuff his glare.

"Me?" Snigdha laughed, and I expected the sound to hiss, but it didn't. Her laughter rang high and clear like a set of crystal bells. "Whatever would I do with it? Only a human can use it."

"But if it can't be sold," I said slowly, "and only a human can use it, why does the Rajah want it?"

"Who can explain the Rajah?" Snigdha shrugged again, and this time the movement resembled the way a snake expands and contracts its body to move. I felt realization dawn on my face, which brought a curious look from Snigdha as she continued, "Perhaps he wishes to keep it on a shelf. Or perhaps he wants it to spite Mr. Scratch."

Nelson and I both shuddered at the mention of that name. Mr. Scratch was the biggest, baddest warlock from Monterey to Sacramento. And I don't mean witch. I've met plenty of witches, from the religious types who wouldn't know a real spell if it were cast in front of them to the sorts who would end up in urban legends if they let people know what they could do.

But Mr. Scratch and his ilk were the real threat that generated the Inquisition and the witch trials. Modern people can make all the noise they want about politics or land grabs. The truth was that villages and churches got wind of powerful, demonic spell-slingers like Nicholas Scratch and fear overrode their good senses until they killed enough innocent people that they felt better.

Oh, they were shooting for the right targets, but I don't doubt that they missed. Guys like Mr. Scratch didn't end up burning on stakes or at an *auto-da-fé*.

Nelson and I looked at each other and our fight from earlier went out the window. If we were competing against Mr. Scratch for the Djinn's Tear, we were going to need a united front. And maybe a battalion of marines. And air support. And maybe a nuke.

Snigdha watched us with something close to pity. I tried to think of something to say, but I was still stuck on the idea of trying to outmaneuver a warlock who had bound at least one major demon that I knew of.

I don't know if Nelson was as depressed by our prospects as I was, but he at least thought of something to say to Snigdha. "I don't suppose you would share any thoughts that would help us."

"I have no love for the Rajah, nor any particular desire to see him get what he wants, but I have no call for urgent vengeance against him." She tilted her head, considering. "And you both have always shown me proper respect."

Her nostrils flared as though she sighed, but I swear I never saw her torso expand. Not that I was watching her torso.

"I will tell you this: like most granted wishes, the acts of the Djinn's Tear follow the path of least resistance. The owner has promised a demonstration this week that will leave no doubt in the minds of the wise as to the item's veracity. The demonstration will undoubtedly be large and showy, but the key is that it will likely center on the Tear's location. That should narrow your search."

A management seminar once advised me to thank someone seven times for any charitable donation. If that's a good rule, then Nelson and I must have tripled it as we left, and I swear that I saw actual humor in Snigdha's smile before she closed the office door.

Maybe the Mahabharata exaggerated the nagas' reputation after all.

THE POLYNESIAN PLACE NEXT TO DEAD TREE SOCIETY HAD TABLES OUT front by the sidewalk, but Nelson and I always skipped them. This time was no exception. We pushed through the glass door and into the place that was far too upbeat and colorful for our current mood.

But it smelled savory, with meats and peppers and oils filling the air. That was what mattered most to us right then: food.

Without a word to each other, Nelson and I followed the young hostess to a table. She left us menus, but we had eaten there enough times that we didn't need them. As soon as our waiter showed up we ordered lunch: mesquite grilled turkey with broccoli, green beans, and pad Thai noodles for me, barbecue pork loin with the same sides for him.

After the waiter dropped off our water and coffee, I looked up at Nelson and said, "So...."

"You're not off the hook." He spooned sugar into his coffee. "But we can't afford to be at each other's throats right now. There's too much at stake."

I chose not to point out that I wasn't at his throat. See, I can keep my mouth shut sometimes. I could also tell that Nelson had more to say, so I let him sip his coffee until he was ready.

"Until this whole thing is over, I've got your back, just like always. We can wait until this is all done to hash things out between us."

He set down his coffee cup and held up one finger. I was struck by the sudden image of Nelson addressing his children the same way when they were in trouble.

"One thing. No more backtalk out of you. No hospitality bullshit. We know the Rajah won't offer, so don't ask. In fact, no challenging the Rajah at all. Nothing." He curled that finger down to join the others in a fist. "I swear to the Almighty, you curb that damned mouth of yours or I'll shut it faster than the Rajah, and I'll cook your corpse for him myself."

"You really believe in God? Big 'g,' watching over all of us, mysterious ways and all?"

"Why?" Nelson set his jaw. "Are you saying you don't? After everything we've seen?"

"That's just it. Lots of monsters, and fair folk, and petty demons, but no angels. Not one benevolent entity out there keeping us safe."

"You think you deserve to see an angel?"

I laughed. "Good point."

"No wonder you have a death wish. Your world isn't worth living in."

"I don't have a death wish."

Nelson stared at me.

"Not letting a bully push me around is hardly the same thing."

Nelson continued to stare. I felt warmth grow under my collar. Where was our food already?

"All right," I said, getting worked up. Frustration came out of me in harsh gestures as I spoke. "Maybe I don't believe the Rajah intends to ever let us go. Maybe I think I was an idiot to ever get in debt to him and that he's just amusing himself until he's ready to kill us. And maybe eat us."

"He would eat us. Don't doubt it."

"You don't think that's just—"

"I've seen it."

That stopped me. I settled down in my chair and leaned forward, ready to hear the truth, ready to hear what secret horrors Nelson had witnessed. I didn't want to. My personal horror tank didn't need any more fuel. But I needed to know this about the Rajah, and I had the feeling that Nelson needed to say it.

"The first time he gave me an assignment." Nelson stared into the distance, his voice growing quiet as he spoke, so I could barely hear him over the clattering of dishware in the background. "The first time the butler ever brought me to that little room where he meets with us. The Rajah was already there, stripping the last raw flesh off of a human femur with his teeth, blood covering his face and hands, a pile of bones behind him in a basket on the floor."

Nelson looked away, out the front window onto the street, as though watching leaves fall from the maple trees.

"The smell was too much for me. I fell to my knees and threw up everything I'd eaten for the last three days."

He shook his head. "The Rajah didn't react, didn't say a word. I wiped my mouth on my sleeve and looked up and there he was, lounging in his chair the way he always is. No blood, no femur, no basket of bones, not even the smell remained. It was like the whole thing never happened, except for the pool of vomit on the floor and the fact that I was on all fours."

Nelson's last words came out just above a whisper. "He just pointed to a chair, and I sat, and he told me what I had to do for him. But his eyes, Roland." Nelson's shoulders shook, as though the memory had shivered up his back. "His eyes. Without a single word his eyes told me that he had shown me the truth, and my fate if I disobeyed him."

I had no words for this. No comfort. No commiseration. Nothing.

"I don't know what the Rajah is," said Nelson in a stronger voice, "and I don't want to know. But I do know this. He isn't someone you challenge."

He looked at me once more, but this time I didn't see anger, fury or desperation. I saw fear. Fear that cracked a tiny thread in his voice as he finished. "That's what I think of every time you talk back. Every time you mouth off. Every time you ask for more than he wants to give you. This isn't some stupid game. You and I are cavemen. And the Rajah is that thing outside the firelight waiting to eat us the moment we let our guard down."

No wonder Nelson could barely speak in front of the Rajah. No wonder he hated that I did. Nelson had been broken back before I ever met him.

"I'm sorry, Nelson. I never meant to—"

"It doesn't matter."

"Nothing you've said makes me believe he's ever going to let us go."

"You missed my point." He pressed one palm down on the table between us and leaned in close. I could smell fear sweat mixed in with his coffee breath. I could see desperation in his eyes. "You and I,"

he said, "we're not working for him so he'll let us go one day. We're
working for him so we get to live to see tomorrow."

The waiters brought our food, so hot they had to warn us not to
touch the plates. I couldn't tell you if it smelled good. I'd lost my
appetite. And from the lost look on Nelson's face, so had he.

WE DID MANAGE TO EAT IN BITS AND PIECES THAT AFTERNOON AS WE
chased down another couple of possible information sources in the
heart of suburbia.

That wasn't laziness, by the way, or any trepidation on our part
about hitting the urban centers. Fight a couple of ghuls and
revenants and pretty soon you stop worrying about muggers and
other criminals.

Truth was, suburbia had more people with the time, money and
inclination to come together in groups and try their hand at serious
occult practices.

But we got nowhere that day. Most of the small timers we knew
either had either not heard of the Djinn's Tear or lied to us about it.
In most cases I was pretty sure they lied: shifty eyes, tight voices, that
sort of thing.

I swear, if I could get most small-time occultists into a poker
league, I'd earn enough from them in six months that Karen and I
could retire to the Bahamas and live like royalty.

Nelson dropped me off at around five, so he could get home in
time to keep up the pretense of a nine-to-five job with occasional
overtime. And we both knew this assignment was going to require
some late hours.

Speaking of which, we really did get time-and-a-half when we
worked more than eight hours in a day or forty hours in a week,
because the Rajah really did pay us. That always seemed weird to me.
I mean, we were in no position to refuse any task he set for us, even if
our only payment was not being eaten, more literally than I
had hoped.

Of course, there may have been some metaphysical explanation for why the Rajah paid us. Possibly even for why he continued to give us tasks and maintained at least the pretense that we could work down our debts to him and earn our freedom. Since I didn't even know what the Rajah was, I had no way to guess what rules he played by.

Nevertheless, he gave us 1099s and paid us a pretty good wage on a per-hour basis through direct deposit, plus overtime, health and dental coverage, and the occasional bonus. He even covered our mileage.

He didn't require us to fill out time sheets, either, though his estimations of the hours we devoted to each job never failed in their accuracy down to the quarter-hour.

Maybe that was why he paid us. It was another way to prove how thoroughly fucked we were. Every week he showed us that he knew exactly how we spent our days and nights, even when we didn't tell him. He even knew how far each of us drove, which meant he knew where we had gone, and when.

Just a little reminder that he had some means of keeping tabs on us, in case we ever thought about trying to run away. It worked, too. I know I thought about running away at least once a week, but never believed I could get away with it. I'm sure Nelson felt the same way.

Then again, maybe the Rajah just wanted us to be on call anytime of the day or night. And if we had to work regular jobs — I can't even say straight jobs, because if Nelson and I had worked straight jobs in the first place we would never have ended up in debt to the Rajah — we would have had periods of unavailability that he could not have complained about.

Instead, we were beholden to the Rajah for not only our lives, but for the money that fed, clothed, and housed us.

God, I was depressed.

The first thing I did on arriving home — after I double-locked the door and checked the schedule on the fridge to confirm that Karen was working the swing shift again — was feed Lance. This time I got to watch as his sticky tongue snatched cricket after cricket until his little belly was full. I always found it soothing to watch Lance eat. Something about the clarity of the natural order, or maybe the fact that I provided the food he enjoyed. My own life might have been out of control, but this I could do. I could feed and care for my gecko.

If only my life were as orderly as his.

If I ever got clear of the Rajah, the first thing I would do was marry Karen. Then we could have a kid or two, live like normal human beings. Join the natural cycle of life, instead of this unnatural cycle that trapped me into dealing with things like nagas and warlocks and whatever the hell the Rajah was. Maybe Nelson didn't want to know what we were working for, but I did.

And on that note, I put Lancelot on my shoulder, tuned the radio to one of my evening talk shows, and sat at the kitchen table to read my nightly homework.

Tonight's book was *The Foulness Out of Araby* by Giovanni di Mateo, a small press folio from the nineteen twenties. I had hopes for that book. It was the one that taught me how to hunt ghuls, even though old di Mateo would rather I had steered well clear of them, if the warnings in his text were any indication.

It was tiresome reading though, with its rants about the "Old Ones" and references to the "Mad Arab," who, as far as I could tell, learned things Man Was Not Meant to Know and had the gall to write about them. Not that di Mateo had any stones to throw on this one.

If I ever got my hands on this *Al Azif* by di Mateo's "Mad Arab," I'd read that too. And I knew there was an English language version of it our there, translated from Arabic by way of Greek. Apparently it was the per project of an Elizabethan sorcerer, and published under a title that horror movie buffs would love.

Sure, if I read it I might get "torn apart in the marketplace by invisible demons," but how much worse could that be than being eaten by the Rajah?

The Foulness Out of Araby was half a story of di Mateo's travels and half a taxonomy. Like a tourist's guide to supernatural Iran and Iraq. I hoped to find hints in there about what the Rajah might be. Yeah, he looked Indian, and had a slight English-Indian accent, but that could have been an act. Anyone who could appear out of nothing and make a pile of dead human vanish right in front of Nelson, putrid smell and all, could probably look like whatever he wanted.

So why look for clues in a book about monsters of the Middle East? Because the easiest lies to pull off over a long stretch of time are lies that come close to the truth. If the Rajah hailed from the Middle East, he would have had an easier time pretending to be Indian — at least to a couple of ignorant Americans like Nelson and me — than he would have had if he pretended to be Norwegian. Besides, I'd already gone through every Western book I could find, and I'd run out of Indian books for the time being.

All right, so the Rajah's magic meant that maybe none of these details mattered. In that case, I had nothing to go on. He could have been anything.

After several hours of banging my head on an outdated writing style filled with racist assumptions, and teasing out what little bits of useful information I could discern, the Rajah still could have been anything.

Oh, it wasn't quite that bad, but I didn't find much. The Rajah could have been a djinn, in which case Nelson and I were seriously outclassed and had no prayer. That didn't sound right to me. Djinni might eat a human, but they didn't tend to have a whole lot of patience for games. Still, the Rajah wanted the Djinn's Tear even though he couldn't use it. Maybe the name had significance?

The same held true for marids and ifriti, which, as far as I could tell from di Mateo's details, appeared to be other words for djinn, functionally synonymous.

The Rajah could have been a ghul, which in some cases might grow as powerful as a baby djinn, but I didn't think so. A ghul might have pulled the appearing out of nowhere stunt, and a ghul would definitely eat a human, but a ghul could never have pulled off the disappearing remains trick.

The only other option even remotely plausible from di Mateo's book was a manticore, but di Mateo said nothing about shapeshifting manticores. I slammed the book in disgust. Maybe the Rajah really was an Indian monster after all. Was I overcomplicating this?

I heard a key in the lock, and reflexively glanced over at Lancelot, back sunning himself under his lamp. The gecko looked untroubled, so I hoped that meant Karen was about to come in, not some kind of doppelganger.

Maybe Nelson had a point about me reading too much.

Somewhere around eleven-thirty, with Lancelot back under his sun lamp, the talk show host ranting about the impact of hybrid cars on gas tax revenue, and my neck complaining from the way I leaned over di Mateo's thick text, the front door opened and in came Karen.

She looked beautiful as always even in her faded peach blah uniform with its white trim. Although it helped that her "ten percent" button was undone. That was what I called it anyway, because when she left that not-quite-the-top button open her tips from male customers went up: fifteen percent became twenty-five, and twenty percent even swelled to thirty.

The Rajah paid me pretty well, but I thought Karen still made more money than I did. Not that it mattered. She had made more than I did at our old jobs too, and in those days she wasn't expected to declare her tips on an income tax form.

Karen stopped dead one step inside the open door. "God, you still look like hell. You didn't take another beating, did you?"

"Same beating." I stood and closed and double-locked the door, planting a quick kiss on her lips as I did. She smelled like bacon and pancakes. Was it wrong that I found that arousing? "Just won't look pretty for a few days yet."

"Does it hurt?" She tenderly prodded my face.

"Nah," I lied. "I feel like I could go ten rounds with the champ."

"You're moving like you already did. And went down in the first."

"Sorry, I've been hunched over my book."

"That's it." She grabbed me by the collar and led me into the hallway bathroom, the one with the tub, and cranked on the hot water. She dumped in some kind of bath salts. "No arguments. You soak until the water's cold. Give your poor muscles a break."

"You could rub them?"

That got me a smile. "I'd love to. And maybe rub something else while I'm at it. But playtime will have to wait. I missed my afternoon meeting."

"You could go tomorrow."

"No. I need a meeting right now."

I had my shirt halfway off, but those words froze my world. "Are you all right?"

"Not really." Only then did I notice how her breaths were shallow. Barely there. "I caught a customer snorting in the restroom. She ... offered me some." Karen must have seen the look on my face because she was quick to add, "I said no and walked straight to the kitchen and called Shelly." Her head twitched back and forth in a quick, irritated shake. "Eddie almost fired me for making a personal call."

"That son of a bitch!"

"I told him to do it and he backed off. He knows I'm his best waitress." She blew out a breath. "I hate this job, Roland. I really hate it."

"I know." I wrapped my arms around her and she put her head on my shoulder. "But if we really want to move away from here when we can, we need to sock away as much as possible."

"I know...." She stiffened up and stepped back. "I need to go to my meeting. You hit the tub and rub some life into those muscles. I want you ready for action when I get home."

She left and I slipped into the near-scalding water, slowly so I could get used to the heat. My muscles already began thanking me, not quite relaxing all at once or anything like that, but easing in a way that felt grateful. Before long, steam and sweat matted down my hair, and a pleasant languorous sensation had my thoughts drifting.

Worried as I was about Karen's near miss with cocaine that day, I admit that a selfish part of me hoped that her last words meant she was finally coming out of her slump. Karen and I would have wild sex every night for months. Then some part of her would close down, and she would barely let me kiss her for weeks at a time. I always figured that she loved sex, but she needed to cut me off once in a while – or maybe cut herself off – so she could prove that I was with her for more than just great sex. That I really did love her.

That was the other reason I wanted to marry Karen. I wanted to make sure she understood that my love was not going anywhere. She and I would be together until death did us part.

Of course, if I didn't come up with a way to get free of the Rajah, that death might part us all too soon.

4

——————

I WOKE THE NEXT MORNING ALONE IN TANGLED SHEETS AGAIN, BUT THIS time I smelled bacon and butternut squash pancakes. Was I dreaming? Karen had not cooked me breakfast since she started waiting tables. Not that I could blame her. If I had to spend eight hours a day serving breakfast foods, I sure would not want to go home and prepare them.

I reached for the ground and walked myself out of bed and onto the floor with my hands. My muscles all felt better than yesterday. Note to self: stiff, sore muscles can be combated with ibuprofen, a hot bath, and three sweaty rounds of sex.

Yes, three, and it wasn't our biggest night by any stretch. Don't get me wrong, I was never some great sexual athlete. It's just that Karen had ways of making a man rise to the occasion.

I grabbed my plush, red-striped robe from my fifth of the closet, but stopped short of the door to the bedroom. I turned back and made the bed, then tied my robe and headed down the hall. As I approached the kitchen I could hear Karen singing a pop song from our high school days, "Top Down Lover" by Honey Childe.

Breakfast and singing? Much as I'd like to have attributed her good mood to my masterful performance in bed last night, I'm just not that arrogant. Something had to be up. Was that why she was so eager last night? Was I so self-involved I missed the key signs?

I could feel my jaw clench and my brow knit. I paused in the doorway, trying to wipe clean the outward signs of stress through deep breaths. She might just have felt happy. It could happen. It even did, from time to time. But after her temptation last night…

"Admiring the view?" Karen's tone was playful, but she knew she looked good, standing at the stove in a sheer negligee minus the matching bra and panties intended to be worn underneath it.

I didn't try to keep the interest out of my tone as I said, "Love it, but don't let the bacon get you."

Karen flipped two pancakes onto a pile of four more and waggled one finger at the other pan, making sure I saw the spit guard, a mesh cover intended to catch any hot grease that popped off the bacon.

With the practiced grace of a dancer she slid the pancake pan into the sink, shuffled the bacon onto a different plate where a paper towel soaked up its grease, ran water into the first pan, set the second on top of it, also in the stream, and finally added the spit guard to her dish stack.

She turned, gave me a wicked smile, and strutted to the table with a wiggle in her hips that made sure I watched her and not the plates. As she passed I said, "Keep it up and our food will get cold."

"Ah ah ah," she said as she sat. "Must keep up your strength. But if you're a good boy and clean your plate, maybe we'll talk about dessert."

I practically jumped into the empty seat, noticing for the first time that our dishes and flatware were already set up, and that she had poured us both glasses of water and orange juice. No syrup for the pancakes, but that was a concession to her job. Karen could no longer stand the smell of maple syrup.

"Today's a magic day, Rollie."

Karen was the only person allowed to call me "Rollie," and I suspect that I would not have let her do it if she had not given me a great deal of … positive reinforcement. "Why's that?"

"Oh, I don't know." Her smile hid a secret, like she had some big surprise planned for me and did not want to tip her hand too early. "I just think something wonderful's going to happen today. Ever feel like you're going to win the lottery or something?"

"No."

"Never?" Her hand stopped with a forkful of pancake halfway to her mouth. "Never ever?"

"Not since high school." I poured a sip of orange juice onto my plate, then took a drink while Karen continued eating. "If luck is a real thing, mine is all bad."

"Can't be all bad. You have me."

"And I think you used up my lifetime supply of good luck. Maybe more. So I had to take extra bad luck to make up the difference."

I meant that to come out playful, but Karen's smile faded. "I brought you bad luck?"

"No, I mean—"

"You mean your life was better before you ever met me."

"No! I mean you are the single bright spot in my life, and your radiance is so intense that everything else looks bleak in comparison."

Karen stared at her plate, thinking. To give her time, I tried a piece of bacon. It was crunchy with just enough juice to have tender spots. Perfect bacon, but it was wasted on me at that moment.

"I know things look bad right now." Karen spoke slowly, still staring at her plate. "Our jobs are hell and we have a mountain of debt to some sort of gangster. But you'll see, Roland." She looked up at me, desperation in her eyes. "You'll see. Everything's about to turn around for us. Today *is* magic. You'll see."

I dropped to my knees and took her in my arms. Karen clung to me like I was a stuffed animal saving her from a thunderstorm. Half to herself she said, "You'll be glad you met me yet, Roland."

In that moment I would have given anything to hear her call me Rollie.

THE DAY STARTED OUT OVERCAST AND COOL, WHICH SUITED MY MOOD. It was my turn to drive, so I picked up Nelson at his usual spot and started us up toward 280 North and our next series of sources to hit. Along the way, Nelson tried to engage me in conversation and speculation about the Djinn's Tear, but my thoughts were still on Karen. That look in her eye. The desperation in her tone. Why did that seem familiar?

The memory hit me as we passed a copse of evergreens near the freeway entrance. December. Two years ago. Karen and I had just moved in together, seeing the futility in maintaining separate apartments when we ended every night in the same bed anyway.

We had figured out how we could blend our possessions together with some small amount of wrangling and bargaining. For example, she had agreed that I needed one of our bedrooms for a library, and I had acceded to barely getting any closet space to call my own.

The deal was a trick, by the way. She needed the library space as much as I did, with her books about chess and game theory and logic. But that was all right. I didn't have all that many clothes that needed hanging up.

We were just about done with our token attempts at decorating for the day. I had arranged the furniture at least a dozen different ways before collapsing on the couch and announcing that we were ordering pizza for dinner. I had no intentions of cooking, or leaving the apartment, or even changing out of my faded Golden State Warriors tee shirt and paint-stained jeans.

Karen laughed at the seriousness of my proclamation. She plopped down next to me, wearing paint-stained jeans of her own, along with a red and black felt shirt hanging open over a plain white tee shirt. Her hair was tied back in a short pony tail.

I had that tiredness in the limbs that comes from physical exertion. A pleasant sensation, that could have continued all evening as far as I cared at that moment. But my mind was not so tired as all that. So I asked what I thought was an innocent question. "What do you want for Christmas?"

"Christmas!" Karen jumped up and ran out of the room.

My arms, legs and back begged me to stay right where I was. Surely she would come back and tell me what was going on, what was so very important that she had to go digging for it right when we were just settling in for the evening.

My curiosity got the better of me. I dragged myself to my feet and slumped into the spare bedroom — soon to be the library — where we had our remaining unopened moving boxes. Karen had already cut two of them open and was digging through a third.

"Karen?" I said. She didn't look up, or even pause. "What are you looking for?"

"I can't find your Christmas stocking. I found mine" — she held up a long, dark green, hand-knitted piece of work that had her name in white large letters down the front — "but I can't find yours."

"You can stop looking. I don't have one."

She turned to me, the look on her face saying I might as well have told her that my puppy was run over by a semi.

"Dad's a lapsed Catholic, and Mom's kind of a lapsed Muslim, so we never really celebrated anything except the days off." I shrugged. "I mean, they got us kids something each December so we wouldn't feel left out, but we never decorated."

"You have to have a stocking, Roland. Full of little wrapped presents." She sat back on her knees, and that desperate look came into her eye and tone, like I'd never heard before.

Like an idiot, I misunderstood.

"No, really. It's all right, Karen."

"No. It isn't. And you need a tree. A real tree." Tears started trickling down her face. Her voice got shaky. "With shiny stupid ornaments on it. And tinsel. And presents waiting underneath it. One from me and one from ... Santa Claus. These... these things matter, Roland. And you've never..."

She started crying and I went to her and dropped down on my knees beside her. I just hugged her while she cried. I wanted to ask why it mattered so much, but we were too new as a couple. So I held her. And as soon as she stopped crying I took her out to buy a tree, and shiny stupid ornaments, and tinsel, and garlands, and mistletoe, and finally a stocking for me. Not that we had a fireplace to hang it from.

It was months later that I found out about how her dad left when she was eight, about how he disappeared one December night and never came home. How her mother took down all the decorations the next day and told her that Christmas was canceled.

Her mother threw it all out, down to the last strand of tinsel. But Karen and her sister snuck out that night and dug through the garbage looking for their stockings. They put them up in secret in their closet, hoping that Santa would find them anyway.

But Santa never came.

"Now why would you be thinkin' I'd know anything about a trinket like that? Not at all my sort of thing at all, is it now?"

I hated talking to the fae. They lied, their conversations ran in circles, and by the time we were done they usually got something out of me without telling me anything useful at all. What was worse, half the time they pulled some kind of trick on me for my trouble. But Nelson and I had gotten nowhere in another day of searching, so we hit the only faerie ring in the area where I knew I would always find someone to talk to.

Of course, to get there we had to trespass on private property, some sort of paddock off El Monte near or in Los Altos Hills. Mind you, in that area, a "paddock" consisted of more square acreage than some neighborhoods I'd lived in. But in this case, it meant that no one was likely to spot two wandering idiots stopping by a ring of toadstools in the late afternoon sun, enjoying the smell of dry grass and horse sweat and talking to a person most people refused to see.

The person in question looked like a man two feet tall, in a bright green frock coat and top hat, complete with monocle and cane. I doubted that was his actual appearance as much as I doubted that "Ridges" was his true name, but that was what he wanted us to call him.

"I know the Djinn's Tear isn't from your part of the world," I said, "but I figured that such a powerful object couldn't possibly come to the Bay Area without the Good Folk hearing all about it."

"Ah, but you do have a softness to the tongue, don't you boy. McCreedy, isn't it? Irish, are you?"

"On my father's side," I told him, as I told him every time we spoke. Nelson fidgeted, but he always let me take the lead when we spoke to the fae. He said my bloodline would get me more respect. I told him that my Irish blood made no difference. It was not as though I could claim Thomas the Rhymer as my grandfather.

But Nelson insisted. Probably just trying to keep his profile low. I could have told him it wouldn't help. Hold your tongue around the fae and they assume you're guarding secrets. Sooner or later one of those fae will decide to dig those secrets out of you, one way or another.

"And what about your mother," continued Ridges. "What is she then?"

"Kurdish."

"And yet you say your name is Roland McCreedy? How is it that your mother had no say in your naming?"

"She gave me my middle name, but that is not yours for the asking."

"Ah, you do learn, boy, don't you?" Ridges smiled like a proud grandfather, odd to see on someone a third my height. "Read all about this sort of thing in those books of yours, haven't you now? Well, my book-learned bucko, the sprites tell me that you set a fine bowl of milk, so I guess it behooves me to tell you as much as this, seeing as how I can't have my own fine people going hungry if something unfortunate were to happen to you. So, I'll tell you this much, and maybe you'll listen, and maybe you won't. I'm betting you won't. Your type never does listen to good sense when they hear it, even when it comes from the mouths of those who know better than you do, and who have a great deal more learning and experience than a gobdaw like yourself could ever hope to amass in a dozen lifetimes full of your books. No, I'll tell you this anyway, even though I'm sure my words will slip slide past your ears as though I'd never spoken a syllable in your presence, and no doubt your final words will be, 'Ridges was right. I should have listened to him when I had the chance, that noble, brilliant person whose boots I'm not worthy to lick clean on a rainy muddy day the like of which you never really see in this new dry land, but you saw all the time back in old Eire.' No, I'll tell you because I'm a right good and noble person who tries so hard to go through his life doing good and noble things, however rarely sleeveens like yourselves might let him. So here you are, good, simple advice, more than you deserve, but less than you'll accept, I'm sure: Forget the trinket. Grab that girl of yours and run far away. Enjoy what little life you've got left to you."

I drew a breath to respond, but Ridges was gone. The faerie ring itself felt ... shut down. When we got here it felt vibrant, like the tremor that causes an avalanche, if the tremor is sustained and the avalanche doesn't start. Now it just felt like a circle of mushrooms.

"I guess that's it," I said to Nelson.

He shrugged and led the way back to my car. We opened the doors and were overpowered by the smell of at least a thousand pounds of horse manure. We let the doors hang open and popped the trunk, trying to air out the Camry, but the smell refused to budge. I held my breath and searched the car, but found no sign of a cause, which meant only one possible answer.

"We might as well get in," I said. "The smell isn't going anywhere until sunset. That's the trick they played on us for coming."

Nelson didn't budge. "Does the bus come through here?"

"Like I know the bus routes?"

"Maybe we could walk to a diner or coffee shop?"

"At least six miles round trip to Suzette's Crepes, which is the nearest place I know of."

Nelson kicked a rock. "I hate the—"

"They can hear you!"

"—walk down this hill." He squeezed his next words past a jaw clenched so tight his cheeks jutted out like he was storing nuts for the winter. "Fine. Let's drive. But if that smell sticks to my clothes, I swear...."

We closed the trunk and extra doors and got in. I put all the windows down before I even started the engine. As we pulled onto the street, I muttered, "When you say something like that, they take it as a request."

Nelson growled.

⸻

Nelson growled for the rest of the day and well into the evening. The fae had been listening, as I warned him every time we went to that ring, and were kind enough to grant his request: the smell faded from my car with the setting sun but remained just as fragrant on Nelson's person.

The smell also meant that talking with Ridges had been the research highlight of our day. We could not have dared to show our faces to any major player while carrying the literal stink of a fae prank. That would have destroyed what little credibility Nelson and I had established for ourselves.

So the rest of our conversations had been of the all-but-wasting-time-with-the-small-timers variety.

In short, the day stank like Nelson.

Because Nelson insisted on maintaining the illusion of a nine-to-five job, he had to leave his house every morning at eight-thirty like clockwork. Me, I refused to kowtow to his lie since most of our tasks involved seeing people who were not available to visitors until at least noon. If they slept late, so could I.

I never asked what Nelson did with his mornings, for fear that he would try to drag me into his a.m. activities. But since he left so early every morning, when it was my day to drive I had to meet him somewhere. At first we picked different diners or coffee shops, but finally we settled on Hollenbeck Park in Sunnyvale. It was central for both of us, and had plenty of nearby spots where he could park safely all day without inviting questions from curious locals.

I did wonder sometimes if part of the reason Nelson maintained his lie was to keep me away from his family. After all, once he cleared his debt with the Rajah, assuming that ever happened, he wanted to leave the whole experience behind. I was part of that experience, so I had no doubt that if that day came, I would see my partner for the last time.

That might mean the Rajah would assign me a new partner. There was a disturbing thought.

It was around eight when I dropped Nelson off at his Taurus. They sky had stayed clear and the evenings were still warm enough for a windbreaker. Hollenbeck Park had a couple of joggers making the rounds, and one kid trying desperately to squeeze in a few more shots with his basketball. Otherwise the street was pretty quiet.

"Hey," I said to pause Nelson as he got out of my car. I almost didn't finish the thought, because the sooner he was gone, the sooner I was free of that smell. Still, when he looked back, I asked, "Did you have a partner before me?"

"For a while. His name was Greg."

"Greg cleared his debt?"

"Not the way we hope to. G'night, Roland."

I think I said something inane in the way of a good night, but my thoughts were elsewhere. Had anyone ever survived a debt to the Rajah?

When I got home, Karen's Jetta was in her spot and all the lights were on with the shades drawn. I checked over my shoulder to see if I had been followed. I listened hard for sounds that didn't belong, but heard only the normal background stuff: neighbors, mosquitoes, and cars in the distance zipping down highway 280. Odds were decent that I had not brought a threat home with me.

Another car was pulling in down the back alley, but I recognized the red sedan as one that often parked out back. A couple of houses down, a middle-aged man wrestled with children and groceries while his wife — pregnant again — made her way up the stairs.

Nothing out of the ordinary. I pulled out my keys and let myself into my apartment.

"There he is!" Karen bounced off of the couch, turning off the television and dropping the remote. She wore her hair down, freshly washed and dried by the look of her curls, and her short, black silk robe with nothing underneath. She almost hummed with energy. My stomach clenched. Was she doing coke again?

She spun in circles on her way to me, too bouncy, like she used to be when she got high. I couldn't even enjoy the way her robe rose and exposed her with each turn. I wanted to cry. That morning desperation had been a warning sign and I'd ignored it. The pressure on our life was too much for her. She'd gone back to cocaine and it was all my fault.

"Tell me I'm brilliant," she said, wrapping both arms and one leg around me.

"You are," I choked out, wishing I'd been smart enough to tell her that this morning. That I hadn't left with her believing she had brought me bad luck. "You're brilliant and beautiful and far too good for a loser like me. I'm so sorry."

"What are you..." Then she caught me checking her pupils and her puzzlement dissolved in a huge smile and a peal of laughter. "I'm not high!" She showed me her un-dilated pupils, then tilted her head back so I could see that there were no white flakes or blood in or around her nostrils.

"Check my heart rate while you're at it," she purred, and placed my hand on her bare left breast. I could not resist giving it a squeeze before sliding my hand over to her breastbone.

"If you keep groping me, naughty boy, my heart rate won't prove my innocence."

I couldn't tell, but I admit she had me kind of flustered, and much of my blood was rushing away from the thinking part of my body.

"You swear you're clean?"

"Cross my heart," she said, exaggerating the gesture so her robe fell open completely.

"That's all I needed to hear."

I tried to tell Karen everything I felt for her in a single deep kiss, but the message must not have come through because she required lengthy elaboration on the kitchen floor, and then against the sink, and once more on the couch.

When I thought we might pause long enough for conversation, I said, "Although I have never doubted your brilliance, why did you ask me to confirm it today?"

"Because I was right." She raised herself up on one elbow, smiling as though she'd won simultaneous chess matches against Kasparov and Fischer. "Today was magic." She untangled herself and padded into the kitchen. This time I let myself enjoy the view. She got something out of the refrigerator, and I heard glass clink, and she came back into view carrying a bottle of champagne and two flutes in one hand, and a small slip of paper in a sandwich bag in the other.

"Behold," she said, holding up the slip of paper. "The winning lottery ticket. All five numbers, plus the special number, all one hundred percent right. As soon as we get this baby processed, lover, you and I will be about twenty-eight million dollars richer, after taxes."

I had not thought it was possible for her smile to get brighter. She proved me wrong as she bounced onto the couch and handed me the bottle to open.

"Money enough to square us with the Rajah and let us live like royalty somewhere where the weather is perfect year round and we don't have to do anything but play all day and fuck all night. We can be free now, Rollie."

She tilted her head, almost smug.

"Now tell me I'm brilliant."

I WOKE UP ALONE, MY LIMBS SNARLED IN THE SHEETS AND MY HEAD

pointing the wrong direction. Of course, since the pillows were on the floor, alongside the pile of blanket, it didn't matter which way I faced.

The clock on my nightstand insisted that it was ten a.m., not four a.m. like my body tried to tell me. My mouth was dry. My skin itched with old sweat. My hair knotted together in limp strands. I needed about two gallons of electrolytes plus an i.v. bag or two of saline. If Karen planned to celebrate like that every night now that we were rich, in six months I'd either be in the best shape of my life, or three months dead.

My legs and hips refused to assist, so extracting myself from those sheets took a good five minutes. When I finally managed to stand on my feet, albeit unsteadily, I stripped the bed. Those sheets needed washing worse than I did. They might just have to get thrown out. There are limits to what a modern washing machine can achieve, especially in our building.

I stumbled into the bathroom. It's spring rain scented freshness made me feel downright dingy. I took stock. The bruised side of my face had faded from purple to sickly yellow, but no one would think I had jaundice thanks to the darker spot on my left cheekbone. Most of my body felt sore and exhausted, but for the first time this week, I was pretty sure the ghul was no longer to blame.

Still, I popped a handful of ibuprofen and stepped into a shower hot enough to scald away the top layer of skin. I scrubbed and rinsed and repeated until I felt clean enough for public display, and stepped out of the shower like a new man.

As I brushed and flossed my teeth a thought occurred to me: I never actually checked the ticket. Much as I loved and trusted Karen, doubt crept in. She had no reason to trick me. Such a ruse would accomplish nothing beyond one night of fun – which she would know would have been enough to earn forgiveness for what was essentially a harmless joke.

But that sort of joking was not Karen's style. A joke like that would have been the sort of thing Karen would have mocked in Cosmo. "Want to have a hot night tonight? Tell your man you've won the lottery and let the sexy celebrations begin!"

I debated the possibilities in my head as I threw on my robe and followed the smell of coffee into the kitchen. I poured myself a cup, splashed the first swig into the sink, took a sip of warm comfort, and turned to see about my breakfast. I found a note on the fridge:

Rollie,

I'm meeting with a lawyer to try to claim our money anonymously. Start thinking about where you want to live out our life of decadence. I'm thinking Bermuda or Argentina, maybe Brazil or Greece. Oh, and decide what kind of new wardrobe you want. You need new clothes worse than I do.

Love always,

-K

Well that settled that. Last night was definitely no joke. We were rich. I let that sink in as I ate my toast, re-reading Karen's note with a stupid grin on my face. I didn't need my small-time occultist poker league after all. Karen won the lottery. We were rich. We could go anywhere. We could do anything. I just had to iron out one detail first.

I checked the clock. I still had almost two hours before Nelson expected to pick me up. Just enough time, if I left right away.

I had to go talk to the Rajah.

5

———

Nelson did not take my news well.

"You did *what*?"

Nelson screeched his Taurus to a halt in the middle of a suburban Mountain View neighborhood, throwing me forward against my seatbelt.

It was around twelve-thirty. Cloudless. The beige sedan behind us blared its horn as it weaved around. A couple of young guys in a nearby driveway looked up from under the hood of their old Mustang. They had sheets and oil-blackened parts all around them.

Nelson ignored the world outside his car as he turned to me in the passenger seat. "Tell me you're joking. Tell me you didn't."

"I did. I went to see the Rajah."

"Idiot," he grumbled as he found a parking space at the end of the block next to a row of apartments. He even stomped on the emergency brake pedal, though we were on level ground. He turned to face me again, cheeks flushed and jaw contorted in rage. I slipped one hand near the door handle, in case he went for his billy club. He said, "We see the Rajah when he sends for us. That's the arrangement."

I couldn't help making sure the young guys paid us no special attention, but they had turned back to what looked like rebuilding their carburetor.

"I had exceptional circumstances."

"Don't you get it? There are no 'exceptional circumstances.'" Nelson shook his head, nice and slow to make his point. "There are no exceptions. *We're not exceptions.* You and me, we're down on the battlefield and the Rajah has swords under our chins. We live exactly as long as he decides we live, and not one second longer."

"Fuck that." I saw Nelson clench his fists, so I pushed ahead. "Seriously, Nelson, fuck that. Look, I'm going to do my job and try to get that damned Djinn's Tear, not that we're having any luck so far. I'm not going to do anything that will endanger Karen, or you, or your family."

"You already have, you selfish prick. You put all our necks on the line for this one." He glowered at me and I swear his voice got deeper. "Even. My. Kids."

"I get it! I fucked up! And I'm sorry I put your kids in danger, and Tish, and Karen. But fuck the Rajah and his rules. Maybe you want to lick the Rajah's boots for a few more seconds of life. Me, I want to find a way to take that sword and cut his damned head off."

Nelson laughed, a sincere, slightly hysterical sound. "Try not to take me with you when you go down."

I got caught up in his laughter and shook my head helplessly. As his laughter petered out, Nelson seemed to deflate a little.

"So tell me, oh ye of high aspirations, what was so important that you had to see the Rajah?"

"I tried to buy my way clear of the debt. Karen won the lottery last night."

"No joke?"

"She's meeting with a lawyer right now."

"How'd the Rajah take it?"

"Laughed me out of his house. Even Jeeves gave me a condescending smile."

Nelson shook his head again with a puzzled, disbelieving grin. "I can't believe you thought money would help. As if the Rajah doesn't have enough."

Nelson started his car again, released the emergency brake, and pulled us back onto the street. He sighed. "Think this coven will know anything more than the last one?"

"If they do, you think they'll tell us?"

Nelson didn't bother to reply. We drove for several minutes in silence. At a stoplight he glanced at me out of the corner of his eye. "Congrats on the lottery. Hope you live to enjoy it."

In an undertone to himself I heard him add, "I hope we all do."

***

THE COVENS WERE MORE DEAD ENDS. SMALL TIMERS AND WANNABES covering their ignorance with arrogance. Nelson and I had figured this would be the case, but we had to make sure. Four-fifths of our legwork for every assignment came down to crossing off dead ends and false leads.

Besides. If a major player scooped us, that was one thing. But if a minor player did? That would be the sort of mistake that would have ended in the Rajah picking our guts out of his teeth.

After a wasted afternoon, Nelson and I grabbed dinner at Meat for Your Beast, an up-and-coming fast food restaurant. We even ate in the "dining room" to give us a break from the car. Meat for Your Beast had a circus theme, decorated inside with paintings of lions and tigers, elephants and monkeys and even a team of zebras ridden by a mob of meerkats. The workers all dressed like lion tamers, complete with hats on their heads and toy whips at their sides. No clown imagery in the restaurant though. Probably afraid of a trademark violation.

Big cushy seats, high wire music playing, and the best fast food I'd tasted in years on my tray, but still the place smelled like any other burger joint: fat, greasy and fried.

Time was I would not have splashed the first sip of soda onto the floor or into a drain. I used to reserve that for coffee, milk, and alcohol. But lately I felt that I needed all the help I could get, and I expanded my list of offered drinks to include everything except water. So I splashed a little bit of Dr. Destroyer into the soda machine's drain before I snapped the plastic lid into place.

Nelson and I didn't talk much during dinner. We tried to make noises about the state of the Forty-Niners, but the topic didn't hold us, so we lapsed into a tense silence. No clues, no hints, and way too much in the balance.

Worse, we knew that the world around us would be more dangerous when we walked back to his car. The sun had set. Twilight was upon us, and all the things that hid themselves from the light of day would be out prowling and hunting and generally menacing.

We had walked into the restaurant like two hungry men impatient for dinner. We walked out like two soldiers behind enemy lines. I held my refilled soda in one hand, but my other hovered inside my jacket near my Ka-Bar. Nelson didn't risk the soda and kept his hand on his knife hilt, also in his jacket.

We held a regular pace, side-by-side like any pair of co-workers heading back to the office. But we craned our necks every step to cover the area behind us in an alternating pattern that had taken us days to practice when we first started working together. As a result, we could walk casually while constantly sweeping the area for threats, eliminating our blind spots as thoroughly as humanly possible.

Full dark hit before we reached the car. The moment it did, fire lit up the cloudless night. I staggered back a step, but Nelson looked up so fast he fell over backwards. Letters of red flame stretched hundreds of feet long, high in the sky. They read: "HERE IS YOUR PROOF."

I dropped my soda.

"COME ON!" I DRAGGED NELSON TO HIS FEET AND INTO HIS CAR. I sprinted around to my side and leapt in. "Somewhere northwest of us," I said. Nelson fired up the engine and peeled out of the parking lot. He weaved us through traffic like a running back sniffing a touchdown. I turned on the radio and scrolled through his preprogrammed channels of music to find one of my local talk shows.

"...visible over the entire Bay Area and seen as far away as Santa Cruz to the southwest and Vallejo to the northeast," said Willy Wallace of Wallace Walks, the kind of show designed to teach you things you didn't know about your own cities and neighborhoods. Not good enough. I needed a real news station.

"No one has claimed responsibility for the display as yet," said a female announcer on 102.3 The Scoop, 'We Don't Just Report the News, We Dig for More.' "We've just heard that the FAA is grounding all air traffic out of San Francisco, Oakland, and San Jose, citing passenger safety. All incoming air traffic is being re-routed to Sacramento. This is going to throw a real monkey wrench into business travel, Bob. Want to give us a look at... Wait, this just in. Witnesses near Travis Air Force Base report that fighters are taking to the air. We've seen no official statement from the base as yet, but you listeners know us, we're going to push. In the meantime, Jim, any chance this is a fluke of the weather, like some kind of twisted ball lightning?"

"Well, Susan, if it is it's not like anything we've seen before. For one thing, those letters are still there, raising the question – what are they burning? You can't have fire without fuel, but fuel has mass and mass is affected by gravity. That fuel should be falling, and the fire coming with it. But those letters just hover there in the sky above Palo Alto..."

"It would be just our luck if the Tear were at Stanford," muttered Nelson, leaning on his horn and cutting off an old Buick tank. "No way anyone's going to believe I'm a student."

Ah, bad jokes. The mind's first line of defense against situations no sane person would seek out.

"He might not be keeping it at Stanford. He might have used it there is all." I blinked. "Of course, that would mean that he found a virgin on a college campus. Head for the engineering department."

"Geez, stereotype much?"

"You have a better idea?"

Nelson shrugged. The announcers were going on about the possible religious implications of the fiery skywriting. They had calls out to various churches, but were moving on to the likelihood that this was a terrorist action when Nelson said, "Turn it off."

"We need information."

"That's not information. We know what caused it, and it sure wasn't a terrorist cell." He shrugged. "Not the kind they mean, anyway."

"You never know when something important will slip out without their realizing it."

"Turn it off."

"What if there's a police investigation? We need to know who else is hunting."

"Turn. It. Off."

I gave the button an irritated stab. I confess I did not expect the newscasters to give us a detailed look at police movements on the ground in Palo Alto. I just found the prattle of talk shows soothing.

We pulled off 280, zipped down Page Mill Road, waited a seeming eternity at the left-turn light on Junipero Serra and dropped down to just under the speed limit as we cruised onto the Stanford campus. The letters still burned above us, bigger and brighter as we got close, but what did that mean? Had they really been centered above the Djinn's Tear at the time of the wish?

The letters might have looked brighter here, but the sky around them and the campus around us could have been any other night. Just as dark where the glow from street lights and buildings didn't reach.

The Stanford campus always looked like money to me. First there was the huge undeveloped hillside that belonged to the University. As we continued up Junipero Serra that was on our left and what looked like hoity-toity neighborhoods went past on our right. I thought those were faculty housing, but I didn't know why I thought so. Just one of those things you hear along the way somewhere and accept. There may not have been any actual school housing until we pulled onto Campus Drive.

The campus itself had green grass, colorful flowers, and lush trees year-round, something else I associated with wealth. The neighborhoods where I grew up saw grass die in the summer and trees denude themselves in the winter. All right, that latter part had nothing to do with money, but it meant those neighborhoods looked bleak while everything around me on this campus was downright verdant.

The buildings here had been designed by attentive architects with styles and curves beyond the simple box-shapes that dominated most houses, businesses and rental properties down where I lived.

Wait. I was rich now. Should I have been looking at these buildings and gardens with an eye toward planning? Maybe after we finished here I could talk Nelson into cruising through Atherton or Portola Valley, where I could see how real rich people lived and designed their houses.

Then again, maybe Karen should be along for that drive.

"Crap," spat Nelson.

I shook my head and looked at the world outside my thoughts again. Students. Everywhere. Dressed in sweats and jeans and robes and suits, it seemed that every student on campus had stopped eating and studying and having sex long enough to run outside and look up at the sky. And once out there, they all stayed, talking about it and what it meant, I suppose, or just staring as though the letters would change messages, or scroll and tell us all the prologue of the next Star Wars movie or something.

And the pedestrians weren't the worst part. Cars flooded the campus streets, and they were the minority compared to the bicycles. Ten-speeds and mountain bikes and custom jobs with long front forks and even the odd bicycle built for two. Bike riders mobbed the streets and the walkways and what seemed like every free square inch of space.

It was a wonder we could inch along as fast as we did.

"Think there's a game tonight?" I asked.

"Don't be cute."

"Seriously. The traffic might be unrelated."

"Look again."

I did, and realized that the bicyclists spent half their time looking up, as though they were riding around … looking for … the source. And in the cars, the drivers or passengers craned their heads, likely doing the same thing, whether they drove deeper into campus or tried to flee it.

"The Tear is gone," I said.

"How do you know?"

"Whoever has it escaped during the confusion. It's what I would have done."

That earned me a scoff. "You're some genius strategist now?"

I shrugged. "Either this guy's an idiot or he isn't. If he is, then he's in the middle of a huge crowd, caught literally red-handed over a dead virgin. If he isn't, he's gone. What do you think? Think an idiot could have held the Tear for hundreds of years without getting killed or robbed?"

"So what do we do, Sun Tzu?"

"We cruise the campus and look for cops. If this guy's so good he made the body disappear then we're wasting our time, and the Rajah's going to eat us before the week's over. If the body's there, then someone in all this crowd spotted it and called 911. By the time we get anywhere in this mess, cops will be on the scene."

"So what?"

"So maybe we can learn something about where the deed was done. Or maybe we can come back tomorrow and spot something the cops didn't know to look for. Or maybe this is all a waste of time and we should just slit our wrists now."

"Drama queen." Nelson chuckled, then brightened. "Guess what that means." He gave me an evil smile. "You get to drag yourself out of bed before noon tomorrow."

"How do you figure?"

"Think we're going to be the only ones who want a look at the scene? We need to get there early. I'm thinking six in the morning."

"Six in the morning is a rumor. It doesn't really exist."

"Don't worry. I'll bring water balloons to help you wake up, in case you aren't ready."

We went back and forth like this on the long, slow drive through the streets of Stanford. It gave us something to do, I suppose. For better or worse, Nelson did have to admit I was right. Before we were halfway across the campus we heard sirens to follow. As we passed Oval Park on Palm Drive, the main route onto campus, I spotted flashing red and blue lights.

Some hour or so after we first turned onto Campus Drive we reached the rubberneckers' Mecca. A police cordon had been set up to hold back the throngs along the periphery of the Rodin Garden, a part of the Cantor Arts Center's complete Rodin collection: all of his statues cast in bronze, wax, plaster, and terra cotta.

"We should have guessed," said Nelson. "Once we knew it was Stanford, we really should have known."

"He might have been more creative than that. For all we knew, he might have been a baseball fan and done the deed on the pitcher's mound at Sunken Diamond."

"No chance of that. This is a statement after all. What would have been better for a statement?"

"The Winchester Mystery House?"

"Roland," he began, then trailed off. Laughter shook him. "All right, maybe you have a point. But, you know, the Mystery Spot down in Santa Cruz would have worked too."

Nelson kept moving, pushing the traffic to let us back off campus so we could head for home. We entertained ourselves by coming up with other locations that might have been good for a statement. We started with more serious possibilities, like the Rosicrucian Egyptian Museum, but before long we got sillier and sillier. I think my favorite suggestion was either the buffalo run in Golden Gate Park or the Google campus in Mountain View.

Instead the current owner of the Djinn's Tear had chosen a more traditional symbolic location for his sacrifice: at the foot of Rodin's sculpture, *The Gates of Hell*.

6
———————

My alarm began its buzz at the obscene hour of five-thirty. I was wrapped in Karen and sheets following a second night of celebrating our good fortune. I tried to reach for the alarm, but had to struggle to get my arms free of the sheets. I didn't move fast enough. Karen lurched to sitting position, grabbed the baseball bat she kept beside the bed for protection, and smashed my alarm clock in a single swing.

I found myself grateful that she hadn't grabbed the .38 from her nightstand.

"No alarms before ten," she grumbled, eyes still closed and hair like a blow-dried cat. "It's a rule."

She collapsed back down into the bed and wrapped herself around me. I tried to detach myself, but she gripped tighter, grunting a sound that clearly indicated that I was not to even think about getting up.

"I have to," I said. "It's for work."

"Quit. Rich."

"Can't quit yet."

I swear she growled, but rolled over and slammed her head into her pillow. "Owe me."

I smiled and kissed her shoulder, which got me a somewhat mollified growl, then slumped my way into the bathroom and straight into the shower. Cold water shocked me awake, warming as I washed so I left the shower feeling human. The mirror told me that my bruise was fading, but I would be stuck with that yellow color on my left cheek for another day or two.

I popped some ibuprofen, to help with lingering soreness not eased by the shower, though my muscle complaints stemmed more from my exertions with Karen than yesterday's legwork. I choked down enough tap water to avoid dry swallowing the pills, and considered again getting a filter for the bathroom tap. Then again, once the lottery winnings came through, we could afford to move somewhere with drinkable water. What a luxury.

Nelson knocked as I finished my breakfast toast. I ran him through my ritual checks, and when I opened the door, he had a water balloon in his right hand, cocked and ready to throw.

"Throw it and I swear I will retaliate with napalm."

"Where would you get napalm?"

"Found a recipe online. Some of the things we deal with hate fire you know."

Nelson's face crinkled in skepticism. "How would you store it?"

"Tanks." I was bluffing, of course. Karen would never have allowed me to keep napalm in the apartment. She didn't even let me touch her .38, which was probably a smart decision. I wasn't the one who went shooting.

"You can find anything on the Internet if you look hard enough. The trick is making sure the seal is airtight. Almost took my hand off with the first batch."

Nelson continued to stare, something like pity shading into his eyes. Then he shook his head. "You don't have any napalm."

"Throw that balloon and find out."

"Oh." He snorted with a smile that said that he had forgotten he was threatening me with a water balloon. He carried it past me to the kitchen sink, held it up with an air of performance, and ritually slashed it open with his Ka-Bar. "Happy?"

"Much better. Now I'm ready to go see a murder scene."

"You don't think you look conspicuous?"

I was wearing my usual khakis, black this time, I admit, and my long-sleeved shirt happened to be black. All right, so maybe I thought a modicum of stealth was in order. Nelson wore his usual short-sleeved work shirt with a blah tie and boring pants. You can take the accountant out of the office...

"Yeah, you're going to blend on the Stanford campus."

"*I* look like nondescript authority. The professor of a class you aren't taking. *You* look like an unmasked ninja."

"So you get to take lead on any interviews. Let's go."

As I double-locked the door behind me, I turned to Nelson and said, "Wait, why aren't you waiting at Hollenbeck? This is my day to drive."

He grinned, and I flashed on the image of Nelson as a mischievous twelve-year-old, the kind of kid you didn't expect to cause trouble in class, but always did. I grimaced.

"Really? Just for the water balloon?"

"And I'm sure you really have napalm."

He was fishing for an answer. I could hear it in his tone, the hint of question behind the statement. My turn to grin, but it didn't go beyond my lips. Inside, I felt my guts tug downward. Just a couple of days ago I would have laughed and assured Nelson that I didn't have any napalm and painted a mental image for him of Karen's reaction if I did.

But now I had to worry about what Nelson would do after this assignment. Let him wonder if I had napalm ready to use.

WE FOUND A PLACE TO PARK ON CAMPUS AROUND SIX A.M., A GOOD hour or so before sunrise. Well, a solid hour anyway. I refused to see anything good about it. Nelson, on the other hand, was whistling a bouncy tune.

"Stop smiling, you smug bastard."

"Someone's crabby in the morning. Should've brought your own thermos."

Nelson was never without his sixty-four ounce thermos of coffee. I'd never seen anyone chug it down the way he did. He even had a refill deal with some of the local coffee shops. He knew not to offer me any though. Can't pour out the first sip of someone else's drink.

As we walked over from the car, we seemed to have the place to ourselves. I didn't see any joggers or drivers or even bicyclists. The closest people I could hear were the drivers on El Camino, their tires a distant sound only audible because of the pre-dawn hush. I smelled cut grass and evergreen trees.

Stanford displayed *The Gates of Hell* on a dais, set against a wall of large, burnt-beige blocks. Flanking it as though cowering before the gates stood two more of Rodin's eerily lifelike statues.

As if the scene weren't creepy enough, floodlights lit it from the ground in front, throwing disturbing shadows on the block wall. Completing the picture was the blood of some poor virgin, a dried puddle on the dais. I guess the crime-scene cleanup crew didn't take midnight calls.

Bravado-filled jokes aside now, I understood why the thief chose this location for his statement. Or her statement. Whatever. Either way, it made for a dramatic setting.

Surrounding the dais was crime-scene tape. No police on watch though, at least none that I could see.

"Think we need to pass the tape?" asked Nelson.

"I'd rather not." I glanced left and right. I didn't see anybody and I was starting to wonder if I should have. "We don't look like the most innocent pair."

"You could've changed—"

"The activity, doofus, not our outfits."

"Still, we might need some of her blood."

"His blood. His name was Eric Collingsworth." I shook my head at the amazed expression on Nelson's face. "Try listening to something other than music sometime. It's been all over the news."

I sighed. "And the blood won't help us. It's dry, for one thing, it's probably been stomped all over, for another, and worst of all the guy's dead. What do you want to do, call him back from the grave and ask who killed him?"

I swear to God, Nelson tilted his head like he was thinking about it.

"You sick fuck. You won't crack a single book, but you want a call up the spirit of a murder victim?"

"Just a thought. Hey!" He looked at me, eyes wide. "Can you *feel* anything here?"

I scowled at Nelson. He knew I wasn't psychic. I never had any special powers. Nothing like that. But one thing I learned from all my homework is that most people don't notice strange things because they don't want to. The supernatural is not just super, it's *unnatural* — maybe it came into existence in this same little world of ours that we humans did, but the supernatural was not a part of the natural order of things, the cycle of life and death and whatnot.

That was what drove me nuts about the wanna-be witches and pagans out there, all spewing modern equality garbage about the supernatural as though it applied. 'Oh, fae spirits are a part of nature, just like we are. We're all a part of one big organic wholeness, like a giant ball of light.'

What a load of crap. Fae spirits aren't born. They don't die of old age. Kill one and its body won't decay, it will fade away. I've seen it. In fact, 'kill' is the wrong word, because you can only kill something that's alive.

Supernatural things aren't alive. They aren't undead. They just *are*, until someone figures out what rules they follow and makes them stop existing. These things may sometimes look like us, but they are not us, and we suffer when we forget that. Like when I expected the Rajah to let me buy my way out of debt. A human would have set a price, even if one too high for me to pay, but the Rajah wasn't human.

Anyway, because the supernatural is ... wrong, because it doesn't really belong in this world the way we do, most humans refuse to see it. Their eyes will track right past it unless it presents an immediate threat. But make no mistake. We still notice. We get little chills, or creeps along the back of the neck, or an odd fluttering in the stomach, an itch in the palms. It varies from person to person, and sometimes creature to creature. Usually the signs are tiny, easily dismissed.

Unless you train yourself to notice them, like I did. I worked hard at it for months, until I got to the point that I could take a deep breath, relax, and feel if something unnatural was nearby. That was how I first found the faerie ring where we spoke to Ridges, and that was what Nelson was asking me to do now.

Nelson, of course, refused to develop this sense. He argued that noticing these things made them more likely to notice me. I found it irritating that he believed this, but still wanted to exploit my practice at every opportunity.

Not that I saw many options here. Visiting the scene of the crime sounded like a great idea last night, but Nelson was an ex-accountant and I was an ex-motel manager. What were the chances we'd find something that trained forensics officers missed?

I took a deep breath and puffed it out quickly. When I first started learning to do this, I would have closed my eyes and taken that breath as slowly as I could have. But then it occurred to me that I needed to be able to notice things in a hurry, and speed became a key part of my practice. By now I would notice anything active around me and recognize that it was supernatural without even trying, not that sensing it meant that I could automatically identify it. I would just know that it didn't belong.

But this was different. Something awful happened here, but the murder itself, sick as it was, was natural. What that murder wrought, though, was not, and that was what I strained to feel: the leftover wrongness of a powerful artifact and the magic it worked.

When I pushed myself to actively pay attention to those things my human nature begged me to ignore, my heart beat faster and the nerves in my skin tingled. Especially in my fingers, as though I had been awakened in the night by the sound of a thump from the next room. Everything in my being focused on sensing the next change I could pick up. A sound. A movement. Anything. Even my breathing stilled.

There. A whiff, then a foul reek assailed my nose and tongue, made my eyes water and run. I gagged and fell to my knees rocking back and forth with my face in my hands.

"I hate this," I said as I rocked, trying to control my rising nausea. "I hate it I hate it I hate it."

Suddenly Nelson was beside me, crowding me without meaning to. "What? What did you learn?"

"Oh, God, Nelson, this is..." My stomach rebelled and I threw up, barely getting my hands out of the way in time.

"What? Talk to me."

"Don't know what kind of amateur detective club you boys came from," said a deep, amused voice behind us, "but if you puke at the sight of dried blood you ought to leave this to the professionals."

I wiped sweat from my forehead with the back of my hand and unclean saliva from my mouth with my sleeve, then looked back over my shoulder to see two thuggish representatives of the campus police force.

All right, so they were young, fit and clean-cut. Just then they looked thuggish. Maybe it was the way the taller one had his hand on his night stick. I hoped he didn't draw it. Ours were in the car, and pulling the Ka-Bars from inside our jackets might not have gone over well.

"Sorry," said Nelson, in a smoother voice than I expected him to manage. He placed one hand on my shoulder, fatherly. "When we heard where it was, we thought it might have been a ritual killing. My friend and I are armchair occultists, and we thought maybe we could spot something the police wouldn't know to look for."

He gave my shoulder a pat. "Obviously we're a little over our heads here. We're sorry to trouble you. We'll be on our way."

"How about you show us some I.D. first."

"Sure, of course." Nelson pulled out a driver's license and I used my clean hand to fish one out of a pocket in my khakis as I stood. I kept my breaths shallow and through my lips, so the smell of what I'd just done didn't invite repetition.

The licenses were both fakes, of course. The Rajah knew that some things he asked of us were illegal, and though Nelson and I avoided breaking the law as much as we could, sometimes having top-notch falsified driver's licenses and credit cards came in handy.

The credit cards under false names actually worked and had two thousand dollar limits, but if we used them for anything other than an expense the Rajah considered legitimate, he docked our pay. The cheap bastard.

The campus cops took down our pseudo-information and let us go with a warning not to show our faces again.

By the time we were back at the car, the first hints of predawn began to glow in the east. I started hearing bird songs, and wondered what was the exact moment of dawn for magical purposes. Did the birds begin singing because the lingering magic of the Djinn's Tear had been chased away by the rising sun? Did that glow, that hint of sunlight I thought of as predawn, represent the true moment of dawn? The magical reset button that broke some kinds of spells?

I wished I'd been paying more attention. Maybe I could find out more about the phenomenon in one of my books.

Nelson grabbed me a bottle of water from his trunk and saved his questions until we were inside, giving me the chance to rinse and spit first, then down a few swallows.

I never offered the first sip of water. That would have been an insult.

"So?" asked Nelson.

I breathed fast and shallow. I needed to focus on what I had felt, but I didn't want to vomit again. "I've never felt anything so sick. Like moldy, rotten meat fermenting in my head, but still alive."

Bad image. I managed to shove the door open as I fell out and to my knees, throwing up bile now because I had nothing solid left to expunge. I shivered, sweaty, until the second wave hit and passed. Then I sat back, butt on my heels and knees on the ground, and rinsed and spat three times to clear the taste out.

"Thank you for getting out of the car in time." At least Nelson had the good grace to sound guilty. "Need another water?"

"Please." I sipped from the water bottle until the first one was empty. I smirked that Nelson handed me the second bottle from behind, but I couldn't blame him for not wanting to dirty his patent leather shoes.

I stripped off my jacket and tossed it onto the car seat. As I drank a little more water, I tugged the sweat-stuck parts of my shirt loose from my skin. After a minute or so, I felt good enough to stand, albeit with somewhat shaky knees. I leaned against the hood of the car. "Maybe we ought to review this out here, just in case."

Nelson pulled out a small, battered notebook and a half-length pen. He must have considered this information important. I'd only seen that notebook a few times in our six months of working together.

"You've already mentioned that the Djinn's Tear is the most foul thing you've ever ... sensed. What else did you learn?"

"First of all, I'm going to recognize that feeling if we find it again, and from some distance away I think. So we have that going for us." Gee, the thing could nauseate me at range. Yay. "It overwhelmed everything else, though, so I couldn't tell you how many were involved, or whether the Tear-holder had any supernatural nasties along as bodyguards. Couldn't have been easy to get poor Collingsworth up on that dais and cut out his heart, so we have to assume that our target has help."

"Can you tell which way they went? How far away it is?"

"No." I sighed. "I can tell that it's gone, because that smell was fading when I noticed it. The sunrise will probably wipe it out." I paused to let a wave of memory-induced nausea pass, then sipped a little more water. "Looks like you were right though. We had to get out here before sunup."

"Yeah."

There was that guilty tone again. Maybe he had begun to under-stand what price I paid to...

"Crap."

"What?" Nelson dropped his pen and drew his Ka-Bar. "Trouble?"

"Yes. No. I don't know." I wiped my face with my hands. "I just realized. This sensing thing. It's magic, isn't it?"

He put his knife away and bent to retrieve his pen. "Figured you knew."

"So simple I never thought about it." I smacked myself in the forehead. "Should have thought about the book I got it out of."

"You're not casting any spells." Nelson spoke with a firm tone, considering he had recently contemplated hiring someone to call us up a spirit. "What you're doing is tiny, and passive. Shouldn't draw any attention."

"Yeah, but it still has its price." I looked at the puddle of bile on the asphalt. "Worse, I did it without realizing what I was doing."

"Get rid of those damned books. We don't need them." When I started to scoff, Nelson swore and pushed ahead. "No, Roland, we don't. You just put yourself through hell and all you know is that you'll recognize this hell when you smell it again. As opposed to all the other hells."

"We're into something big this time, Nelson." I rubbed my neck and cheeks, wiped more sweat from my forehead. "We've only been talking to the small-timers so far because we don't want to admit it. You didn't lie to that cop though. We're in over our heads. Once we bump up against a major player, like Scratch, we'll need more than a little detection magic to survive."

"I'd rather you die than start casting spells." Nelson slapped the flat of his knife against his hand. "Roland, there are worse things than dying, and if you play with your books too much it won't matter if the Rajah lets you go — the rest of the supernatural world won't."

"Northwest," I said, standing up.

"You think there aren't nasties in Alaska?"

"No. I mean the Tear went northwest." Arguing with Nelson must have given me enough mental space for that little bit to process. I realized I caught a whiff of that foul smell leading away from campus to the northwest. "May not be there now, but that was the direction it was going when it left *The Gates of Hell*."

"Impressive work," said a strange voice that hissed like a straight razor on a leather strop. "No wonder Mr. Scratch wants to see you."

Nelson and I turned, Nelson combat-ready with his Ka-Bar, but me still holding a half-empty water bottle. I recognized the speaker from its reputation, and I would have bet that Nelson did too.

Facing us was Carnifex, the favored pet demon of Nicholas Scratch.

7

———

Dawn. The new day. Movies would have you believe that living to see the dawn meant that you were safe, that you had weathered the worst that the supernatural world could throw at you and the rest was smooth sailing. Experience had taught me that there was some truth to that notion, even beyond the dawn's effect on some kinds of magic, that whole legions of otherworldly nasties had to hide from the sun's rays.

But there in a little parking lot on the Stanford campus, in the pale light of the rising sun, Nelson and I looked upon a demon.

Carnifex stood five feet tall, with indigo scaled skin and the head of a hooded cobra. The demon looked so thin that it might have been able to use one long, skinny finger to pick a modern lock. Its eyes were vivid purple with snake-slitted pupils that glared hatred for all living things.

I slammed closed that part of my awareness that noticed the supernatural, but my skin still itched from this thing. Worse, my bladder wanted to let go. I squeezed everything south of my waistline to keep that from happening. I assured my body that the demon was not going to kill us. Its master wanted to talk. It just told us that. Mr. Scratch wanted to see us. My bladder considered that grounds for another attempt to let go, but my clenched muscles at least kept me from soiling myself.

I choked out, "Does your boss have an appointment?"

The words slipped out before thinking part of me realized what I was saying. I closed my eyes and resisted an urge to smash my head through the door of Nelson's Taurus. I snapped my eyes open a moment later, unwilling to forgo my sight with that thing around.

Apparently I opened my eyes just in time to see Nelson give me a look that told me he'd have been happy to help me put my head through his car door.

Carnifex crouched, a slight side-to-side sway of its head making the movement threatening. It rasped, "No, he does not have an appointment. But I have permission to hurt you in delightful ways if you refuse."

The demon's hood spread a few inches. "Please do refuse."

My body decided that if the bladder couldn't let go, the stomach would. I retched and lost a bottle-and-a-half of water onto the asphalt, Nelson's front right tire, and his shoes. A wave of gratitude passed through me that the bile pooled just short of Carnifex. I didn't want to find out what that thing would do to me for puking on its bare, scaly feet.

Without taking its eyes off me, Carnifex darted its forked, mottled purple tongue into the pool of vomit, and my stomach clenched a warning. Not that it had anything more to void. The tongue's twin tips slithered through the slime before returning into Carnifex's mouth.

"I know the taste of your insides now," said the demon. "Your stomach, your throat. Your sweet misery. Please, refuse my master so that I might taste more."

"We're coming!" said Nelson. He stood there sweating as bad as I was, with his Ka-Bar dangling forgotten at his side. "Sh ... shall we take my car?"

The demon's body stretched and warped into ribbon, twisting its way past me through the air and into Nelson's back seat. I flinched as it passed, and the tail end whipped across my face – not painfully, but wiping another taste of the vomit from my lips. By the time I turned, Carnifex sat in the back seat, staring at me as though I were a dessert topping.

Nelson glared at me and shook his shoes with each step as he moved around the driver's side.

I did not want to get into that car. Every instinct in my body told me to run, to avoid getting closer to that demon — although my instincts would have said the same about any demon — and to certainly not put my back to it.

I closed my eyes and thought of Karen, the way she smiled when she beat a higher-ranked chess player, the way she threw an extra wiggle into her walk when she knew I was watching, and most of all the look of amazed joy when I told her she was free of her pimp.

I got in the car.

ON THE DRIVE OVER, CARNIFEX ONLY SPOKE TO GIVE DIRECTIONS, AND even then said the bare minimum: "Right. Left. Right." It gave little warning about turns, but Nelson seemed to expect that. Still, even in silence I felt its menace — its eyes watching the back of my neck, its tongue tasting me in the air.

We took city streets from the Stanford campus, and it pleased me at least a little that we turned left onto El Camino Real, heading further up the Peninsula. That meant more distance between where Scratch lived and where I lived.

All around us flowed the self-involved driving of the morning rush hour. Cars going too slow, cars going too fast, none of the drivers thinking about where they were, what was around them. No doubt they all had their minds on the day ahead of them, projects they dreaded, meetings they hated, lunchtimes they loved, or whatever it was that normal people thought about as they went through their days.

Me, all I could think about was the demon in the backseat. The demon that wanted to taste my insides because I had mocked it within seconds of meeting it.

In a moment of weakness at a stoplight, I swore that I would never get flippant with a demon again. I regretted the thought immediately. Carnifex, the Rajah, Scratch, even Ridges – these things all counted on my fear. Maybe they even fed on it, I didn't know. But if I gave into that fear then they would win and I would become nothing but their toady, their sniveling servant. Nelson was halfway there, maybe more. I refused to let them break me.

The light changed and I said, "So, Carney, how long have you been working for Sir-Scratch-a-Lot?"

Nelson flinched as though I'd struck him, making the car lurch as it moved through the intersection. We were on a slow stretch of El Camino, passing through "downtown" Menlo Park. If we kept going, Atherton would be next, then Redwood City, then San Carlos.

Carnifex did not respond, unless its rasping hiss was a response. Maybe it was a laugh?

Soon we turned right into the neighborhoods somewhere around the Atheron-Menlo Park border, probably on the Atherton side because the quiet streets all had huge, lush trees and the houses had high stone walls, some covered in ivy and most of them gated with wrought iron.

Karen and I could have bought one of those houses now. But anyplace that had a neighbor like Nicholas Scratch held little appeal, however pretty the area might have been. Maybe the Bahamas. Karen looked good with a tan...

Nicholas Scratch lived on a dinky corner lot. Well, at least it looked dinky compared to the rest of the block. I guessed the lot size at a fifth of an acre. It was surrounded by two rings of sequoias, both inside and outside what I thought was a solid wall of gray stones. But as we pulled into the driveway at the sole gap in the sequoia rings, a section of the wall swung back like a gate revealing a single-story, dark blue house with black edging in the center of a well-trimmed lawn.

The house, like the lot, was smaller than I expected. Maybe two thousand square feet, not much more than double the area of the place I shared with Karen, but with plenty of windows. No blinds or curtains, but after a moment I realized I could not see inside the house through those windows.

I tried not to think about how that was accomplished — no reflections or colors, just transparent windows that failed to display what lay beyond them. I shook my head and my shoulders tried to twitch up.

Ahead of us down the driveway was a separate single-car garage, also dark blue with black trim and a roller door that looked like mahogany.

We passed through the stone gate and all my body hairs stood at attention, as though from static electricity that didn't reach my scalp. Magic, strong enough that I didn't have to relax to notice it. A warding spell most likely. That would explain why Scratch's was the only house on the block to not have the warning sign from some security firm planted in plain sight.

I glanced back and saw sigils etched into the stonework of the wall. It was a testimony to my studies that I recognized two of them: suppression spells that made anyone nearby treat all odd sights, sounds or smells as normal and not worth noticing. A soft whistle escaped my lips.

Carnifex tilted its head as it regarded me. It made that rasping sound again, but the quality had changed. It sounded almost ... contemplative.

Nelson parked in front of the garage. I opened my door first, and Carnifex — once more in its ribbon shape — twisted past me through the air and vanished toward the house. I started to get out of the car, but Nelson stopped me with a hand on my shoulder. I looked back and found myself staring into the business end of his billy club. I looked past it and into Nelson's glare.

My Ka-Bar was inches from my hand, but the grip Nelson had on his club meant he could break my nose or ruin one of my eyes before I could draw my knife.

He knew that. And he knew that I knew it.

Adrenaline jagged through me, told me the door was open. Told me I could dive backwards out of range and make this a fight.

But I didn't want to fight. Not here. Not now.

"I thought we weren't going to be at each other's throats," I said.

"I thought you were going to rein in that tongue of yours."

"If we let them cow us, they win."

"If they kill us, this has all been for nothing."

We stared at each other. I knew Nelson was waiting for an apology or a promise. But Nelson had surrendered to his fear. "How long shall we keep Scratch waiting? I'm sure he's a patient man."

Nelson swore and pulled his billy club away, slamming it into the pocket in the driver's side door. I blinked, sighed, and left my billy club in the car too. He had a point. If we had to fight our way out, we were not going to make it.

I did keep my Ka-Bar though, because as Machiavelli wrote, "Among other evils which being unarmed brings you, it causes you to be despised." I had started reading the likes of Machiavelli and Sun Tzu around the same time as I started on the occult texts. Figured they might help me understand these creatures that are all about power and control.

Nelson got out of the car, and I think he slammed his door even louder than I did. As we approached the front door — mahogany like its garage cousin — it swung open for us, held by a young blonde who looked like the kind of eighteen-year-old sought by men's magazines for centerfolds. Except she was missing the innocent vibe. This blonde had a hard, used look in her eye that spoke of a rough life. Her dress was short, tight, and aggressively red. Her feet were bare.

"Mr. McReedy, Mr. Milner, welcome," she said in a whisky-soaked contralto. "Mr. Scratch instructs me that you are to wait in the sitting room. If you will follow me."

"Should we take off our shoes?" That earned me an approving look from Nelson. I half-expected him to pat me on the head and offer me a cookie.

"Take off anything you like," said the blonde with a sinful smile.

Nelson took off his shoes. I kept mine on.

By the light of an early October morning, with birds singing and lawn mowers mowing in the background, Nelson and I entered the Atherton home of the most powerful warlock in the greater Bay Area: Nicholas Scratch.

I stepped past the front doorway through spells strong enough that I shivered for the first three steps, but my partner didn't even flinch. Of course, that might have been because he was watching the backside of our blond greeter as she led, but that was his business.

I was more interested in the interior of the house. I'd been expecting something out of a horror movie: black candles, creepy grandfather clocks, dusty smells and creaking boards. What I actually saw was the kind of exaggerated opulence that the Rajah might have appreciated. The indigo wall-to-wall carpet was so soft and plush that my shoes sank into it. The walls were cerulean, with subtle patterns swirling in the paint that might have served occult purposes. A teak wardrobe stood in one corner, eight feet tall — which left it a good two feet shy of the ceiling — and six feet wide. The walls displayed orgy scenes from different eras, all original paintings, and each with its own spotlight.

A second glance showed that not all the orgy participants were human.

On our right was an open doorway, and despite the extensive natural light from the windows, I could not see into the room beyond. It didn't matter. Our guide led us through a door on the left-hand wall.

When she opened the door, I got only the barest glimpse of the room ahead of us before agony jabbed through my temples. I doubled forward, clutching my head.

"Are you all right?" I heard the girl ask, a sharp sound underlying her voice that hadn't been there before.

I pressed my palms to my temples. Rubbing seemed to help. Long seconds passed, then I could unclench my jaw. I opened my eyes and saw and Nelson had drawn his Ka-Bar but not yet threatened the blonde, who stood near me as though to help, but without touching.

More time. Me forcing air into my lungs until the pain subsided. I stretched myself upright.

Nelson's eyes narrowed and he flicked his chin toward the front door, in case I'd lost my bearings, but he knew better than to ask any questions and admit his own ignorance in a dangerous place.

Through the now-open door ahead of me lay the source of my pain. The room was huge, easily forty feet on a side. But there should not have been forty feet between that doorway and the outer wall. My mind had held a rough idea of the boundaries of the house as I entered, and at least half of this room should have been on the lawn. But it wasn't. And my body had rebelled at the inconsistency.

I kept rubbing my temples as I looked around. The room was all soft blue and green splendor, with huge bay windows admitting plenty of sunlight and a tan, backless, circular couch surrounding a round, white oak table. The cushions stretched five feet across all around the circle, except for two three-foot breaks that allowed foot traffic to and from the table in the center.

The couch alone was too big to fit inside where the walls should have been, and its pieces were too wide to fit through either doorway leading into the room. My temples pounded again and I kept rubbing, but my stomach threatened to ditch its scant supply of water.

"Are. You. All. Right?" The blonde, still close beside me, sounded serious now. Underneath her supposed concern lay undercurrent of fingernails on a chalkboard. That was new.

I looked at her and saw an outline of tiny horns on her forehead, a hint of bat wings shimmering in the air behind her.

I licked my bone-dry lips and said with a slight croak, "You're good. I almost didn't see you for what you are."

Nelson finally pointed his Ka-Bar at our greeter. Better late than never, I supposed. But then, I was just glad to know we were both armed, even if my knife was still sheathed.

The blonde smiled, and the horns and wings that weren't quite there faded as though they never had been. Worse, sex seemed to ooze out from her.

The pounding in my head abated, but I thumped my forehead before it vanished entirely. Better to keep the pain than let her get to me like she did Nelson. Even now my partner's knife hand dangled useless by his side and his jaw grew slack with wonder.

"Enough," said a man's voice. The word was soft, but it broke the spell. The extra sex-boost faded from the air, and Nelson regained control of his faculties.

My headache came raging back, but under the circumstances I considered that a good thing.

I turned to see the speaker. Nicholas Scratch stood about six-and-a-half feet tall and lean with muscle. His weathered face might have made me guess his age in the mid-forties, but his reputation claimed that he had been born in the early eighteenth century. The bowl cut of his short brown hair, flecked with gray, worked with his simple, comfortable dark brown shirt and pants to give him a monkish look.

His eyes ruined the effect: one was hazel, but the other dead, cloudy. The hazel eye showed life and movement, but the dead eye stared always ahead, unblinking.

Stories conflicted about that eye. Some said it was a gift from a demon, and that it saw the future. Some said it was his devil's mark — the sign of his pact with evil — and that his familiars fed from it. Still others suggested that it was a demon itself, bound into his body to make him immortal.

I just knew it creeped me out.

The blonde — succubus? — draped herself around Scratch like a cloak, rubbing muscles and kissing his neck, but his good eye stared at me as though reading answers in my entrails.

A moment later he nodded and said something in his clear tenor voice that sounded like, "Zix rachna."

The pain in my head eased, and my nausea faded, but what made me feel better was that I didn't relax. If anything, I felt edgier, which meant that whatever Scratch had done, he had not tried to control me.

"Better?"

"Yes."

My thank-you died before it reached my lips, and by Scratch's smirk he heard it die. He waved one hand toward the couch, to all appearances oblivious to the ministrations of his attentive blond demon.

"Please sit. I can have food brought if you are hungry."

Nelson trudged ahead of me to sit. I joined him, turning my back for no more than a second, but when I faced Scratch again the blonde entered the room carrying a silver tray laden with sardines, three cut-glass bottles of brown liquor, three tumblers, and a small dish of ice with tongs.

My stomach clenched and my balls tightened, trying to reassure me that they were still there despite the wave of fear that coursed through me.

A moment ago that demon had clung to its master. I hadn't even seen it leave the room and it could not have been gone for longer than an instant.

I didn't know about Nelson, but I was getting righteously sick of feeling outclassed everywhere I went.

"Cognac, brandy, bourbon," said Scratch pointing to the bottles in turn, then pouring himself a generous helping of cognac. The blonde returned to caressing and massaging him.

I spoke before Nelson could move, my voice loud over the rumble of my unhappy stomach. "No, thank you."

Nelson glared at me. I had just refused hospitality, which would have ensured our leaving there alive. And since I refused he couldn't accept without looking weak, which was never a good idea around monsters.

Well, Nelson could get as mad as he wanted. There was no way I was going to drink strong alcohol on an empty stomach in the house of a warlock. Hospitality rules would not have prevented me from making a drunken error or striking a bargain, and might have obliged me to accept the attentions of Scratch's sex demon, if he offered.

Scratch did not look pleased or displeased at my refusal. He merely lounged on the massive cushions, leaning on one side. Nelson and I sat ramrod straight by comparison, across the huge white oak table from him.

"So." Scratch paused for a sip of cognac, then swirled his glass. "Carnifex tells me that the Rajah has you chasing the Djinn's Tear."

Nelson looked down. I held my expression as blank as possible. Scratch smiled, a more jovial look than I expected.

"He also tells me that you" — the dead eye never wavered but I would have sworn I felt it stare at me — "sensed the direction it had gone."

"Just a detection spell." I flicked my hand to indicate the layers of magic around us. "Nothing you couldn't have done, I'm sure."

"Detection spell?" Scratch laughed, a warmer sound than it should have been. "Fool, magic cannot track the Djinn's Tear or I would have it already. Did you never know that you had the Sight?"

"I don't. I just taught myself to notice things, the things people usually miss. Like that this room is wrong."

"Don't think about that," Scratch said, his tone cracking like a door slammed too hard. "I have eased your discomfort. Do not require me do more."

"Sorry." I guess it said something about my attitude that my apology made Nelson look at me, and this time I was sure he would pull out a cookie.

Scratch accepted the apology with a nod and said, "Perhaps you have the Sight, and perhaps you do not. But if you can track the Djinn's Tear then you are uniquely qualified to find it." He tipped his glass to us. "And that is just what the two of you will do for me. You will find the Djinn's Tear and bring it to me."

"We're not for hire."

"I never said you were."

"We work for the Rajah. If that's a problem for you, bring it up with him."

"Actually, that's a problem for you." Scratch sat up and the blonde smiled over his shoulder. "Because if you don't bring me the Djinn's Tear, your pretty Karen will be going to hell."

"You're bluffing," I said.

Scratch gave me a lazy smile. His dead eye looked through me. His blond demon snuggled in behind him on that huge white couch.

He raised the hand not occupied with his cognac, fingers pinched as though holding something. Then a yellowed piece of parchment appeared, dangling from those fingers. The page was covered the slanted loops of archaic handwriting.

Except at the bottom, where a different hand, a modern hand, had written a name above the line in something like red ink. Something I suspected was not ink at all.

"Recognize the signature on the bottom line?" asked Scratch. "Bring me the Djinn's Tear and not only will I leave you two gentlemen in peace, I'll tear up the contract. I'll even let your dear Karen keep the money."

Money?

I bolted.

I leapt to my shaky legs and ran for the front door as fast as I could manage. I could hear Nelson huffing and puffing two or three steps behind me as we crossed Scratch's entryway with its obscene paintings.

My shoes still sank into that damned plush carpeting with every step. Fear spurred me forward, made me hyperventilate. Fear for Karen, and fear that Scratch would stop me, that he was not yet done with us.

But Scratch let us go. In fact, from the contralto screams behind us, he had moved on to banging his sex demon.

I ripped open the front door and propelled myself across the lawn.

"Wait, damn it!" yelled Nelson. "My shoes!"

But all I could think about was Karen. I had to get to Karen.

I was almost ready to break a window on Nelson's Taurus and hot wire it when he unlocked it. Then we were both strapped in and moving.

To his credit, Nelson drove like a speed freak the whole way through light late-morning traffic, never once asking a question or sniping a remark. He just kept up a running tally in a soothing voice, telling me how much closer we were getting.

I could hardly hear him through my stress.

I jumped out of his car while it was still moving, not even pausing to check if I'd been followed. I just barreled my front door open and cried out, "What did you do?"

My head whipped around, but it took my eyes a moment to spot a surprised Karen at the kitchen table, fingers on the keyboard of her old laptop.

I left the door standing open behind me in my haste to get to her.

"Karen, what did you do?"

"I haven't bought anything yet." She held up her hands as though guilty. "I've just been bookmarking things for after the payment clears and the money is ours. In fact, I have another appointment with Roderick — he's the attorney who's helping us claim the money anonymously — and he's hooking us up with an investment broker over at—"

"Karen!" I felt tears leak down my face as she met my eyes. I fell down to my knees, panting for breath.

Karen hurried from her chair to crouch down and take my head in her hands. Soft concern filled her face, knitted her brow.

"How…" My voice broke and I had to start again. "How did you know we would win the lottery?"

She looked away. Her lips twitched as though with embarrassment. "It's no big deal." She stoked my cheek again, wiping away the tears that continued falling.

"A few weeks ago this old man had two big breakfasts, drank about six cups of coffee, flirted as though he might have a chance, and then stiffed me on the tip. Made a lot of promises about it though. Said that money was tight then, but he'd just made a deal that would make him rich. Knew a guy called—"

"Mr. Scratch."

"Yes, how did you know?" She paused to stroke my head before continuing, "Anyway, the guy swore that when Mr. Scratch came through he'd make it up to me. But everyone gets stiffed on a tip sometimes. So I gave the deadbeat lech a little stank eye and forgot all about it.

"But a couple of days ago the old man came in again, this time in a fancy suit with a gorgeous redhead on his arm. He ordered a single cup of coffee. He didn't even stay to drink it, but he tipped me a hundred dollars and gave me Scratch's phone number, in case I 'ever wanted to ditch that dive.'

"He drove away in a Ferrari. An honest-to-God Ferrari." Karen shook her head in wonder.

"So you called that number." My heart tried to sink down through my torso, but my stomach was way ahead of it. "And Mr. Scratch offered you a deal."

"Old fashioned folktale shit. 'Sign this piece of paper in blood, granting me your soul in exchange for worldly wealth for all your days.' Like I believe in souls."

"But you signed the paper."

"Hell yes! Souls aren't real, but money is! How could it hurt? Even if it didn't work, I wasn't out anything."

She smiled. "But it did work! We won! And the promise is money 'for all of my days.' If something happens to our money, we'll get more."

Then she noticed my reaction.

"Honey, why are you crying?" She cradled me in her lap as I sobbed, hushing me and stroking my face. "Rollie, with the lives we've lived, even if we have souls they aren't worth toilet paper. At least mine isn't. And if you have one, well, it's still safe."

I hated the tone that came into her voice then, as though she blamed herself for everything bad that had ever happened to both of us. Maybe Karen was no saint, but I had earned plenty of my own problems.

And I had made my own deal with the devil. A deal that hadn't even gotten me material wealth.

Worse, Karen's arrangement was all my fault. I had thought I was keeping her safe by not telling her the truth about the Rajah, by not telling her what Nelson and I did to pay off our debts, by trying to hide her from a world full of unnatural creatures that would sooner eat her than look at her.

"I'm so sorry, Karen." My tears began to flow again. "This is all my fault. I should have told you everything from the beginning. You see—"

"Touching," rasped the voice of Carnifex from the doorway. "But you have a job to do. Now."

<hr>

KAREN SCREAMED AND BEGAN SCRABBLING BACKWARD INTO THE kitchen.

I reached out with my foot to slam the door, but Carnifex said, "Close that door and I will kill your partner."

"You need us to find the Djinn's Tear." I rolled to my feet, positioning myself between the demon and Karen.

"You are the one who can follow the Djinn's Tear. It is your beloved to whose soul my master holds title. Mr. Scratch does not need your partner."

"Then give me a moment or I will kill you." I narrowed my eyes, glaring hatred with as much intensity as I could muster. And I had a lot of hate for this this damned thing and the warlock it represented.

"And after I finish with you, your master."

Carnifex rasped that hissing sound again, the one that might have been a laugh. It turned its back and I slammed the door, kicking myself inside for being so sloppy as to leave it open in the first place.

I turned to see Karen cowering, huddled in a ball on the linoleum against the cabinets under the sink. My turn to crouch beside her, wiping tears from her cheeks and hushing.

When she recovered enough to meet my eyes, I hated the fear I saw there, but thanked any gods that might have been merciful enough to look in on a bastard like me that her fear was *for* me, not *of* me.

"Rollie..."

"That was a demon. It works for Mr. Scratch."

"Then that paper..."

"Yes, you really sold your soul." I brushed a stray lock of hair behind her ear. "But I'm going to get it back. Scratch promised to tear up the contract if I get him something, and you even get to keep the worldly riches."

"Fuck that." She clutched my arm. "Let's run, Rollie. Right now. Grab the ticket and go, get as far away as we can."

"He owns your soul. He can find us anywhere we run."

"And," rasped a voice from behind me, "his demons have license to enter anyplace you call yours. Your time is up, Mr. McReedy. Leave with me now or face the consequences."

I kept my back to the demon. "There's more, honey." I sighed. "More than I have time to tell you now, but I swear to you. I'll tell you everything tonight."

"Now, Mr. McReedy."

I kissed Karen softly on the lips, stood, and went out to hunt for an ancient relic, alongside a man who wanted to kill me and a demon who wanted to eat me.

8

Outside my apartment the world looked disturbingly normal. Pale blue midday sky, a bright sun that others would find cheerful, a few clouds, cars looking for parking spots. I could even hear my neighbors arguing about laundry. Not Norman Rockwell normal, but close enough.

Safe bet that not one of these people ever struck a deal with a monster.

The moment my front door was closed and double-locked behind me, I whirled on the serpentine demon.

"Listen up, Carney. You never come near Karen again. Ever. You stay the hell out of our home, stay away from her work — just keep your damned distance from her."

The demon's hood expanded to full indigo width and its purple eyes narrowed, their slitted pupils expanding. Carnifex said, "Or what?"

"Or I'll tell your boss to fuck himself. He needs me." I slowly tapped my chest with one finger. "I'm the one who can find this thing. He needs me, and he needs Nelson. The two of us have been in the acquisitions business for some months now. Together we're good enough to find the Djinn's Tear and snag it."

I leaned in as close to those purple eyes as I dared. Nice and quiet I said, "But if you come near Karen one more time..."

"Please do refuse. Then my master will claim the girl's soul and I get to eat you."

The demon's head moved even closer without the rest of the body budging an inch. Those slitted pupils so close that my lashes might brush them if I blinked. I could smell blood, and bile, and other people's fear.

My heart raced. Heat under my collar. Sweat on my brow. But I would not look away.

Finally Carnifex said, "And I would so enjoy eating you."

"Get in line." I spat on the ground to give myself an excuse to lean back, to look somewhere other than those evil eyes. I knew I would only get one chance at this bluff and I couldn't afford to blow it. "That won't get your master his toy, now will it?"

By the time I looked back up, the demon's eyes had narrowed further, and begun to glow just on the edge of ultraviolet.

"That's what I thought. So you stay the hell away from Karen while Nelson and I do our job. And afterward Scratch promised we'd be in the clear, so you'll have to stay away then too."

I wondered what the chances were that Scratch could be counted on to keep his word. It was part of a deal, right? He had to uphold it, right?

"In fact, why don't you leave Nelson and me alone to work? We don't need you breathing down our necks."

"I am here to watch and remind. This is not your option."

"So watch from a distance. We'll call you to check in twice a day while we're searching, and, of course, when we find it."

"Three times a day."

"Done."

"Watch for me over your shoulder, Roland Adar McReedy. I will never be far away."

With that, Carnifex twisted into a ribbon and vanished around a corner.

I took a moment to breathe and let my shoulders ease. I rubbed sweat out of my eyes. I'd done it. I'd gotten us a little breathing room from Scratch's demon.

A car horn triple-honked, and I recognized the tone and pattern: Nelson and his Taurus. He must have stayed nearby, known our work day wasn't done.

I wanted to ignore him, go back inside and comfort Karen. Even just hold her one more time. But I had monsters to appease.

Before I headed out to where Nelson waited, though, I glanced over my shoulder after the angry demon that knew my full name.

If Carnifex was nearby, I couldn't see it. But that didn't make me feel any better.

I SLIPPED INTO THE PASSENGER SEAT OF NELSON'S TAURUS AND HE started to drive before I even had the seat belt fastened. "Don't you even want to know what—"

"Shh," he said.

We cruised away from my apartment and onto Stevens Creek Boulevard, which meant we could have been going anywhere. I tried to think of the nearest Meat for Your Beast location, in case he was after lunch, but came up blank.

Nelson looked serious. His brow was low and tight. He had both hands on the steering wheel. He even leaned slightly forward in his seat, instead of easing back the way he usually did.

"At least tell me where—"

"Shut up, damn it." Nelson pulled us onto 280 North, matching the lunchtime traffic speed of seventy-five. "No talking until we get there."

I started to ask where, but he shushed me again before I got the words out. Nelson had something in mind, but I couldn't tell what, even when he hopped onto 85 toward 101.

When we got off on El Camino toward Mountain View I gave him a suspicious glance, but he kept his eyes on the road. Busier around here. Lots of restaurants dealing with the lunch crowds. Even the fast food joints got backed up, and not just the top tier places.

By the time Nelson turned onto Castro Street I knew where we were going: New Dawn Books. Snigdha's. I sighed to let him know I'd figured it out, but even that earned me another shushing.

So I fidgeted, and drummed my fingers, and stared out the window at the lunchtime pedestrians, and worried about how poor Karen was going to handle this afternoon.

All right. I'll admit that last thought dominated my mind.

It occurred to me that I might get home to find that she had left me. I couldn't blame her. This was all my fault. All of it. She hadn't even wanted to stop hooking. She did it for me. I dragged her into this supernatural mess, and now her soul was in the hands of that foul diabolist.

I slammed my fist into my thigh. I needed focus. Even if Karen left me I still needed to get her soul back. She deserved that much before the monsters ate me.

"Wake up," said Nelson, pulling into a spot in a parking lot I knew all too well, right next to that Qi Gung place. "We're here."

As the wave of Nag Champa welcomed us inside New Dawn books, I called a greeting to Therese behind the counter. I started to tell her that wearing her dreads bound up atop her head like that made her look like she was wearing a bowl of blond snakes as a hat.

Impatient, Nelson never gave me a chance to finish. I got as far as "Hi, Therese. You know—" before he pushed me on through the store, and into the hall where the meeting rooms were, and finally into the smallest one, on the right just past the bathrooms.

The décor represented everything I hated in New Age garbage. The basic decorating scheme had been cribbed from some 70s self-help movement: soothing green walls, pale beige carpeting, bean bag chairs and throw pillows in primary colors. Bad enough, but it was the charts and posters that really got me. Astrology and palmistry and Kabbalah and runes and Chinese Zodiac and chi meridians all next to each other as though they somehow belonged together.

Oh, and there was a big white board that tempted me to write "THINK FOR YOURSELF" in big block letters.

Nelson stepped into the room with me. He shut the door behind us and leaned back against it.

I folded my arms, starting to feel almost as angry as he looked.

"All right, Nelson. What the hell is so important that you don't have two seconds for common courtesy?"

He sighed out so much tension I thought he would collapse. His knees did buckle for a moment, but he recovered without falling.

I felt my building anger totter but I held onto it. In a gruff voice, I asked, "You all right?"

"No time for that." He pushed himself back against the door until he was standing straighter, but he stayed leaning. "Snigdha promised me a protected place for a private chat."

"A private chat that only she can hear?"

"Who cares? As long as Scratch and the Rajah can't hear us." Nelson puffed out another breath. "Scratch doesn't change anything. The Rajah gets the Tear."

He saw my jaw open to respond and yelled over me. "It doesn't matter! Karen's a big girl and she made a deal. That's on her. You and me, we made deals with the Rajah and with each other. Those are on us. Scratch can't bully us out of them."

"You selfish bastard. Carnifex almost killed you this morning, just to prove a point. That's how little you matter to Scratch."

"Scratch wouldn't dare cross the Rajah like that. The Rajah's too tough."

That got a laugh out of me, but there was no humor in it. "Scratch might have to offer reparations, but you'd still be dead. And you would be. Except *I* talked the demon out of murdering you."

"So we go to the Rajah right now and get Scratch off our backs."

"If you believed that would work we'd be at the Rajah's right now and not at Snigdha's."

We stared at each other. The look in his eye made my fingers itch for my Ka-Bar.

I sighed, and something deflated inside me. What was happening to me? I never used to be a violent man. Now I was ready to kill the only real friend I had, outside of Karen.

"Look," I said. "Until we find the Djinn's Tear, this is all academic."

"Yeah," Nelson said with a bitter laugh. "Maybe we'll get killed trying to swipe it, and none of this will matter."

"No more of that," I said in tone so sharp it shocked both of us. "We're coming out of this alive, *and* we're getting Karen back her soul."

My turn to interrupt Nelson before he could reply. "I don't know how yet, but I know the first thing we have to do is find that artifact. Until then we're just spinning our wheels."

"All right, but I want to talk to the Rajah first." Nelson shrugged. "He considers us his. Maybe he'll take offense at Scratch trying to steal his toys."

Nelson and I stared at each other, the way I imagined soldiers staring at each other while hiding from mortar fire in a foxhole.

"You really believe the Rajah will let us go one day?" I asked. "That he'll actually let us work off our debt?"

Nelson smirked, then snorted, then started laughing.

"Yeah, I guess it was a stupid question."

"No," said Nelson, gasping for air. "He will."

More gasping, but I gave him time to recover. I just had to hear his logic. Finally he recovered himself enough to speak.

"After the Rajah ate Greg, my last partner, I started to doubt. I just kept my head down and worked harder so I didn't give him an excuse, you know? But you showed me something."

Nelson waved his hands wide. "All these monsters, they have different rules than we humans do. And their rules are sacrosanct. They can't break them even if they want to."

I saw where he was going. "So you think that, whatever the Rajah is, if he says we have a debt to work off, then one day—"

"We'll be clear! Like in a fairy tale."

Nelson barely had any hope left to cling to. I could see that in his eyes. He knew I was the one who studied. I was the one who could tell whether or not his pet theory would work.

Except that I didn't know what the Rajah was, so the best I could do was guess. I did know one thing though.

"You realize in those fairy tales, the tasks were either impossible or took longer than a human lifetime to complete. Unless the hero got supernatural help."

"And we have Snigdha on our side." He said it like he had no doubt.

Me, I had doubts.

"Is she though?"

"She is."

I rubbed my eyes. Snigdha could probably hear every word I said, but I still had to say it.

"Look. I don't know what happened between you and her, why you trust her so much. And I'll grant you that she's helped us out now and again." I caught his eye and held it. "But, Nelson, she's still one of the monsters. Never forget that."

"Enough about her." Nelson loosened his tie. "What do you think about the Rajah? What are our chances?"

I scratched the back of my neck and thought about it some more.

"Since we don't know what the Rajah is, we don't know what rules he follows. He might just be playing a game with us." I flung my arms out in a helpless shrug. "Until we know that we don't know anything. But when we do, we'll know how to kill him.

"Let's not get ahead of ourselves," said Nelson gently waving a calming hand. "Whatever he is, if we do what he wants he won't eat us today. And if we bring him the Djinn's Tear he won't give the people we love back to the *human* monsters."

Nelson straightened his tie. "Now let's go see if the Rajah'll get Scratch to leave us alone."

THE RAJAH LAUGHED US OUT OF HIS HOUSE.

Even Jeeves shook his head as though we should have known better.

9

"Well, that was productive."

"Shut up," said Nelson, scrupulously adhering to traffic laws as he drove us down through the hills into Los Altos proper. Good thing, too. We had passed at least one speed trap already, and Nelson's car was the cheapest one around us by about ten thousand dollars. A sure target.

"It's a bonding thing," I said in a fake cheery voice. "Now we've both been laughed out of the Rajah's."

"I *will* kill you."

"I'm sure that will give you twenty seconds of great pleasure before Carnifex slaughters you like a Thanksgiving turkey."

Nelson hesitated at a stop sign and rubbed the bridge of his nose. A pack of bicyclists went past in their skintight neon outfits, without bothering to stop. Nelson used them as an excuse to linger. That earned him a blast of the horn from the Lexus behind us, but the cars crossing didn't seem to mind taking our turn.

"So now what?" he said. "We didn't learn anything at *The Gates of Hell*, at least nothing that tells us where to find the prize."

"Crap. What if it's been sold?"

"It hasn't."

Mr. Lexus hit his horn again.

Nelson smiled at my raised eyebrows and said, "One sec."

He crossed the intersection and pulled over to the curb next to a corner shopping center. The kind with an ice cream shop and a fancy local grocery store. Not a supermarket. An actual grocery store.

"I asked Snigdha when I set up our little meeting. They're taking bids through the weekend."

"How are they taking bids?"

"Watch." Nelson grabbed a small notepad and pen from the center console. He wrote, '$200 in unmarked singles' on the paper, folded it twice, and held it on one palm.

He said, "I bid," and the paper vanished in a flash of sickly green fire. I caught a whiff of the power of the Djinn's Tear as it did. Nelson said, "Just takes intention. Must have been set up with a wish."

"So we dig around for another heartless body?"

"I doubt it would help. If one's even been found by the police, that gives us two problems. One, the cops will be watching the details of that crime like a croupier watching bets, worried about a serial killer. And two, everyone else who's interested in this thing is going to think to look for that body. That means we're hours behind on that lead, at best."

He turned to look at me, as though expecting miracles. "We need an angle none of them have thought of. Any brilliant ideas? Any tricks from your books?"

"Yeah, let's resort to spells and buy ourselves even bigger problems."

"Like things could get worse."

"Fuck!" I punched Nelson on the shoulder before I could think to stop myself. "Want to dare the fucking universe while you're at it?"

To his credit, Nelson looked chagrined as he rubbed his shoulder. "Sorry." He dug around under his seat and came up with a fast food salt packet. He tore it open and dumped the whole thing over his left shoulder, onto the seat and rear floorboards. "Think that'll help?"

"Technically, you should have knocked on wood to avert the omen, but it'll have to do." I snorted a laugh and shook my head.

Nelson reached over and knocked twice on his billy club, then turned to me with a worried grin.

I shrugged and said, "All right, enough superstitions for now. We need to figure out who was close enough to have learned something when the fiery proof hit the sky. Who are the players close to Stanford? The Sons of Morning run around there, don't they?"

"I hate those guys. They give even Satanists a bad name."

"Yeah, but they're it among the Palo Alto players big enough for this game."

"Not quite. The Texan is back on the hiking trails."

That was enough to give me a shiver even though I don't hike. "I thought he moved down to Alum Rock Park."

"He's back for the school year. He prefers his joggers college-age."

"The Texan isn't human. He couldn't use the Djinn's Tear. Why would he want it?"

Nelson gave me a significant look. "Why does the Rajah?"

I hung my head. "I hate this job." I rolled my shoulders and sat up. "Sons of Morning first. At least they're human."

"Agreed," said Carnifex from the back seat.

Nelson and I had our Ka-Bars drawn and menacing with speed that would have done us credit, if not for the fact that we had missed the demon's presence until it spoke.

Nelson let out a breath, but he must have decided that the demon did not pose an immediate threat because he lowered his weapon.

I did not.

"You're not supposed to show your face unless we call you."

"But you did." Its rasp sounded amused. "You said, 'I'm sure that will give you twenty seconds of great pleasure before Carnifex slaughters you like a Thanksgiving turkey.' You called. I came."

It flicked its tongue as though tasting the air, then added, "A small correction, by the way: neither of you will enjoy a fast death. When I kill and eat my prey I make it last for weeks." Its hood flared a few inches as its violet eyes met mine. "Weeks."

"You've heard our report then. Piss off until we call you again."

Carnifex hissed and a blast of its breath hit me, once more

carrying the scent of bile, and blood, and others' fear. But the demon twisted into its ribbon shape and vanished through an air vent.

Nelson looked at me and shook his head as we sheathed our knives. Neither of us spoke. Nelson put his car in drive and pulled away from the curb back into local traffic.

We were Palo Alto bound, heading for an occult lodge with a reputation so sinister that even Aleister Crowley had refused to go near them.

At least, that was the rumor.

THE SONS OF MORNING HAD A LODGE BUILDING ON RAMONA STREET IN Palo Alto, a block off University Avenue, as though they were any other innocuous group like the Oddfellows or Masons.

Yes, the Masons are innocuous.

No, I won't tell you how I know.

The Sons of Morning had bought the land decades ago, when prices were cheap, and the property included a parking lot that would have made them a mint if they'd opened it to the public.

They kept that lot for their own private use though, and employed a guard who asked us twice for our business before allowing us to park. Even so he took our names, Nelson's photo, and wrote down the license plate number.

Heck, he probably wrote down all the car details, including the VIN, while we were inside. These folk seemed the type. Not that I had any room to talk on the paranoia front.

The building itself was two stories of ignore-me-gray, weathered enough to look uncared for, like an old box with a pointy shingled roof. But that roof was in good shape, if any passerby felt interested enough to notice.

The front door was a faded white, and a tarnished brass representation of their symbol rested above it: the half-risen sun, eight rays extending at length.

"Are we supposed to use a special knock?" asked Nelson.

"Yep." I turned the knob and pushed the door open. "The they-know-we're-here."

The interior of the building gave the lie to the exterior. The walls and even the floor of the entryway were Brazilian cherry hardwood. The coat racks — cloak racks? — were fashioned from some polished, gleaming dark wood I didn't recognize, as were the single doors to our right and left, and the double door in front of us.

In the corner of the entryway was a gorgeous, antique oak desk with a leather writing pad, an inkwell and quill, and a sleek, stream-lined laptop.

Sitting at the desk was a fresh-faced kid, the kind who would be legally buying beer before he would ever need a shave.

No wards on the entry, which worried me a little. In fact, no spells I could notice at all. Except one...

I caught Nelson's eye and did the long blink, signaling him about an important detail. A fresh-faced detail.

"Can I help you?" asked the kid with an eager smile. I would have felt sorry for him, if he were human, for what we had to do next. But groups like this one didn't hire college students, and required special handling on approach.

"It dares speak to us?" Contempt dripped from Nelson's words.

"Fetch your masters, servitor," I added, matching Nelson's tone. I turned to face the left-hand door. "Your very presence offends us."

The door I faced opened, and in stepped a woman whose cruel good looks spoke of a life of pleasure and power at the expense of others. I had seen women wear skirt suits like armor, but this one wore hers like a weapon. Steel gray and aggressively cut and styled, with black pumps that clicked on the wood like a knife locking open. She wore her midnight black hair shoulder-length and trimmed with precision, and her eyes were so dark they almost matched it.

Even her perfume smelled aggressive. I didn't recognize the scent, but I decided it was hemlock.

"By all means, take offense," she said, her tone soft enough to fool the unwary. "You're no better than servitors yourselves, running about at the whim of the Rajah. And you come without invitation."

"The Rajah pays us," I conceded, "but we work for ourselves, and we were drawn here by power and opportunity."

"The Sons of Morning will not clear your debts. You must bring power, to gain power. We have no room for weakness." She turned to leave, and I heard the servitor stand up behind us.

"We didn't come to join you," said Nelson. "We came to discuss something that would benefit us both."

"You have nothing we need." She walked through the left-hand door and began to close it behind her. "Begone before I return or I shall destroy you."

"Fine," I said. "We'll just handle the Djinn's Tear on our own then."

"The Djinn's Tear?" She halted mid-step, her grip tightening to stop the door from closing. She looked over her shoulder at me. Her eyes ran calculations.

She turned back around, and gave us a knowing smile that made my stomach want to run and hide behind Nelson.

"Perhaps you should have mentioned that detail sooner. But then, it is not a subject for lobbies or foyers, and certainly not for servitors. Let us discuss it in more appropriate surroundings. You may call me Sapphira."

***

Sapphira led us to a small meeting room, maybe ten feet wide and twelve long. The heavy, ornate teak table could have seated six, and its chairs were carved to match, but the hardwood seats were mitigated by soft leather pads that felt more comfortable than they had any right to. The walls were painted sunrise yellow, and the wall opposite the door showed off a mural of their half-risen-sun symbol.

Sapphira sat at the head of the table, under the mural. Nelson and I took chairs flanking the table's foot. Always conveniently near the exit, that was us.

The servitor from the lobby — or maybe they made more than

one from the same specs — brought in a small silver tea set, and poured us each a cup of tea. Even the saucers were silver.

Sapphira took the first sip, establishing the drink's safety. My brow crinkled when I failed to recognize the aroma of the tea, and Sapphira said, "African Sunrise, a blend of honeybush, orange peel, and vanilla."

Nelson shot a warning glance at me and took a sip, accepting hospitality and ensuring nonaggression between the Sons and him. At least for the duration of this visit.

Nelson could have saved his glare. I knew this was important. I had to drink the tea or risk not leaving the building alive. Hospitality rules were one of the few things the whole supernatural world agreed to. Even the worst bastards wouldn't break them. And most of them couldn't try. Literally. Most supernatural creatures could no more violate the rules of hospitality than I could have flown across the room under my own power. Or kissed my elbow.

And if this woman was as steeped in magic as I suspected, she qualified as a 'supernatural creature.'

That's right, I said 'most' couldn't try, but I didn't say 'all.' My policy was not to trust any creature's rules until I knew them for certain.

But hospitality had never failed me yet.

Hospitality was the reason I asked for something to eat or drink every time I had to visit the Rajah, and it was also the reason Jeeves never brought anything. The Rajah would never offer us hospitality. He wanted us to know that each time we entered his house might be the last.

I could feel Sapphira watching me, noting my hesitation as I stared at my cup. Hospitality itself was an easy call, but tea, in an office setting, presented me another problem.

"Mr. McReedy," our hostess reminded me, "hospitality is an individual commitment from each guest."

"I don't suppose you have any biscuits to go with the tea. I'm more of a coffee drinker."

"I'm watching my figure," she said in a mocking tone, her eyes steady on me.

She knew who we were, probably knew why I hesitated. Wanted to see if I had enough brass to spill my chance at safety. To give her a reason to declare that I rejected hospitality when she knew damn well what my offering represented.

"Screw your first sip rule, Roland," muttered Nelson, as close-mouthed as he could manage. "Drink it."

I did the only thing I could think of: I picked up the cup without using the handle, jumped as though it were scalding hot instead of warm-verging-on-hot, and made sure to spill the first sip with deliberation in my thoughts. I righted the cup quickly, grasping the handle this time, and took the second sip.

Strong herbal rubbish. Probably fine if you liked sweet tea.

Sapphira laughed, a more pleasant sound than I expected. Perhaps it reflected real amusement instead of haughty cruelty?

"I suggest you leave the acting to your sister. You have no talent for it."

I bit the inside of my cheek, hard. I tasted blood, but managed to hold a neutral expression. This bitch knew about Colleen? But Colleen had moved down to L.A. after college, while I was still in high school. The only reason Sapphira would know about Colleen...

"Yes, Mr. McReedy, the Sons of Morning became curious about you after you appeared on the scene. Much as we did about you, Mr. Milner, when you first began working for the Rajah. Which reminds me, I do hope little Gina is over her cold."

I heard Nelson's chair rustle, but kept my eyes on Sapphira. Her nostrils flared displeasure. "Oh, do sit down, Mr. Milner. I have not offered threat to you or yours, and you have accepted hospitality so I doubt you are foolish enough to do more than posture."

She smiled at us over her cup, the smile a trapdoor spider has when it senses approaching prey.

"I merely wished to clarify our positions. If you have come to trifle with the Sons of Morning, you will regret your folly."

Threats to life and soul aside, I needed to get out of this lousy business just so I could stop listening to people throw around words like 'consequences' and 'folly.'

"You've made your point, Sapphira, now let me make mine. On the scale of threats in the Bay Area, you, personally, don't even register. Nelson and I didn't know you existed until we met you a few minutes ago. You weren't important enough to notice."

I set my tea cup down on the raw wood next to the saucer, and watched Sapphira's eyes follow the movement.

"But now we've noticed you. If you're stupid enough to start something, we will dig up weaknesses you don't know you have, find every secret you think you hold safe, and I personally guarantee your last words will be, 'but they're only human. How did they...'"

I cut off the end of the sentence, took another sip of tea, and set the cup down on its saucer. "Now are we going to waste more time making faces at one another, or shall we talk business?"

***

The Sons of Morning were the worst kind of anarchists. They claimed to want limitless freedom for all, but only after they had enough power to bully the weak and disorganized into worshiping them as gods. They wanted to set up hell on earth, with them running the show. If we met them with anything less than strength they had to respect, they would have bulldozed us.

Besides, my threat was only half a bluff. These occult-types always seemed to forget about the sheer volume of mundane resources readily available these days. For less than the cost of a night out I could get my hands on her legal name, date of birth, social security number and whatnot. She'd find out we humans have some magic of our own, and we call it technology.

And anyway, I would have enjoyed taking these bastards down a peg. I didn't know if they still counted as human, or if the vile magics they practiced made them something else. But they started their lives as human beings, and traded their humanity away for power. To my way of thinking, that made them the worst kind of monsters: willing converts.

"Very well, Mr. McReedy. You wanted to talk about the Djinn's Tear. So talk."

"By now you have to have figured out that your spells aren't going to find it."

"You assume we're looking for it."

"You were ready to kick us to the curb before I said the magic words. Now we're here in the inner sanctum drinking your tea."

"This is hardly my inner sanctum, but your point is made."

"So enough bullshit already."

With all the practice he was getting, I started to worry that Nelson would figure out how to actually hurt me with one of his vicious glares.

"No," said Sapphira, "our spells have not found it, and I have been forced to conclude that it is concealed through the use of its own power."

"My research says that magic cannot track it."

"So you believe your mundanity gives you an edge."

I jammed my thumbnail into the flesh of my index finger to stop myself from saying, 'No, our *humanity* is what gives us an edge.' Much as I would have enjoyed antagonizing her, the conversation was starting to get somewhere. Instead, I said, "Exactly, and as the only two human players in the game, we figure that gives us the best chance of winning."

"You aren't players, you're pawns."

"A pawn that crosses the board becomes a queen."

"A queen is still just a piece. More valuable, but ready to be sacrificed if necessary."

Did I mention that Karen was the chess player in our household?

"Fine. But if Nelson and I grab the Tear, we figure that gives us leverage. Maybe it means we come here without debts, that we bring power."

Sapphira laughed, and this time the sound carried a cruel undertone that scraped along my spine. "All the power of the Djinn's Tear at your command, and you allege that not only would the two of you share it, but that you would wish to join our ranks?"

"Yeah," said Nelson, setting down his tea cup. "Even I can't pretend that's not bullshit. Chances are good that one of us will kill the other and use the power of the Tear to disappear from the game board."

"True," I chimed in, seeing where Nelson was going. "But there's that moment of opportunity, isn't there? When we have the Tear, but before we've offed each other. Maybe someone like you could move in and take it from us."

"Not that we're offering you that chance," said Nelson. "We're going to do everything we can do to avoid it. Far as we're concerned, either Roland or I get that power. The rest of you can fuck off and die."

I don't know how I kept the shock off my face that Nelson could speak so brazenly to someone who terrified him — which I believed included any supernatural power we met with. Snigdha excluded.

Still, I kept up the patter, spinning my cup slowly to hear the ceramics scrape. "But here's the thing, if we fail to get it, we're dead."

"One of two ways really. Both nasty."

"Terrible." I stopped playing with my cup and looked up at Sapphira, but could read nothing in her cool expression. "So, we have no choice. We need to get our hands on that relic. And while we're pretty sure we're the only ones who can do it, we're equally sure we need a little more information to get started. That's where you come in."

Nelson and I stared expectantly at Sapphira, who borrowed time with a slow sip of her tea.

"Perhaps the Sons of Morning are confident that our bid shall win the prize."

"You expect us to believe that you can offer absolution?" I let the look on my face give my opinion of her chances.

"No one can offer that." She added tea to her cup, but didn't offer any more to us. As she poured she said, "But we can ensure ... shall we say ... a cushy position in hell."

"Let's go," said Nelson, standing up. "They've got this locked up."

"Yeah," I said as I got to my feet. "I doubt anyone will top that bid. It's not what the owner *wants*, but second-best is good enough, right? I mean, what's the guy going to do? Not sell it? Vanish for another few hundred years of decadent self-indulgence?"

"Sit."

The command tone in Sapphira's voice impressed me. Shook me out of my bravado-fueled patter. I sat, and so did Nelson.

She continued, "What exactly is it you want and what do you offer?"

"We want information," I said, as cards-on-the-table as I could get. "Anything you can tell us about what you picked up the night the fiery letters hit the sky. The Sons of Morning were the closest major players. You had to have noticed something."

I needed courage for the next part, so I gathered what I could through another sip of that awful tea.

"As for what we're offering, well, we all know that after we leave here you intend to hit us with some kind of a trace spell, so you can follow us and swipe the Djinn's Tear out from under us."

Sapphira smiled and inclined her head.

"Spells like those work better on the willing." I swallowed. "Give us enough useful information, and we won't fight the trace or get it removed. You'll get a fair shot at stealing the Tear from us before we can use it."

"That's your offer? Key information in exchange for a slim chance at the prize?"

"No." I pushed my saucer and the rest of my tea forward. I had drunk enough for ritual purposes anyway. "Your information won't be the key. It'll be a single step on a longer path. And we're offering you a better chance than you have without our deal."

Sapphira finished her tea as she considered, then set down her cup. She didn't seem ready to speak, so I tried to close the deal.

"This is the best offer you'll get from anyone, and your best shot at the prize."

"Surely the Rajah will kill you for your failure."

"Yeah, well I'm pretty sure we're dead either way. Why not spit in his smug face one last time before we go?"

Sapphira laughed again, this time the pleasant, amused sound. It still creeped me out because both of her laughs sounded natural for her. Not a very human trait.

"Your rationale is almost enough to persuade me, but my answer is no. The Sons of Morning shall claim the Djinn's Tear as they claim everything they desire: directly and through strength. If you understood us at all you would have known we would never deal with the likes of you."

I almost bit down my response, but I saw the same question on Nelson's face, so I asked it. "Then why talk to us at all?"

"Fool. The key to solving a puzzle might be found in any piece. Now leave."

The servitor entered the room then, and escorted us out. The condescending expression on its face would have done Jeeves proud.

"I can't face the Texan today," I said as I slumped into the passenger seat of Nelson's Taurus. "I'm done."

The afternoon sun was hanging low, starting to paint the blues and whites of the sky and clouds with reds and purples. Twilight would hit soon, with full dark hot on its heels.

"Too late in the day anyway," said Nelson as he fastened his seat belt. "No way we want to run into the Texan after dark."

"Hell no. In fact I want to be safely home with Karen when full dark hits."

"Mind if we stop for food first?" Nelson fired up his car. "If I don't get something to eat soon I'll gnaw through my steering wheel. I don't think I've had anything but coffee since before dawn."

My stomach rumbled agreement.

"Meat for the Beast?" asked Nelson with a laugh.

"Whatever."

Nelson waved at the narrow-eyed guard as we left the Sons of

Morning parking lot, and three backstreet blocks later he parked at his favorite fast food joint. I would have sworn he'd memorized every Bay Area location they had. Not that they had many yet. They were still spreading out.

The parking lot was just this side of empty. Just us and one lone pick-up truck. I could hear cars in the background, but none of them seemed anywhere near us.

I could already smell the food though, beef and potatoes and grease enough to rumble my stomach again.

Nelson started to get out of the car, but I said, "Wait. We better report in first." I waited until Nelson settled back in and we both had our Ka-Bars drawn before I said, "Carnifex."

The demon twisted into the car through an air vent and resumed its serpentine form. I told him of our failed efforts with the Sons of Morning, and it rasped that sound that I had decided was its laugh.

"Very well," said the demon. "I shall convey the state of your failure to my master. Perhaps he shall lose patience with you."

I scowled at the thing's hopeful tone as it stretched into its ribbon form to slip out of the car and vanish. Half-starved and stressed near the breaking point, I got out of the car, looking forward to a few minutes free from demon oversight to enjoy a little food in peace.

The late afternoon air felt good on my face, cool. Sometimes when the air is like that you can feel it slip in under your collar and up the cuffs of your pant legs. It was a little thing, but it made me smile.

I called over my shoulder to Nelson, "Was it me, or was that meeting room kind of stuffy?"

I turned to shut the car door.

Naturally, this was when I got jumped.

10

I shoved the car door closed with a heavy click, my thoughts all about a King of the Jungle burger with a side of shredded potatoes. I started to turn...

...and heard the Howl.

The awful sound tore through my eardrums like broken glass. Ripped down my nerves. Nestled in my soul. The mournful cry of a mother wolf watching her cubs flayed and eaten alive. My heart sped. Tried to burst. World gone red around me. Limbs twitching. No control. Mind splitting. Overwhelmed.

Despair.

Two years ago. Motel back office. Stack of cash. Drug money. Pimp money. All I would ever be...

Sorrow.

Me at twelve. Dead winter backyard. Fresh broken dirt. Here lies my puppy...

Horror.

Me at six. Dusty attic. Cracked old chest. Toys? No. Spiders. Thousands. Babies. Adults. Everywhere. All over me...

A thump broke the spell. Pain spilled in through the side of my head. My back was on the asphalt. I tried to move. Tried to rub my head. Tried to stand. Nothing worked right.

Nelson shouted. Couldn't hear him over the ringing in my ears.

Red eyes glowed above me. Dark shaggy fur blotted out the afternoon sky. Smelled like tombs. Old death.

Wide, snapping jaws. Saliva dripped. Burned my cheeks.

My arms and legs like dead weights. My chin failed to tuck. Lolled.

The jaws darted down.

Sharp, tearing pain. Hot gushing fluids. My scream a gurgle. The world went black.

11

———

WHEN MY EYES NEXT OPENED I STOOD ON A LUSH GREEN HILLSIDE under a sapphire sky. Not a single cloud, but where was the sun? The air was still, a pause between breezes. The smell of grass and clover a subtle perfume to my nose.

Memory hit. My hands leapt to my throat. Probed. Prodded. But my flesh was whole, untouched. My neck and chin didn't even show signs of stubble, much less having been torn out by...

Someone spat. I turned to see Ridges standing to my left, but this Ridges stood more than six feet tall and solid as I was. His emerald green suit, frock coat, and hat matched his monocle and walking stick. The whole ensemble shaded only a touch brighter than the soft grass beneath me.

"What are you doing here, you great sleeveen? And at your tender age? Who's going to be lookin' after me sprites then? Have you gone and thought of that at all, you selfish gobdaw? And that sweet girl of yours? How d'you think she'll be getting along without you? Did you stop and think of her for a moment even? You may not be much to look at, but you've got the blood of the old country flowing in your veins and there's not a girl alive who can resist that, and if you leave them, oh, if you leave them, well they'll just never be the same again, will they? How can they see the world as anything but black once they've known the brightness of love with a boy of old Eire? But no, good, dear old Ridges warned you, told you what you needed to do like you were my own kin, my own flesh and blood, my own great lumbering nephew, but no, not a hint of attention did you pay to the true and hard won wisdom of your elder and better who told you what you needed to do before things got out of hand. No, you went and did just exactly what you like without a moment's thought for the future and what it all meant. No, and a great skinny thing like you can't even blame it on the *ríastrad*."

"*Ríastrad*?" My mind needed a moment to catch up. I'd heard that word from my grandmother... "Warp spasm?"

"Warp spasm?" Ridges mimicked in a sour voice. "Leave it to the English to steal our majesty and make it ugly. No, you can't even blame it on the 'warp spasm,' though you don't listen to the brilliant advice of good, dear Ridges, whose monocle you are not worthy to polish, any more than that Setanta boy did, even before he got his airs and they started calling him 'dog.'"

Setanta? Dog? "You mean Cú Chulainn?"

"He knows a name! The McReedy boy won't hear the tiniest hint of sense from the lips of old Ridges, but he knows a famous name."

"Where am I anyway?" The colors were so clear and vivid, the smells so sweet. I reached down and touched grass as soft as cat fur. I couldn't place any of it, but... "There's something familiar about this place."

"Oh!" Ridges dropped his walking stick and buried his face in his hands. He mumbled, too soft for me to hear at first, but he must have realized that because he grew louder until I could make out his words.

"All the boy's book learning, all the nights he's wasted with hands on musty old tomes when they could have been on that lovely girl of his, and he learned not a single useful thing, did he now? Reading from all over the world and ignoring his own people, his own blood."

"My blood flows from the east as well."

Ridges' fingers spread and I saw his eyes. I saw deeper into his eyes than I had ever seen before, and fathomless depths of ancient power shone back at me.

I had always thought of Ridges as comical for a fae. I knew the fae were dangerous and tricky, but what I saw in Ridges' eyes then dwarfed all the posturing of Carnifex. Ridges might have played the little sprite, but he had to have been a *Daoine Sidhe*, one of the fae nobles.

Nelson had gotten angry that Ridges made him smell like horse manure, but with the same amount of effort Ridges could have cursed the entire Milner family line for generations. He could have answered our questions at his faery ring and returned us a century later. That was the kind of power I saw in those eyes.

Ridges watched my jaw drop and smiled, which didn't make him less terrifying.

"Maybe your eastern relations have some claim on you, my boy, but you're here, aren't you now? Maybe you should think about what that means."

I TASTED CARDAMOM, SWEET BUT STALE IN MY DRY MOUTH. I BLINKED tired eyes open and saw the roof of Nelson's car. I sat with the front passenger seat reclined until I was almost lying down, giving me an excellent view of a dried, dark stain on the beige molding above the back seat. Spaghetti?

A stolen red airline blanket covering me. It smelled of old tobacco. It must have been the blanket from Nelson's trunk, the one he used to conceal a carton of cigarettes from his wife.

"I thought you stopped smoking," I croaked. My throat felt raw, like I'd been gargling with broken glass and chasing it with whisky.

Wait. My throat was whole? But those jaws... That *thing*...

I sat up, sweat breaking out on my forehead, heat racing over my skin, my breaths shaky.

"Sit back. Rest," said Nelson. "You're all right."

I started to sit up again, but Nelson insisted, "Rest. *You're all right.* I'm taking you home."

I looked out my window. Freeway traffic, but not much. Dark skies above. Light from the tapering hillsides on each side, businesses and apartments starting to replace the fancy houses behind us. We were on 280, somewhere around the Mountain View border.

Not in a Meat for the Beast parking lot. Not in Palo Alto. Safe at the moment. Safe from...

"What—"

"It was a sending. I'm pretty sure it was an actual black dog. You know. Spectral equivalent of an attack dog. Went for you the moment we got out of the car." He glanced at me over his shoulder. "I had to take you to the Rajah."

"No!"

"I called Snigdha first, but got the machine." He shook his head. "You were dying! In fact, I thought you *were* dead there for a minute."

"I was. Or I might have been. I don't know." I shook my head, thought of my throat, and brought my hands up to pat it all over, feel for any imperfection. Something felt different, but not about my throat...

"The Rajah didn't add to your debt," said Nelson, and I could hear the bad news fighting not to come out. "But, well, he took partial payment as a warning."

My hands!

The little finger from each hand was gone, bitten cleanly off. The skin had healed over, but each stump bore the unmistakable impression of teeth. Sharp teeth. Teeth that did not belong in the mouth of any human.

"For what it's worth, he didn't just heal the throat. He also took care of your bruises and stuff."

"He bit off two of my fingers."

"I know. He made me watch." Nelson shuddered.

Silence stretched between us while I stared at where my lost digits should have been. I wiggled my remaining fingers, felt my last knuckles try to wiggle what was no longer there.

The silence proved too much for Nelson. "At least you're still alive."

"Yes, and thank you." Nelson tried to dismiss my thanks with a shrug, but I didn't let him. "I mean it. I'd rather lose two fingers than let Karen lose her soul."

Brave words. And I did mean them. Mostly. But fire burned in my gut, flowed through my veins. Anger. Anger at whoever had sent the black dog. Anger at myself for being too slow. Anger at Nelson for not finding a better way. Anger at the Rajah for taking my fingers, for demanding so much debt for that favor in the first place. Even anger at Karen for selling her soul. What the hell was she thinking?

I sat and stewed for the rest of the drive. But I was not going to let all this anger go to waste. Before this was all over, I had to find some way to channel it, to make the right people pay. I just had to figure out how.

***

AWAKE!

I bolted upright, grabbed the armrest and Nelson's wrist.

"It's all right," his voice said, soothing in the reddish darkness. "We're here."

My gummy lids pried slowly open, let in bright sodium light. Outside my window was my Camry. Looked better than I felt.

More sights. The alley parking behind my apartment. Nighttime. Neighbor cars in neighbor spaces. No Jetta. No Karen. Gone?

Did she leave me?

Exhaustion flooded my muscles, ached me head to toe. Too much strain. Too long. I dropped back in the seat, eyes closing. Ready to sleep. Maybe ready to die. Again.

My door opened. "Come on," said Nelson, standing outside the door. When did he... "Let's get you inside."

I didn't move.

I heard him sigh, like he wasn't surprised. Nelson's hands unbuckled my seatbelt. He grabbed my wrists. Started to pull.

"You have to help me," he said. "If we get jumped while I'm carrying you—"

"Gone," I mumbled. "Blew it."

I had to force those words out three times before Nelson said, "Karen? No. She's a tough lady. Probably went to buy silver bullets for her .38 or something." He tugged again. "Now come on. 'Cause you sure as hell aren't coming home with me."

Between us we managed to get me out of that car. But only just. I moved like a marionette with cut strings. All dangly dead weight, leaning heavy while Nelson half-dragged me across the concrete and past our dumpster.

As we passed the back apartments I heard televisions, conversations. No threats. I smelled chocolate. Mrs. Johnson baking again. Probably chocolate chips cookies for her nephews. I loved chocolate chip cookies. Right from the oven, when they're so gooey they start to collapse in your hands and you have to blow on them just to keep them from burning your tongue, and they do a little bit anyway but you don't care because you can taste the butter and the sugar and the chocolate, most of all the chocolate, like molten drops of heaven on your—

Nelson's hand, patting my face just this side of slapping.

"Wake up, Roland. I'm not fishing for your keys."

Keys. Hand. Which pocket again? Oh. Yeah. Right front. Into my jeans. Easier with missing finger. Missing finger. Missing fingers. No piano lessons for me. Sorry, Mom, I—

Nelson pulled my wrist, got my hand out of my pocket, my key ring hooked on my index finger. He leaned me against the pale blue stucco while he tried keys. Gave me a good view up and into the apartment across the way. That girl was working out with her curtains open again. Zumba or something. Dancy. Lots of jiggling. *Moving.* Not supposed to notice the jiggling. Not supposed to notice her at all. Karen would... Karen. My Karen. Gone? Come back, Karen. I'll make it all right. Find a way. Have to—

"Jesus, Roland." Nelson grabbed my shoulders and started hauling me inside. I had no help left to give. I was crying. He dragged me to the couch and managed to drop me on the saggy cushions. He tossed my keys on the coffee table.

"I'm taking off now," he said. Too loud, like he thought I couldn't understand. "You sleep. I'll see you tomorrow."

Sleep. Sleep sounded wonderful. Blissful oblivion. Maybe a dream where Karen and I...

After two false starts, I opened my eyes. There was Lancelot, sunning himself in his terrarium next to the television. Have to feed him later. Above his terrarium was that cartoon painting of a dog. *Karen's* cartoon painting of a dog. Hers. She was gone, but not *gone*. She'd come home again.

I settled back into the cushions, exhausted muscles rejoicing, encouraging me to give up consciousness, to let them rest and heal. Good idea. I nestled in.

No. Not yet.

Something poked at the back of my brain. Told me I wasn't safe. I stared at my keys. Something about my keys...

The top lock. If Nelson left my keys, then he could only lock the handle, not the deadbolt. That second lock was like superstition for me, but superstitions have power of their own.

I had to lock the door.

My muscles wheedled and cajoled me to let it go just this once, but my gut and my brain told me that was a bad idea.

One at a time, I forced my feet off the couch until I had both shoes on the floor, more or less flat. I dragged myself to a sitting position. Deep breaths for support, but they grew regular and I started listing to the right. Hands onto the cushions to brace me. Arms shaking. No good.

Down I went, onto the floor.

More aches. At least it was progress, of a sort. Except that now my limbs tried to tell me that our thin renter's carpet was comfortable. The lie of the desperate for sleep.

Why so tired? Healed. Oh. The Rajah. Must have used my own life force. Cheap bastard.

Hand by hand, knee by knee, I forced my body to crawl the eight endless feet between where I fell and the front door. Each movement took focus and set off a series of crying complaints all through me.

Finally, I reached the door. I had to grab the handle in both hands and push and strain myself upright, leaning against the plain white paint of the front door. On the third try I got the deadbolt set. I let myself lean and rest up for the marathon trek back to the couch.

I promised my body hours of sleep if it cooperated. I promised it a solid meal when we woke up. I just kept up a stream of promises, trying to make myself believe I could do it, that I could get back to that soft, soft couch.

But leaning against the door was bliss. Leaving it meant moving and moving was a bad thing. Moving took effort. My body didn't want any more of that. I started to wonder if I could sleep in my current position, but my knees told me no. They started to shake with their own desire to collapse.

By an act of will alone I propelled myself far enough to fall over the arm of the couch and back onto the cushions. Sleep took me before I could even reposition for comfort.

I WOKE TO THE SOOTHING FEEL OF A HAND STROKING MY HEAD. MY EYES fluttered open to reveal Carnifex, sitting on my coffee table, with its long, bruise-purple tongue retracting into its mouth. Disgust quivered through me, forced me back deeper into the cushions as though I could slide into the cracks and disappear.

Carnifex rasped its ugly laugh.

So much for the power of superstition.

"You aren't supposed to come in my apartment." My voice sounded sluggish, but stronger now after some rest. Speaking didn't even hurt. "We agreed."

"I agreed not to approach Karen Falk nor enter this place in her presence." The demon swung its head back and forth. "She is elsewhere. And in your turn, you were to report three times each day."

Its indigo hood flared and relaxed. "And yet you rest from your day's labors owing me a report. Does this mean you accept defeat?"

"No. I'm recovering. While you were off telling Scratch what we'd learned, a black dog tore my throat out."

"I find your report incomplete." Those slitted pupils widened as the demon leaned closer. "Provide details. Slow, lingering details. Begin with the pain."

"I'm not doing this to give you your jollies. The point is that someone attacked us, someone who knows what we're after."

"Perhaps they simply do not like you."

"Lots of people don't like me. But no one's ever sent a black dog after me before." I sat up, grateful that I still wore my jacket, which meant my Ka-Bar was in easy reach. "No, we've been making a lot of noise about the Djinn's Tear, and someone wants to stop us from getting it."

"Suspects?"

"Got to be the Sons of Morning. They've got the weight to handle a black dog. Must've believed Nelson and I could snatch it out from under them so they tried to take us off the game board."

"Only you were attacked."

Anger helped me meet its eyes without flinching. "You were watching?"

"I was elsewhere, but you live. Ergo, Nelson Milner dispatched the black dog while it was focused on you and had you healed." It rasped a sound I couldn't interpret. Perhaps a sigh? "A weakness of the breed. They handle multiple targets poorly."

"So the black dog wasn't after us. It was after me."

My day just kept getting better.

"Then you must be guarded."

I didn't like the sound of that.

Carnifex extended its forked tongue into the air and another bout of revulsion shuddered through me. The demon clamped its mouth shut and bit off a six-inch section of purple tongue. But the bitten off chunk did not fall to the ground. It squirmed and writhed in the air, smoothing and shaping. Two little eyes opened and I suppressed a scream. A jaw opened and closed. The whole body stretched and rippled, a tiny purplish snake floating in the air.

Carnifex hissed at it. The snake bit its own tail, spun in a circle, and vanished. Carnifex turned back to me and said, "I shall stay close and guard you—"

"No. Nonononono."

"—and my tongue shall update my master for me. It is settled."

"Not settled. Not happening. Get the hell out of here."

"You cannot be left alone. I shall guard and watch you until you find the Djinn's Tear."

I yanked out my Ka-Bar. "I will cut my own throat. Your master will never see his toy."

"You will not abandon Karen Falk to her fate."

I pressed the sharp knife against the skin near my jugular, felt its keen edge. "I'll do it!"

The front door opened and in stepped Karen.

KAREN'S JAW DROPPED AND SHE STOPPED WHERE SHE WAS, ONE STEP inside our front door, on the kitchen linoleum. Her keys still dangled from her fingers. I had a moment to notice that she wore her 'stress clothes' — loose jeans, old sneakers and a bulky gray sweatshirt — before I turned back to see memory of our agreement flash in the demon's eyes. Carnifex hissed displeasure, but twisted into a ribbon and vanished.

"Lock the door!" I leapt my feet, only barely aware that I still held a knife to my own throat. "Quick!"

Karen slammed the door, twisting the handle lock and top lock with impressive speed. But before I could speak she whirled on me. "Drop the knife."

I held up one hand, calming, and started to slide the Ka-Bar back into its sheath. "It's all—"

"I said 'drop it.'"

That startled me into standing straighter. I dropped the combat knife and held up my hands to show that they were empty.

Karen closed the distance between us with three fast steps. She grabbed me by the shirt collar and dragged me into the hallway bathroom. I was too stunned to resist. She shoved me to a sitting position on the toilet while she rummaged in the medicine cabinet.

Her glare kept me silent as she shook isopropyl alcohol on a cotton pad. The smell of antiseptic filled the bathroom, overwhelmed the air freshener. But her fingers were gentle when she pressed the pad to my throat. The sting made me twitch, but I kept quiet. I had a feeling that Karen wanted to be the one to break the silence.

Karen cleaned the cut I had to have given myself. She eyed her work from two different angles, but must have decided that I hadn't maimed myself sufficiently to require a bandage. She leaned the small of her back against the counter and regarded me, her gaze sharper than my Ka-Bar and twice as deadly.

"I'm not going to ask what the hell you were thinking, because whatever it was isn't good enough. Not for this. You and I have been through a whole lot together." She rubbed her wrist. "I've given more of myself for you than I've ever given for anyone or anything, even me. If that's not enough to fight for, no matter what we're fighting, you need to tell me right now."

The pain in her eyes made me cry. I fell to my knees a blubbering fool, but before I could wrap my arms around her legs, she pushed me away, her jaw set.

"You tell me, Roland. You say the words."

I needed three tries to get anything coherent past my sobs. "I love you, Karen. And I'll fight through hell by your side."

She dropped to her knees, tears of her own mixing with mine while we squeezed each other as though we tried to mesh into one being. I don't know how long we stayed that way, just embracing and crying ourselves out, but eventually our sobs settled into deep, heavy breaths.

I met her eyes, and saw my own terror staring back at me — neither of us could survive losing the other. Not anymore. But in that moment we were alive and together. We tore each other's clothes off. We made fierce, desperate love right there on the throw rug and cold linoleum.

After we finished we lay entwined, Karen snuggled into my chest. I could still smell her peach bath lotion. I heard her breathe a deep, easy sigh, and then she said, "Now I think you better tell me what we're up against."

"Now I think you better tell me what we're up against."

I said those same words to her over a year ago, sitting in the back seat of my Camry. She had just spent three hours trying to dump me and I fought her the whole way. It would have been one thing if she didn't love me, or didn't want me, or there was someone else. But there wasn't.

Well, actually there was. But the other someone wasn't a person. It was cocaine.

Karen needed to quit. She had snorted through her savings and started "borrowing" from me just to make rent, leaning on me to keep her fed.

Everything came to a head on a daytime date. We'd just laughed our way through lunch at Colby's, this great little organic place that made the best coffee cake either of us ever tasted. Next we were going to hit a movie theater to make snide sotto voce comments during some romantic comedy. She hit the bathroom while I paid the bill...

But when she came back had that little shaky extra bounce in her step, her smile an edge too wide, her eyes darting trying to see everything.

Broke the mood for me completely. Up to that point I understood her drug use, or thought I did. Rough family life, working as a prostitute, yadda yadda yadda. I thought coke was her escape hatch. But in that moment something clicked for me. Coke was her life, the rest was enabling.

My face fell like a demolished building. Karen saw, but didn't get it. "Who died?" she said.

Standing right there in the entryway of Colby's with the hostess and three other couples looking on, I said, "You've got to quit the coke."

I don't know if it was the words or my tone, but I've never seen strangers turn away that fast. You'd have thought they were shunning me. Maybe they were.

Karen started crying. Pushed her way past me. I had to follow her, running, through crowds of happy, shopping onlookers. Some old woman apparently decided I'd done something awful, because she told Karen, in passing, that she was better off without me.

I flipped the old bitch off and kept running.

Karen collapsed against the locked passenger side door my car, shaking and thumping her head on her folded arms.

"Karen?" I said, still ten feet away, as though I needed permission to approach.

She started thumping her head faster.

I came closer. Slowly, step by step, so she had plenty of time if she wanted to stop me. When I got close enough I reached out and put my hand on her shoulder.

She jerked away, face in her hands.

"Karen…"

"I know!" She whirled on me, face red and hands waving wildly as she spoke. "You think I don't know? You think I'm stupid? Just a stupid junkie whore who embarrasses you?"

"I—"

"Well I may be a junkie and a whore but I'm not stupid! You think I don't know I'm broke? Do you think—"

"Karen," I said loud enough to make her hear me even though she didn't stop talking, "I think you need help."

"OF COURSE I NEED HELP!"

People were staring now. A big fortyish Samoan man looked as though he was ready to come intervene. I tapped my fob and unlocked the car.

"Karen, let's talk in the car."

"You think *you* can help me?" Mocking laughter with her words now. "What do you know about it? What do you know about your veins crying out for more? About the shivery goodness of a freeze? About the dark hell of going without? What do you—"

"Tell me what I don't know in the car. Please. Before strangers get involved."

She ripped the door open and threw herself in the back seat and buried her face in her hands. I have the Samoan man an I've-got-this wave of my hand, and though he looked skeptical, he backed off.

I rounded the car and got in next to her. The moment I sat down she said, "I'm leaving you."

"That's the coke talking."

And so the fight began. She railed at me, cursed me, told me she was using me, told me I was a bad lover, told me anything she could think of. She denigrated herself, went on about how horrible she was, how worthless, et cetera. Sometimes she said she was better off without me, other times I was better off without her.

I just took it all, every word, and kept coming back by saying, "I love you. I'm not going anywhere."

Don't get me wrong. It wasn't that easy. It would have been impossible, except I kept one image strong in my head: the first time Karen said she loved me.

She said it with fear and hope in her eyes, as though the half-dozen times I'd said it to her by then might have been lies. She said it just above a whisper, her tone disbelieving. Like she hadn't ever believed she could love anyone.

I knew she meant it. I knew she'd meant it for at least a week before she said it. And sitting in the backseat, I knew that all that stood between us was that cocaine. And while she ranted and insulted me, she never got out of the car. I had done nothing to restrain her. She could have left anytime she wanted. But she stayed.

That was how I could take it. Cocaine may have made her scream at me, but it couldn't make her leave me.

So I took it all until she wore herself out and lay back, sweaty and exhausted, against the seat.

That was when I looked at her and said, "I love you, Karen. Now I think you better tell me what we're up against." At the time I was only thinking about dealers and habits and Joe's influence, and figuring out what methods of quitting she might have already tried.

Now here she was, saying those same words to me on the floor of our bathroom.

I had the feeling I'd gotten the easier end of the arrangement.

12

———

The floor of our hallway bathroom was no place for a long, involved conversation. Besides, that kind of talk needed coffee. So we untangled ourselves, got dressed, and headed for the kitchen.

Along the way, I sighed relief that no demons or other surprises had burst in on us, and knocked on the pantry door in passing.

I stopped and furrowed my brow as I realized how bad my life had gotten. I had just knocked wood to avert the omen over something I hadn't even said.

Karen must have turned at my knock, because she cried out, "Rollie! Your hands!"

I guess it says something about how distracted she was earlier that she only just now noticed my missing pinkies.

I didn't try to keep the weariness out of my voice. "It's been a hell of a day." She started to say something else, but I shook my head. "Let me get to it. I'll tell you everything. Just let me get to it. Coffee first."

We moved in tandem to make the coffee, and the normality of our routine eased something inside me. I washed the carafe and prepared the brewer while she ground her favorite blend fresh from the freezer.

When I saw her measure for a strong pot, reality returned. We weren't sleeping anytime soon. I took advantage of a thirty-second window before her part of the process was done, to slip into the living room where I could feed Lancelot and gather my thoughts.

I came back into the kitchen while the coffee machine perked. Karen sat on the edge of the counter beside the refrigerator. I leaned against the sink, four feet of linoleum between us, closed my eyes, and began.

"All those old stories, the folk tales and myths and legends? Those things were goddamn history texts. And just as accurate. I mean they give you a sense of what happened and who was involved, but the little details, those vary by author.

"Take the Grimms, for example. They put their own stamp on everything, changing stories to fit their style. But if you dig around you can find the truth behind the embellishments."

I took a deep breath, for courage. "And I've needed to do that, because all those things are still out there, and I was stupid enough to ask one for a favor."

Karen shook her head with irritation. "I might fuck a stupid man, Rollie, but I wouldn't fall in love with one. So knock that shit off and catch me up."

No doubt about it, Karen was way too good for me. Her beautiful anger made me smile, but I shook the moment away before she could prompt me again.

I told her my history with the things that go kill in the night, starting with that night I spoke to the Rajah, continuing through my first visit to his house and the extent of my debt.

Karen poured the coffee as I talked, a moment later stopping me. "Wait! That. What the hell is up with that? You never used to do it, but now it's every time."

"What?" I asked, taking my second sip of coffee.

"That spilling coffee thing. Or beer, or whisky. I've even seen you do it with soda. Before you take a drink you slosh some into the sink or on the pavement or wherever is convenient. Why?"

"That's nothing compared to the rest of what I have to say."

"Everything, Rollie." She returned to her perch on the counter and leaned forward with a challenge in her voice. "Everything."

"This one's kind of silly, I guess." I shrugged. "Just something I read, and the source wasn't even the most reputable. Anyway, the idea is that every one of us has a personal angel, like a 'holy guardian angel' or something. It watches over us, even when we're too stupid to watch over ourselves." I saw her eyes narrow and hurried along before she could object. "Offering it the first sip of your drink is a way of saying thank you. It's polite and encourages the angel to stay close and help. The book only mentioned 'the first sip of one's wine,' but I don't drink much wine and I need all the help I can get. So I offer it everything but water."

"Why not water?"

"I'm not sure. The book said water would 'offend' it. I figured, why take the risk?"

That seemed to satisfy her, so I went on and held nothing back. I told her about everything Nelson and I had done for the Rajah, even the bits that involved trespassing, unlawful entry, fraud (sounds bad, but it's just the fake i.d.'s), and theft. I told her about all the things we had harvested, hunted, rummaged for, and dug up. Literally in some cases.

When I told her about fighting the ghul for its venom, she winced and interrupted me.

"Those bruises are gone. I don't mean healing, I mean like they were never there."

"I'm getting to it, I swear."

Finally I caught her up through the black dog, the price of the Rajah's healing, the hillside talk with Ridges, and my latest chat with Carnifex. When I finished I tried to sip from an empty coffee cup. Filling it gave me an excuse to let her think.

I had just poured the first sip into the sink when she said, "You've been lying to me, Rollie."

My turn to wince. "Even knowing about these things is dangerous. The more you learn, the easier they are to spot, and the more noticeable you become to them. I just wanted to keep you safe until I could get clear of the Rajah."

"Have you cheated on me?"

"What? No! Never!"

She stared at me for a moment, assessing. The distance in her eyes gave me a pang in my chest.

"Have you lied to me about anything else?"

"No. Just the supernatural stuff, and just to protect you."

"Worked out well, didn't it." She picked up her coffee cup and set it down. Twice. She grabbed the counter's edge beneath her with both hands. "I went out looking for coke today."

"Karen—"

"Let me finish." She held up a hand to keep me back and refused to look at me.

"That thing. Carnifex? That was too much for me. On top of finding out you've been lying and risking your life, and that maybe I had a soul to sell, that great awful snake thing..."

She shivered and my heart tried to leap out of my chest to go to her, but I rooted my feet in place.

She continued, "I thought I'd made everything right for us. Quit hooking. Got away from the old life. But everything turned to shit again."

She shivered, and I would have sworn it started from her stomach. "The need hit me. Told me it would all get better if I just got high. Not too high. Just a little. Just enough to help me focus on fixing things.

"I went out looking to score. Drove past the old neighborhoods. Down where Ricky used to hang out. He always had the best shit." Her voice got a little dreamy before she shook her head to clear it.

"I parked the car. My fingers jumping on the steering wheel the way they used to." She folded her hands, gripped her knuckles. "I had that old tightness in my arms. In my stomach. Anticipation. And, Rollie, it felt good. I missed it."

Her lips started quivering, but she took a deep breath to stop them. She pulled in her elbows and hugged her stomach. It took everything I had not to run to her, but she still wouldn't look at me.

"I saw Ricky across the street with a couple of cronies. Laughing. Smoking. Wearing that same old stupid Members Only jacket. The one he claims was a gift from a made guy.

"I reached into my purse for my cash, but I *didn't have any. I blew it all on that damned lawyer.*" She shivered again. Pulled her elbows in until they dented her belly. Started bouncing her folded hands.

"The habit reminded me that I didn't need cash for Ricky. He would have been happy to spot me a gram for a blow job. Two if I..."

She looked down now, and I felt the air turn to lead in my lungs.

But she wasn't done.

"I started to get out of the car. Had my feet on the curb. My pick-up smile on my lips...

"But I couldn't do it." Her hands started shaking. "The need was screaming. Sweating through my shirt. Begging me. I could make everything all right with just a little snort. Just this once. No one needed to know. Not even you. No one could blame me. Facing down a demon in my own kitchen. Too much for anyone."

She met my eyes now. "But I couldn't suck his dick for it. I couldn't cheat on you. Not even for a fix."

She looked down again from her perch. Let go of her hands and grabbed the edge of the counter instead.

"I needed an ATM. Started driving. Hard, jerky driving. Swearing at cars. Flipped off a soccer mom, but she saw me. Gave me a look. Pity." Karen glanced at me and back down. "Reminded me of the shoppers outside Colby's that time. You know. Anyway, that pity woke me up. I called Shelley. Blubbered at her. She heard the habit in my voice. Talked me down."

Karen looked up at me again, but this time with a weak half-smile. That's when it hit me, and I mean harder than ever before. I didn't just love this woman. I wanted to marry her. I wanted to give her kids. A life. Get her away from drugs and monsters and give her stupid, boring things to worry about like soccer practice.

I crossed the room and had her in my arms before my dropped coffee cup hit the floor. Karen mumbled the rest in my ear.

"Shelly took the day off work. We went to stupid movies. Ate in greasy diners. Just talked all day."

Karen squeezed me hard.

"No more lies between us, Rollie. I'm not strong enough for lies anymore."

WE DRAGGED OURSELVES INTO THE LIVING ROOM AND COLLAPSED ON the couch together, too physically and emotionally exhausted to talk more despite the coffee. I turned the radio on to some sports talk show and absently twitched my fingers in the air, watching the bite marks where pinkies used to be. Karen and I vegetated while armchair experts ran down what went right and wrong with the Giants season and declared which players had to stay or go, or predicted what would go right and wrong for the Forty-Niners. As always, the A's, Raiders, and Warriors were ignored on this station unless they made it into the playoffs.

We drifted off in there somewhere, snuggled together with our feet on the coffee table. I roused during a news break. Karen was already awake, just staring into space, thinking. Show host Johnny Jay started to give us an update on the latest theory out of Ames Research Center at Moffett Field about the burning letters in the sky. He was saying something about combustible gasses when Karen said, "What is the Rajah?"

When I had heard her intake of breath, I'd expected her to ask about the letters or about the Djinn's Tear, so I was too thrown to answer right away.

"He's obviously not human. So what is he?"

"I've been trying to figure that out for months." I pointed with my thumb to the bookshelf behind the couch where I kept my occult books and notebooks. "Half of what I've written over there is about what I've figured out, what I thought I knew that was wrong, and my working theories." I blew out failure as a sigh. "I don't think I'm any closer to the answer now than I was when I started. At least in the process I've learned some stuff that's helped me stay alive and in one piece."

"But you're not. Not anymore." She gestured to my missing fingers. "Today the Rajah crossed the line. He's not just threatening anymore. He bit off things that don't grow back."

"At least I'm alive."

"He needs you alive." She waved a dismissive hand. "Otherwise he'd — it — would have eaten all of you. But it ate your fingers anyway."

"Doesn't change anything. I still—"

"The hell it doesn't." She turned and faced me and the look in her eye almost made me draw back. "You focus on finding that Djinn's Tear. I'm going to find us a way to kill the Rajah."

13

THE BED SHOULD HAVE BEEN DENTED PERMANENTLY FROM HOW HEAVY I slept that night. When my phone peeped a wake-up alarm from its hiding place under the bed, I must have needed three minutes just to flop my arm over the side and paw around for it. Karen slept right through, but she had stayed up later to get started on my notes.

Nine a.m. I had half an hour before I had to pick up Nelson. I still hated to see this side of noon, but Nelson and I wanted as many hours as possible to search for the Texan while the sun was still in the sky. That was not a thing to meet after dark. Even Nelson knew better than to ask for dawn though, not after the day I had yesterday.

I lay in bed a moment, flexing my hands and missing my lost fingers. I could still feel the nerves firing, trying to flex muscles that no longer existed, except maybe in the digestive tract of the Rajah. Assuming the Rajah had a digestive tract. If monsters didn't have a natural eat-excrete cycle like human beings, what happened to the things they ate? Were they just converted to energy with no waste ejected?

I shook my head and forced myself to get moving, before this job cost me more than two fingers.

A shower helped, but my stomach refused coffee until placated with peanut butter toast. That left no time for a leisurely cup, though, so I filled a thermos for the road. Not a monster thermos like Nelson's, just the sort you might find in a lunchbox, done in olive drab and chrome. Whatever. It was enough to hold a few cups of Karen's home-mixed blend.

Sleep had given me a little distance from my stress, but had the unfortunate side-effect of letting me realize just how awful it was to lose those two little fingers. I noticed their absence in everything I did. The toothbrush felt awkward in my hand, the soap and washcloth moved wrong, slipped through my remaining fingers once. Buttoning my shirt and khakis worked all right, but the balance of everything I held, from a butter knife to a measuring cup to a faucet handle was off. I never realized how my pinkies steadied my grip until I didn't have them anymore. Now everything I picked up felt precarious.

Rather than making me sad, though, I let it worry me. Worry me that I had to watch how I held my Ka-Bar, my billy club. Worry me that my movements might be off if I had to fight. Worry me that I might grab the Djinn's Tear off its owner's neck during a struggle, only to drop it and leave it up for grabs.

Worry was good. Worry could keep me sharp. Nelson may have teased me about paranoia, but the moment I let my guard down, a spectral dog tore my throat out and the Rajah ate two of my fingers. I needed my edge. Maybe worry would help me keep it.

The world outside my door was fresh, and cool enough to make me wonder if I needed more than a windbreaker, and cloudy. The kind of clouds that looked like rain, if they didn't burn off. It was October, so they would probably burn off by around noon. Down here in the South Bay we might see a little rain around Halloween, but I had learned never to expect much before November. Probably late November.

Two steps out my front door I heard Carnifex's voice over my shoulder. "I should kill whoever ate those delicious fingers. They should have been mine."

"It was the Rajah, so by all means, go try."

Carnifex twisted out of its ribbon form in front of me, dark blue and ugly, but the violet of its eyes looked excited. "My master grows impatient. If you surrender, perhaps I will make your death swift."

"No you wouldn't. You'd make it last twice as long, just to mock me."

The demon hissed appreciatively.

"But since you're here, Carney, consider this today's first report. I'm on my way to pick up Nelson. We're going to find the Texan—"

"Avoid the Texan. It is not a power to cross."

"It was the biggest, baddest thing that was close to the Djinn's Tear the last time we know it was used. Maybe it noticed something." The demon rasped as though in thought, but I pushed on before it could speak. "Besides, this is our call, not yours. And this report is finished. Fuck off."

Those violet eyes glowed on the edge of ultraviolet again, and the hood flared to full width. "Every word of disrespect, Roland Adar McReedy, increases your future pain. I shall milk your impertinence from you through tears and blood, and I shall savor each drop before I move on to your tasty flesh. By the time you feel my fangs pierce your skin, the exquisite pain shall seem almost relief beside the suffering you will have endured."

"Let me guess." My bravado was undercut by the crack in my voice. I hadn't realized my fear had room to grow. But I would have consigned myself to damnation before I would have let a single tremor show through to Scratch's demon valet. "You'll make me beg for death."

"Oh, no. Your voice will have long since ground away under the weight of your screams." A hint of satisfaction entered its hissing rasp. "I am far worse than anything your pathetic imagination can conjure."

Then it twisted into its ribbon shape and vanished. Worse than anything my imagination could conjure. But it was afraid of the Texan. And the Texan was what I had to go see.

Terrific.

Nelson must have felt as though I needed a break today. He let my thermos go with a simple, "That's adorable. Did you find it in a box of cereal?" Of course, it might have helped that I responded in a deadpan voice, "Came in a kid's meal. Label must have worn off."

He didn't even object to my talk shows on the drive up to Stanford campus. Not that there was anything interesting on the radio. People were still trying to figure out what the burning letters meant. Must have given more airtime to conspiracy theorists than anything since 9/11.

The hills out behind Stanford were a uniform golden brown this time of year. Every winter the rains turned them green, and every summer the dry heat leeched the green away. It was all wild grass and local foliage, though, so nothing really died, just changed color and kept surviving.

Under the circumstances, I found that encouraging.

Apart from the hiking trails, the hills drew attention for two man-made features and one natural. The man-made features were the Stanford Linear Accelerator and the Stanford Dish, a giant radiotele-scope dish. All right, technically there were two dishes, the giant one that's easy to see and the smaller, older one that you can still spot from 280 if you know where to look.

The natural feature of the Stanford hills that everyone knew about were the cattle, which could also be seen from highway 280. Not that they did tricks or anything. They did what cows do, wander around and eat grass. It's just that while you're driving on a freeway through suburbia suddenly you can see a bunch of cows off to one side. I always found that kind of weird.

One feature most people didn't know about was the Oak. Off of the hiking trails a little ways was this huge, gnarled oak tree. Despite its bends and curves, it still stood over a hundred feet tall, and always seemed to me to loom over its whole hillside,

Just as well that most people didn't know about it. I didn't know what that thing was, but it was more than just an oak tree. I could never get close to it without my skin itching something fearsome and my stomach screaming at me to run. I hoped we didn't have to go anywhere near it today.

Looking for the Texan sounded bad enough. Having to look near the Oak was just too depressing to contemplate.

We found a parking spot reasonably near the hiking trails, fortified ourselves with coffee (I opened my door to pour out my first sip), and started looking for the Texan.

Neither of us knew exactly what the Texan looked like, but by all accounts we would know it when we saw it. Well, the accounts said 'him' not 'it,' but it mattered to me that the Texan wasn't human. I didn't know what it was, and I didn't want to know. I wanted as little to do with the Texan as possible. I just hoped to find the thing, ask it a couple of questions, and leave before it decided that killing me was fair compensation for its valuable time.

We brought the billy clubs along for this one, in addition to our Ka-Bars. Just in case.

***

HARD CALL, TRYING TO CHOOSE BETWEEN THE WIDER, PAVED TRAILS AND the smaller dirt trails. If the weather were worse, almost everyone would stay on the paved parts, but this time of year the weather wasn't a factor.

The dirt trails meant less foot traffic and easier isolation, but a more restricted choice of targets. We just didn't know enough about the Texan to know its hunting habits.

But then, rumor said the Texan had been hunting since long before there was a Texas. Some said even before Rome fell. No hunter survived that long without varying its methods.

So we made life easy on ourselves and started with the paved roads.

After an hour we decided we were being lazy and veered onto the dirt trails.

After another hour we had yet to accomplish more than spooking the occasional lycra-clad jogger.

Then, at just about high noon, we came around a tight curve between shoulder-high shrubs that were fighting valiantly to hold onto their green. The air stilled. The birds hushed.

I felt a shiver in my shoulder blades that arched my back into a steep curve. The skin of my neck tried to crawl inside for warmth and protection. I spun around, right hand on the handle of my combat knife, left hand on my billy club. Nelson was a half-second behind me. He stopped his draw with his Ka-Bar half out of its sheath.

What I saw looked like a grizzled old cowboy complete with a dirty Stetson. The Texan looked like a reject from a John Wayne movie, where he would have played the aging gunslinger, retired undefeated to run a bar ... or something. Clint Eastwood westerns were more my speed, but this thing didn't have that spaghetti look: grizzled enough, but too sepia.

And its wrists and fingers were all too long by at least two or three inches. Its teeth when it smiled an aw-shucks greeting at us were stained brown, as though from tobacco.

But I knew that the Texan didn't chew tobacco.

"You boys kinda jumpy, aintcha?" Its voice was a smooth baritone, like it should have been reciting Shakespeare. Made its accent sound put-on.

"Your reputation precedes you, Texan," I said in as calming a voice as I could manage, more for the benefit of my own nerves than for its. "We only came to talk, but we had to be sure—"

"Awww, you boys afraid of little old me? Do your homework, boys, you ain't my type." The grin grew a little lopsided, and I got the impression that its mouth held more teeth than it should have. "Besides I know the posse you run with. I don't see no reason to start somethin'. Less you do."

Those last three words sent a quiver through my gut that would have made Carnifex jealous of the fear. I needed a moment before I could push words out.

"Actually, from what I can tell you don't have a victim profile."

"'Victim profile.'" The Texan chuckled. "Fancy mouth on you, McReedy. Knew a McReedy once, Colin McReedy. Had a fancy mouth on him too. He was a feebee as I recollect."

It tilted its head in an imitation of thought, but the angle wasn't quite right. Too sharp, and the neck didn't give the way necks are supposed to.

"This would'a been down around El Paso. You got kin down there?"

"No idea." Crap. It was bad enough that this thing knew my name. Worse, I thought I remembered Dad saying something about an uncle in the F.B.I. during one of his spates of complaint about my college major. *Roland, this is not the time to review Dad's Lecture Series About Your Bad Life Choices. Get back on point!* "Though I have a feeling that if I did, I don't anymore."

"Hmm. Anyway, ya'll got me dead to rights." It stretched its wrists and fingers and I must have heard sixty joints crack. "Not too particular about who I play with, but I do like to catch them by surprise."

The grin widened a little, and now I was sure that mouth held too many teeth. And I thought they looked a little longer than they had on first viewing. Sweat began trickling down my forehead, and I tightened my grip on my Ka-Bar, but I wasn't ready to draw it. Not yet.

"So," the thing continued in its butter-melting voice. "Ya'll just come up here to ask me if I'm gonna kill you? Or did you have some deeper purpose in mind?"

Standing there on a lonely hiking trail under a cloudy sky, the scent of dust and wild grass in my nose, I was only too glad to ask the Texan about anything that didn't involve killing.

"A few nights ago the sky lit up with burning letters."

"Ah, that was a good night to be a hunter." The grin got wider still. For just a moment I thought I saw a second row of teeth behind the set that were definitely longer that when the Texan first spoke. "So much panic. No one keepin' track of where anyone else is goin'. Hope he updates his bidders soon."

"He?" Even I could hear the excitement in my voice. I tamped it down as fast as I could. "You know who has the Djinn's Tear?"

"'Less it's been stolen in the last eight hundred years and I ain't heard about it." Even the Texan's shrug looked off, like the shoulder joints weren't really attached at the rib cage.

What the hell was this thing?

It laughed and continued, "That what ya'll are about? Tryin' to steal it from the bidders for — what's he call himself these days? The Rajah?"

"Wait," choked out Nelson. "You know the Rajah?"

"Been everywhere. Know everybody. Even that twisty snake friend of yours, thinks its hidin' over there in the bushes. Don't look now. Got a beef between the two of us, goes back more 'an a few years. Comes over here I might have to see if he tastes like chicken."

"But you're willing to let it sit there?" I wanted to say the demon's name, to have it come over. I wanted to let the Texan rid us of Scratch's mandated shadow. It was a happy thought, removing at least one thing from the growing list of creatures that wanted to kill and eat me. "Even though you have a vendetta?"

"Boy, I do love to listen to you talk. Vendetta. I like that. Sounds all proper and cosmopolitan." The Texan went through a series of too-precise hand movements, as though pulling a cigarette out of its mouth and flicking it away. Except that there was no cigarette. "But I can wait for my vendetta on Carnifex. I got nothin' but time."

"You could tell us who has the Djinn's Tear?" Nelson sounded stronger and more eager than he had since he mocked my coffee thermos, which right then lay forgotten on the ground, dropped when I felt the Texan approach. Nelson continued, "You could give us a name?"

"Might could do." That imprecise shrug again, followed this time by a fingertip adjustment to its Stetson that could have come straight off the silver screen. A picture-perfect mimicry of a human movement.

My stomach revolted at the contrast. Made me look away. I worried about the state of my peanut butter toast.

"The question is," said the Texan, dragging my eyes back to it, "what are ya'll gonna do for me? Notice you're down a couple-a fingers, boy. You tradin' tasty bites for information?"

"No!"

"Pity. I do like the taste of McReedy. Well what about you then?" It turned to Nelson. "Better marbling on you anyway. What's that name worth to you?"

Nelson bit his lip. His hand looked forgotten on his half-drawn knife. Silence reigned in the background. The sun broke through the clouds, but it brought no warmth.

"Nelson, don't do this," I said. "We don't need this thing. We'll find—"

"But will you find it in time?" drawled the Texan. It hooked his thumbs in its belt. "Bids are pourin' in, you better believe that. Sooner or later the rightful owner's gonna figure out that ain't no one can offer absolution. Either he'll vanish or settle for the runner up and they'll vanish. Either way, the prize is gone and ya'll are left holding your Johnsons."

"He's right," said Nelson.

"No *it* isn't," I insisted through gritted teeth. "All these things lie, Nelson. All of them. The more it says we need it, the less we really do."

"Can't say I cotton much ta bein' called a liar. But I'll let that one slide if we come to an agreement."

The grin widened another notch. Too wide, beyond even the likes of Mick Jagger and Steven Tyler. The Texan was abandoning its pretense of humanity, and the shaking of my knees suggested running before it attacked. The teeth stretched to an inch long now, all sharp and pointed, right down to the extra row or two behind them. Like a shark.

"So what do you say, boy? Let me take a little off the side? Your pants'll fit better."

"What do you want for the name?" said Nelson.

Formal tone. Businesslike. Nelson was freaking negotiating with this monster. I needed the last of my nerve not to stare slack-jawed at Nelson, but I held my focus on the monster ready to kill us, not the idiot negotiating with it.

"I'll take the spare tire for you. A little roll of flab you'll never miss."

"Too much. The little finger of my right hand."

I winced at that, but held my silence.

"Too little. The whole hand."

"I need the hand too much. My left ear."

"Make it the left eye and we got a deal."

Nelson looked at me. I shook my head in emphatic denial. He bit his lip again.

"Think about it," said the Texan. "Your part of the world has a long tradition of trading an eye for wisdom. Think of that Wo-tan boy. Did a lot of good for him."

"I don't follow the old gods."

"Then say 'thine eye offended thee' and pluck it out for me. Can't say I care much what your reason is, but the offer is a name for an eye. And if we can't come to an arrangement, then I gotta think ya'll came here to waste my time."

The Texan shook out its wrists and fingers again in that long, waterfall series of cracks and pops.

"No. Can't say that'll sit too well with me. Not at 'tall."

"Fine," said Nelson. "But the name first."

In a flash the Texan's arms stretched six feet to Nelson. Its too-long fingers grabbed Nelson's hair with one hand. His shirt collar with the other. It yanked Nelson close.

I drew my knife and baton. Took a step closer. Raised my Ka-Bar.

The Texan said, "Boy's name is Enoch Abrahamson. The Tear won't let him change it. But he won't keep the Tear on him."

And with that, the Texan leaned in and sucked out Nelson's left eye, chomping down with its brown teeth to sever the tendons binding the eyeball to Nelson's socket. Blood spurted, but the Texan's long, thick tongue whisked across and sealed the wound as it went, leaving only a rough scar behind.

The Texan released Nelson, took a single step back, and closed its eyes with a rapturous smile as it chewed.

Weapons still in my hands, I took another step forward, determined to end this foul thing.

The Texan swallowed and said, "One more step, boy, and I'll kill and eat you both. Truth is, a little taste like that just makes me hungrier. So ya'll better collect your boy and leave before I decide to see about lunch. And be quick about it. Looks to me like something that ate him don't agree with him."

I flicked my eyes for a glance at Nelson, and saw him curled up on the ground, trembling. I stepped between him and the Texan, weapons ready, and said, "Get up, Nelson. It's time to go."

Nelson only whimpered.

"Nelson! Snap out of it!"

Nelson whimpered again. The Texan chuckled.

"Funny thing about bein' et by me, boy. Never said I only eat the flesh."

Every human instinct screamed that I either needed to run like hell or kill this thing. But I knew I couldn't take it down without Nelson. Hell, maybe not even with Nelson. But definitely not just me.

I leveled my Ka-Bar between myself and the Texan. Shoved my billy club back in its holder. Grabbed Nelson's collar with my left hand. I needed a moment to adjust my grip for the missing finger, then started dragging him away. After a few steps, Nelson tried to help by kicking along the ground.

The Texan just watched, its grin wider yet, stretching to nearly its ears. It reached up with one finger and tipped its hat.

"Until next time, McReedy. Until next time."

I HATED TO DO IT, BUT I SHEATHED MY KA-BAR ONCE THE TEXAN WAS out of sight. I loathed not having a ready weapon, but joggers didn't need to see me brandishing a combat knife. By the time we reached my car, Nelson had found his feet, but not much else. I still dragged him by the collar, but he stumbled along with me, sobbing and half-doubled over with his hands still covering his missing left eye.

I knew this job might kill us, but I never thought we would die a piece at a time.

I helped Nelson into the car and clicked his seat belt into place. The moment I closed the passenger door I had my hand on my Ka-Bar and my eyes scanning every direction. The Texan was still nearby, and he said he liked to take his prey by surprise.

He also said there would be a next time. Not if I could help it. I kept my back to my Camry and walked sideways around the car to the driver's side. I reached behind me and unlocked it with my left hand, eyes still watching everywhere, even up. When I had the door open, I slid into the seat and slammed and locked the door in one motion.

"Locks will not help you," said Carnifex from the back seat. "The Texan could shatter that glass before you could draw your knife."

Nelson screamed and huddled against the door. I proved how fast I could draw my knife and held it between me and the snake demon. "I didn't call you."

"You continue to draw that knife on me."

"We need time before we report."

"I want the name the Texan gave you."

"Not part of our deal. You want our report? We met with the Texan. Nelson bartered his eye for information. Our next move is to research that information. Now piss off."

Carnifex hissed at me, but my fear gauge was still redlined from meeting the Texan. Those long fangs just couldn't inspire more. But Nelson started openly crying. Tears flowed fast down his face and he keened from somewhere in the back of his throat.

Worse, the telltale smell from men's rooms and city alleys filled the air. Reflex made me hope he didn't soil my seat, but shame followed fast on that thought.

The demon's hiss changed its quality, almost soothed as though in pleasure. Its pupils dilated and its tongue flicked the air. The look Carnifex gave me then was almost lazy, pleased.

"Out," I growled. I wanted to carve the smug satisfaction off that snake face and I let it show in my voice. "You got our second report, now get the hell out until I call you!"

Carnifex hissed a laugh at me, then twisted into its ribbon shape and slipped out through the air vents.

"It's gone, Nelson," I trying for soothing but settling for not shaky. I tried patting his shoulder as I put away my knife. "The demon's gone, and you're safe."

Nelson huddled tighter into the seat and kept crying.

"What did that thing do to you?"

Wrong question. The keening sound was back.

"Don't worry. We'll get you better. I'll find a way to get you better."

Not that I had any idea of how to do that. And I didn't have time to dig through a bunch of books and hope I got lucky. Nelson needed to be in good enough shape to see his family tonight, to figure out a story for them about how he lost the eye. I needed help and I didn't know where to turn.

No. Nelson needed help. And I knew where he would want me to go.

———

I pulled into a space in the lot at Eagle Hill Park in Mountain View, a pretty stretch of green between Castro and Shoreline. It had a large swath of well-tended lawn — currently in use for two separate soccer games — trees lining the outside to give the illusion of privacy, and a big pool where you could take your children for swimming lessons. It also had something more important to me right then: public restrooms.

I turned off the engine and looked at Nelson. He had stopped crying somewhere along the drive, but he still huddled between the seat and door, his face in his hands.

"Nelson?"

Nothing.

"Nelson, I want to take you to see Snigdha. I don't know how to help you, but she might."

Still nothing. I had to hope he was listening at least.

"I thought you might want to change your pants first—"

He started shaking his head emphatically, hands still over his missing eye.

"I have a pair of sweats in the trunk. No underwear, but clean."

"S-s-s-Snigdha." It came out as much a sob as a word, but I understood.

"You want to go straight to see Snigdha?"

His whole body shook with his rapid nod of agreement.

I shrugged and fired the Camry back up.

I COULDN'T MAKE NELSON WALK THE STREETS OF MOUNTAIN VIEW IN his soiled jeans. Instead of parking in the lot across the street as I usually did, I maneuvered down the narrow alley behind New Dawn Books and stopped in the tight space between a stack of empty milk crates and three overflowing plastic garbage bins.

I had no problem squeezing out of my door, but I had to re-stack the crates before I could swing the passenger door wide enough for Nelson's bulk to wedge its way out. As he passed I caught only a hint of his smell over the rancid odor of decaying leftovers from the health food café next door. Apparently the freshest ingredients, served without preservatives, went bad quickly when they were thrown out.

There was another scent in the air, weaker, that explained why Therese never locked the back door during business hours: pot. She must have snuck back here to smoke sometimes on her breaks.

I half-carried Nelson through that door and came face-to-face with Snigdha, her pupils vertical and wide despite her human seeming. Her nostrils flared and she sniffed the air around us.

I froze. I had to check the impulse to grab my knife. I needed a break from monsters for just a little while, even ones that might help us.

Might.

"What has eaten him?"

"The Texan."

She nodded and gestured for me to bring him into her office. I dragged Nelson until I could drop him into a bean bag chair, both of us puffing from hunger, stress, and effort. Cold sweat matted down Nelson's hair and shirt. I had my first chance to see the stain on his jeans that soaked his crotch and the inner part of both thighs. He must have let go of his whole morning's worth of coffee.

Snigdha retrieved two cups of tea from a flowery ceramic service on her desk. I brought Nelson's cup to his lips and helped him dribble a swallow into his mouth before dumping a sip of my own onto my shirt so I could slug some down. I knew the taste then: Darjeeling.

I relaxed into another bean bag chair. Hospitality. I hadn't expected Snigdha to harm us, but coming wounded to any monster was never a safe plan. I looked over to where Snigdha leaned against her desk, a cup of her own held in both hands where she could savor the aroma. She made her simple white dress look slinky. I might have found her sexy, if I hadn't seen her snake form.

Wait. Three cups were on that desk?

"You were expecting company?"

She looked at me, enigmatic as a portrait.

"You were expecting us?"

"You should move your car. The local police love to ticket." My eyes slid to Nelson, and she smiled. "Why do you think I observed the ritual?"

"I didn't mean—"

"I know. You are frightened of us all. Go park your car, and bring back any spare clothes you might have for him. I shall see what I can see about poor Nelson."

I hustled out to a street spot at the end of the block. I had my remaining fingers on the handle of my car door, ready to hop out, when a cop car cruised past and I was acutely aware of being too well-armed for this neighborhood. I turned back and pretended to look for something in my mess of a glove compartment.

Once the cop was gone I got out of the car, pretending to have some legitimate purpose here, like any of a dozen nearby shoppers or suited people, the latter likely heading for one of the law or accounting offices within a couple of blocks.

But even though I had left my criminal past behind, I in no way considered myself legitimate.

Anyway, I grabbed my sweats from the trunk, locked the car, and jogged back down the alley to the rear entrance of New Dawn Books.

I came back in to see Snigdha swaying above Nelson, her arms waving in a complex pattern. The curves and arcs her body described were not possible for humans. Bones would have gotten in the way of such tight curves, such fluid waves. The dance she did without moving her feet was pure snake.

I stood in the doorway, transfixed by the sight. Part of my mind screamed at my vulnerability, at the knowledge that if she lashed out I could never respond in time.

But my body didn't care. It swayed to her rhythm, even my head and neck flowed back and forth in a pale imitation of her smoothness. My heart fell into the rhythm. I could almost hear the whining notes of a snake charmer's pipe...

Snigdha stopped and the spell was broken. She quirked an eyebrow at me. "I see you liked the show."

I was struck by the sudden awareness that another part of my body had responded to her dance, and had approved. I flushed bright red, more ashamed than embarrassed, sputtering sounds because no words would come out.

"It is as I thought," she said, turning back to Nelson. "The Texan has eaten his courage."

"His ... courage?" My voice cracked, but at least the disturbing idea had wiped away any threat of arousal. "Nelson—"

"Can accomplish nothing more today. He must have his family. And rest." She stroked his cheek with what I would have called fondness, were Snigdha human. "But his nature is brave, and the Texan did not bite deep. He may be well enough to leave his house tomorrow."

"What do you know about the Texan?"

"Enough. Better you had not seen him. Better still that you never do again. He will have your scent now, and he will not forget it."

"When we parted, it said, 'Until next time.'"

"Pray that time does not come." She moved to her desk and finished her tea before turning back to me. "Now you should help him with those clothes and take him home."

WHEN I GOT NELSON BACK UP FROM THE BEAN BAG CHAIR, HE MOVED better. He finished his tea on his own, and he refused help with changing his pants. When he came out of the bathroom wearing my sweats, I realized I would never ask for them back. After all, his underwear had to have gotten it worse than his jeans, which meant that he was going commando in my gym pants.

Time for a new pair.

Nelson trembled nonstop and jumped at every noise and shadow, but at least I didn't have to drag him down the alley. He walked on timid feet, eye darting back and forth, head craning to cover the periphery lost with his missing eye, and arms huddled in against his chest. He clutched his soiled clothes like a smelly security blanket.

I did have to lead him out of the alley, uttering constant reassurances and guiding him with my hand on his shoulder. He made me 'cover him' for the seconds he needed to get in the car and don his seat belt.

We were cruising through light traffic down El Camino toward Sunnyvale when I realized. "You're in no condition to drive."

"Forget it."

"Where do you live, Nelson?"

"In my car. Take me there."

"Don't be stupid."

"Pull over. I'll walk."

"You couldn't walk to the car on your own."

"Catch cab."

"You're already in a car."

"Motel then."

"You heard Snigdha. You need your family."

"I'll call them."

"From a motel? That'll look good to Tish."

Ten more minutes we went on this way. Finally, at a stoplight, I had to drop the bomb. "Do I have to take your phone from you and call your wife? It's not like you could stop me right now."

"Kill you."

"Maybe later, but right now you can't do more than say the words. You need your family, and I'm going to do what I have to to get you to them."

"Bastard."

"Yep."

"Drop me there." He pointed to a chain diner. "I'll call Tish. You can watch."

The guy behind me pounded on his horn. The light had changed while I stared slack-jawed at Nelson. I flipped off the horn-blower and moved through the intersection into the suicide lane that would let me turn into the diner parking lot.

I had nothing left to say. I finally really understood, on a gut level, that Nelson had never been joking about killing me. Not once. He distrusted me, maybe hated me, only worked with me because the Rajah made him. If I hadn't been the one who could sense the Djinn's Tear, Nelson might have let me die yesterday.

Maybe I was overreacting. Nelson feared everything right then. Maybe if this were a normal injury he might have let me drive him home. But I was too hurt, tired and pissed off to care. As soon as I had a parking spot I said, "Carnifex."

Nelson cowered in his seat as the snake demon twisted out of its ribbon shape in the seat behind me. From the smell, Nelson soiled the sweats. Not that he could have had much urine left.

"I have a report for you," I said before the demon could speak.

"Our third and final of the day. The Texan put Nelson out of action. He's going home to rest and will be back on the job tomorrow. I'm going to go see what I can dig up about that name." I saw Carnifex's mouth open, so I hurried ahead. "I'm not telling you what the name is. I'll report on my findings tomorrow. We're done for the day. Piss off."

"You presume too much, mortal."

"I said piss off."

It rasped a hiss at me and vanished ribbon-shaped through the air conditioner. Nelson didn't wait another second to open the door. Before he could slam it behind him I said, "You owe me forty bucks for the sweats."

Yes, I included tax.

I DIDN'T STAY TO WATCH NELSON MAKE HIS PHONE CALL. IN FACT, I HAD to take a couple of calming breaths before I could pull out of the parking space. I turned on the radio and hit one of my preset buttons without caring which one. Either a newswoman or a traffic reporter told me that a semi had jackknifed on the San Mateo bridge and shut down traffic both directions.

The blather soothed my grumbling about Nelson as I waited for traffic to let me pull out onto El Camino. It was around two-thirty, just about the start of rush hour. Like happy hour, rush hour was not so much a sixty minute stretch and more of a section of the day. And with rush hour starting I was better off staying on El Camino until at least Wolfe, maybe Lawrence before I cut over toward Stevens Creek and home.

My stomach bitched that I hadn't had any food since breakfast. I reached for my phone to call Karen, see if she wanted me to pick something up.

Fire lit the sky in letters hundreds of feet long: "Three Days Remain."

I stared, probably missing at least one opening to pull out. The

Texan was right. Enoch Abrahamson was growing tired of fielding bids that didn't offer the one thing he wanted: absolution. In three days Abrahamson would either take the "high bid" — whatever that was — or just disappear again.

I had to find him first. Karen's soul depended on it. Not to mention my life, and Nelson's life, and Nelson's whole family.

I pushed the button to turn off the radio. I didn't need to listen to a bunch of whackadoos rant about proof that the End Times were upon us. I had the feeling that my personal end time was pretty well nigh either way.

I also had the feeling that I would be working through dinner.

14

I DIDN'T RUSH OFF THIS TIME. I HAD NO DOUBTS THAT SMALL-TIMERS all over the Peninsula sprang into action as though this were some zany scavenger hunt movie. Well, let them. Chances were that Abrahamson was nowhere near the center of those letters this time. That first time he needed to leave a trail of evidence as proof. He needed that grisly murder to make headline news right under his announcement because anyone who knew anything about the Djinn's Tear would know what signs to look for.

I thought of it as the supernatural world's equivalent of a polite, time-saving gesture. 'Look, here is the virgin you expect to find, dead under the middle of the announcement with his chest opened."

Worked perfectly too. Every news station ran stories about Eric Collingsworth. Some of Collingsworth's friends lamented at six and eleven that he had taken one of those chastity vows and died a virgin. One of the national cable news outlets even aired recreations of the poor bastard's murder. Made great news copy. I guess.

But this time Abrahamson didn't need the publicity. This time he might have killed the virgin out in the salt flats, or someplace equally deserted, and relied on specificity in his wish to position the center of the fiery display. He had had hundreds of years to practice with his trinket. He had to know all the ins and outs.

So I chose to let others race around to see what little their spells and eyes could tell them. Instead I went home.

A GOOFY, TIRED SMILE SPREAD ACROSS MY FACE WHEN I SAW KAREN'S Jetta in her spot. Daydreams of my incipient hug continued until I reached for my driver-side door handle.

Then I remembered the black dog. The personal murder attempt that almost got me because I didn't pay enough attention getting out of the car.

A tremor ran through my back, shook my shoulders. I drew a deep breath, let it out slowly. I craned my head to look through my car's windows at the back alley parking lot behind my row of apartment houses. Parked cars. More parked cars. A stray black cat.

But there were plenty of places I couldn't see. If anything were waiting for me, it could have been hiding behind any of a half-dozen dumpsters, or tucked behind the stucco of a parking port, or even lay in wait behind a decorative shrub.

I thought about that, my fingers drumming on the hilt of my knife. Places to hide, but I had no itchy skin, no shivery shoulders. No signs at all of Things Man Was Not Meant to Notice.

As far as I could tell, nothing around me was more threatening than Mrs. Dennison from down the street, carrying her empty cat food cans out to the recycling bin. I smirked as I wondered how long that black cat would stay stray. She would probably start feeding it soon if she hadn't already.

If it really was a stray...

I stared harder at the black cat. It had notches on both its ears and its fur looked scraggly, but it seemed feline enough. It even bathed its forepaw like a cat. Probably a real cat.

And Nelson thought I was paranoid before.

One hand on the handle of my Ka-Bar, I opened the door and

slipped out of my Camry, keeping my back to the vehicle. A three-sixty spin didn't show me anything else suspicious. I kept my eyes darting at every shadow and hiding place as I hot-footed it to my front door.

For what felt like the first time in years, I didn't get jumped.

I let myself in and slammed and double-locked the door behind me. Karen looked up at me from the couch. Half of my occult library and notebooks lay open around her. She had a yellow legal pad and pen in her hands.

"Trouble?"

"Always, but I don't think I was followed this time."

"What about..." She shivered and the fear that passed through her eyes made me ache someplace deep in my soul. I never wanted to see that look again, but I had the feeling I would before this was over.

"It's a bound demon and its master wants something from me. So we made a deal. It can't come inside while you're here."

"But it can come in when we're not home?"

"I ... hadn't thought of that." My stomach sank, so I joined it, sliding my back down the door until I could hang my head forward and rest it on my knees. "But it will. It'll probably leave us fucking notes or something."

I sighed.

"I'm sorry. I just wanted to keep it away from you."

"Hey." The couch creaked as she rose but I didn't look up. A moment later I felt her stroke my hair. I shuddered as I remembered Carnifex's tongue. The hand stopped. Karen spoke in a soft voice. "Look at me, Rollie."

Even though she crouched, I had to raise my head off my knees to meet her eyes.

"You never asked me about N.A. or the twelve steps." I must have started to apologize because she gave me a small smile and said, "You were giving me space. I know. And I appreciate it. That's not what I mean."

She crossed her ankles and sat with a grace that made me look club-footed. She put one hand on my arm.

"There are a lot of ways to look at it or talk about it: higher power, understanding, support. But those aren't the things that keep you clean. What keeps you clean is breaking it all down to manageable steps.

"People talk about taking it a day at a time. And that works ... mostly. But when the craving hits and you start fiending, a day feels like an awfully long time. Forever. It feels impossible that you can go so long without that sweet high.

"So you don't try to go a whole day. You take it an hour at a time. You say to yourself, 'I can stay clean for the next hour.'"

Her nostrils flared in an inaudible sigh. "Except sometimes even an hour feels too long. The other day, when I stopped myself from buying that fix, I had to stay clean minute by minute.

"And that's how we're going to beat them, Rollie." She started stroking my arm. "We're going to hold it together. And it starts minute by minute."

I rolled forward to sit on my knees. I slipped my arms around her waist and pulled her into the hug I'd been looking forward to, both of us still sitting on the floor with our backs to the front door. "Minute by minute," I said.

"Now tell me about your day."

***

Karen had skipped lunch too, so we ate delivery pizza at the kitchen table: roast chicken, garlic and peppers with a basil sauce. She washed hers down with Cola Rex and I with Dr. Destroyer.

Karen had spent her day reading as though she had joined an occultism class mid-semester. In fact, she had learned enough now that while we ate at the kitchen table she asked an awkward question.

"I don't like the idea that a demon can get in here anytime it wants. What kind of warding spells do we use?"

"None!" I choked out through a mouthful of my third slice. Karen's eyebrows came together in determination and I had to force down a large swallow in my rush to elaborate. "No wards. Believe me, you don't want wards."

"But without protective magic anything can get in here."

"Yeah, but a lot of things can't come in uninvited anyway, and without wards the odds are good that none of the rest will bother. Wards are like sending up a flare that says, 'interesting things inside!' Makes them all want to take a look."

"But the books say—"

"Those books are written by the types of lunatics who think they can gain power without paying the price. Like this Djinn's Tear thing. Makes the owner sacrifice a virgin every time he wants a wish granted. The current owner's been using it to live a life of leisure for some eight hundred years or more. This is the kind of guy who will use his major artifact just to make public announcements. And he thinks he can trade it and get absolved of all his crimes."

I wanted to spit, felt the need give my mouth a grimace. The thought of Abrahamson was almost enough to ruin the chicken-and-garlic taste on my tongue. But I needed Karen to understand.

"Magic always takes its toll. Even the smallest spell screams at the whole supernatural world, 'Hey, I exist! Come play with me!'" I reached across the table, took her hand and squeezed it. "You don't want to get mixed up in magic."

"Newsflash, Rollie. We aren't just mixed up in magic, we're buried up to our necks in it and the tide is rising. Maybe we need to consider all our options."

"Magic won't solve our problems. It'll just add new ones to the pile. It would be like turning to face that incoming tide with our mouths open. We'll just drown faster."

"Then what good are all those books?"

A fair question, and I bought time to word my answer by eating the final bite of my current slice. Karen's piece of pizza sat on its plate, ignored in the face of our topic.

"The authors may be lunatics, but they understand an important concept: everything in the supernatural world has to follow its own rules. Reading those books helps us figure out those rules, and that will give us the advantage we need."

I stopped for a swig from my soda. "I don't know what the Rajah is, but if he's something in those books then those books have the secret to killing him. That's why we have them."

"There's got to be some way to keep that thing from going through my underwear drawer when we're not home." At my puzzled glance, she continued, "I'm missing the pink, French-cut pair."

"Must be for Scratch, the perv. Wards won't help though. I hate to point this out, but you signed a deal with Scratch. That means his demons can just walk right in, no matter what protective magic you might have up."

"He's right of course. We can," said a sultry voice from down the hall near the bedroom. A whisky-soaked contralto voice I'd heard before.

Without looking away from Karen I snuck my hand toward my Ka-Bar, wished I'd kept my jacket on instead of hanging it on the chair behind me.

"Except that the panties were for me," the voice continued. "I just love the color of innocence."

Karen and I looked over to see the blonde demon from Scratch's house. It hid its horns and wings behind its well-used-co-ed façade. A façade so well-constructed even *my* instincts failed to scream, "Monster!"

A façade that wore only a pair of pink, French-cut panties.

"Oh, honey," said Karen with a laugh. "Pink is not your color. I mean" — she waved her hand in a vague gesture to indicate the demon's whole look — "you've got the porn star thing down pat. But take it from an ex-hooker who's seen a lot of flesh and a lot of underwear. Way too much red in your skin to pull off pink."

While Karen spoke, I snuck my knife from its sheath and under the table, blade flat against my thigh.

The demon stamped its foot in an almost petulant fashion, dropping its disguise as it did. Its skin grew sunset red while its eyes, hair and nipples turned deep maroon. Charcoal-black wings sprouted from its back, and matching tiny horns from its forehead. The pink panties burned away to ash so fine it disintegrated. That hair was maroon too.

The moment the illusion dropped, whatever power hid her from my sense of the unnatural dropped with it. I could feel her presence like cinder and fire ants, almost touching my hands and arms.

I jumped to my feet. I got three steps before the full effect of her power hit me. And despite all the warning signs, my body still betrayed me.

In my head I didn't find this creature the least bit sexy, but lust filled the air like her personal perfume. My breath grew shallow. My cheeks flushed. The room got brighter like my pupils dilated hard and fast. My blood raced. My khakis got painfully tight in the front.

I prayed Karen didn't notice. Glanced to check. She stood next to me now, stock still. Jaw wide in silent shock. Eyes wider, pupils huge. Worse, I could tell that the transformation had ... affected her too. The room wasn't that cold.

"Ah," moaned the demon, giving her body a writhe that compelled me to watch her. "I see you both at least show this form its proper appreciation. If only I had time to play."

I finally recovered my voice, even if it cracked on my first word. "Wha-, what are you doing here?"

"Why I have come to fetch you. Mr. Scratch would like a word."

"Doesn't anyone use the phone anymore?"

"Mr. Scratch prefers to see a man's eyes when he speaks. Myself, I prefer ... other views."

She looked me over like a display case. Drew a breath that made me throb. She licked her lips, showing long inches of bright red tongue.

I tried to raise my Ka-Bar, but somewhere in there I'd dropped it. Not that it mattered. My hand wasn't obeying me anyway.

"Well, maybe I could take a *little* time..."

"Lofaham, Solomon, Iyouel, Iyosenaoui!" Karen thrust her right hand forward like a palm-heel strike. I tasted sand in the air. The demon screamed and vanished, just faded out like she'd been taken out of the shot frame by frame.

"What did you do?" I couldn't keep the horror out of my voice as I whirled to face Karen.

"Got rid of that bitch." She snapped her fingers once at the air. "Teach her to come in here and ruin my underwear. And looking at *my* man like that?"

"That was a spell, Karen."

That earned me a glare. "I've already sold my soul. How much worse could it get?"

"I was hoping we'd never find out. Promise me you won't do it again."

"We can't let these things push us around."

Those words sounded uncomfortably familiar. But still. "I don't want every monster in the Bay Area taking notice of us either."

"You work for a monster. They already know about you. And I sold my soul, so they must know about me too."

"They're not a club." Exasperation puffed out of me, but I could see by the tilt of her head that she was listening. I reached out and took her by the shoulders. Not gripping, just holding her attention.

"These things. They don't share information, but they're all over the place. Seriously. One reason I keep putting out milk for the Good Neighbors is that if I encourage them to hang around, I get the side benefit of discouraging others.

"It's like a freaking ecosystem, except that it's not based on natural ecology. It's all based on their own weird guidelines and power games."

"If they're everywhere we won't be able to avoid them anyway."

"I'm not saying it right." The echo of the cinder-and-fire-ants feeling from the succubus — I didn't know for sure that was what the demon was, but 'succubus' would do until I learned a better term — reminded me of the purpose of its visit.

"Look. I've got to go see Scratch or he'll do something worse than send his bitch to play wah guitar at us." I stroked her shoulders once with my thumbs, then bent to retrieve my Ka-Bar.

"In the meantime, I want you to think about something. The more magic you do, the more you play by supernatural rules and the less you play by human rules. Sooner or later you'll turn into something like Scratch. Personally, I'd rather die as a human."

When I left, Karen was biting her lip in thought.

THERE ALONG THE BORDER BETWEEN MENLO PARK AND ATHERTON THE neighborhood seemed to hush like a librarian. "Don't make too much noise. Don't disturb the rich people."

I swear. I had to pull around an SUV loading up with laughing teenagers dressed up for a dance or something, and the sudden noise shocked me so bad I almost went for my knife.

Still, I made it to Scratch's house before sunset, which encouraged me even though I knew I would be driving home after dark. I had no doubts that the police kept this area safe from human threats, even after sunset. Heck, this area had so much money that even the clean cops probably wore silk uniforms and gold Rolexes.

But cops wouldn't do much good against the supernatural, and it occurred to me that Scratch might not be the only nasty with an Atherton address.

Again the section of stone wall opened for me the moment my tires touched the driveway. I wondered if it would still open if I tried to show up uninvited. I pondered that past the ring of sequoias and parked in front of the garage.

I turned off the engine, sucked in a slow, deep breath and let it out through my nose. Talking to Scratch without someone watching my back was pretty high on my list of stupid-things-that-can-get-me-killed.

No, I didn't actually have a list, but making one might not have been a bad idea.

Still, showing up without Nelson at least removed one bone of contention. The last time I had been here, Nelson and I almost pulled knives on each other over the manners we showed monsters. He believed that the power of monsters demanded placation. I believed clinging to our will kept us human. Not easily reconciled positions. Maybe the only way to resolve the issue was for one of us to die.

Then again, longer lives might provide more accurate results. If we both lived to see fifty, I was pretty sure I'd still be human. But would Nelson?

I knew that practicing magic, like Karen wanted to do, would be one way to substitute supernatural rules for human rules. Scratch was prime proof of that. He looked human, but he was a monster.

And Nelson's obsequiousness might be another form of rule substitution. What would become of him if he continued kowtowing to the whims and manners of the supernatural world? Could he turn into some kind of servitor? Become little better than that fake college receptionist serving the Sons of Morning?

What if the process had already started? Nelson was awfully quick to obey the Rajah...

I shook away the distracting line of thought and got out of the car. Nelson wasn't here to watch my back — if he even would — so I had to stay twice as alert.

Again the mahogany front door opened as I approached, and the succubus — back in her used-up-co-ed disguise, complete with a midriff-baring tank top and bright red short shorts — admitted me into the dark blue, single story house.

"Enter freely and of your own will," she said as she stepped back and bowed me in, making sure to show plenty of cleavage and leg. "And leave some of the happiness you bring."

"You forgot the part about going safely," I said as I stepped past her, turning left and heading for the room where Scratch met me last time. I could smell old scotch and good cigars in the air. Just a hint, like it was a room deodorizer. I felt the spells crawl along my skin as they did last time, but I was ready for them. I acknowledged their tingle without letting them overwhelm me. Over my shoulder I continued, "That's kind of important to the saying."

"Are you sure I forgot?" she said in a mock innocent tone that stopped my feet.

"I have seen enough scary shit," I said as I turned to face her Playboy pout, "that a sex demon playing vampire just can't phase me."

"Oh, if I wanted to scare you—"

"You're a hard man to get along with," said a soft voice behind me.

I didn't have to turn to know it was Scratch. I recognized his clear tenor. I bit back a crack about how, with his look and voice, he should have been singing chants with the Benedictine monks.

"Men usually fawn over Xiom," he continued, "especially those who know what she is and what she can do for them."

"Mr. Milner would have been thrilled to see me in only a pair of panties," the succubus said with a coy look that should not have worked, damn it.

I turned to face her master. Scratch wore a simple, dark blue long-sleeved shirt with comfortable looking gray slacks, but was barefoot like his demon. His dead eye stared through me and I felt a twinge from it, as though it poked at what some of the old writers would have called my 'etheric body' or 'aetheric double.'

"Hard to find interest in your sex demon when you're holding the deed to my lover's soul."

"Fair enough," he said with a small smile. "Will you sit, or shall we talk in the hall like cretins?"

My turn to smile.

"Cretins it is," he said in a sad voice. "Modern America has lost all sense of the simple proprieties of life."

"If you'll tell me why I'm here I'll even get off your lawn."

"The Texan gave you a name. You refused to give it to Carnifex. You will give it to me."

"Sure." I pretended to look over the orgy scenes so I could look away from that dead eye. "Just hand over the deed to Karen's soul, cancel her debt to you, and swear that you and yours will leave me and mine in peace, in this world and in every other, until the end of time."

"That is payment for the Djinn's Tear. This is only a name."

"A name you might use to find the Tear first and cut me out of the deal." I met both his eyes now. "Forget it."

His nostrils flared as he took a deep breath and folded his arms over his chest. I had to admit he looked imposing. I wasn't sure I could take this guy even in a physical fight. Too lean, tall, and probably experienced. But it wasn't his physical prowess that worried me. I could feel that dead eye poking at me again.

Just in case this was some kind of telepathic crap, I started mentally singing the first song that came to mind: the Smurfs theme.

Yes, I watched the Smurfs. I was a kid, all right? I didn't say I was proud of it.

"Have you seen the sky today, Mr. McReedy?"

"I saw the letters go up."

"Then you know that our time is limited. I can help you, help us both, but I need that name."

"You bilk people out of their souls—"

"I make fair deals with honest offers."

"And I'll believe that when I can look back on this, years from now, and say, 'That Nicholas Scratch did right by me. He's not as bad as people say.'"

That got a chuckle out of him, but even that sounded menacing.

"Shall we discuss *your* reputation? It's gotten more interesting with the loss of your fingers."

"My reputation doesn't matter. You have to deal with me. I'm the one who can sense the Djinn's Tear, and I'm the only..."

But I wasn't.

———

THIS TIME SCRATCH'S SMILE WAS SO SMALL IT EXISTED ONLY AS A suggestion near his eyes and the edges of his lips. "Very good, Mr. McReedy. You've realized that you aren't my only option here. And Mr. Milner made no arrangement to keep Carnifex out of his house or away from his wife and children."

I turned and started for the door, but stopped short two feet shy of the succubus. I didn't know where Nelson lived. Poor Nelson who had tried so hard to keep his family safe from the Rajah, safe from the supernatural world, safe even from me. He didn't bring his work home, but work followed him anyway.

"I will have that name tonight, Mr. McReedy. The question is, will I hear it from you or will Carnifex wrest if from Mr. Milner?"

"Call back Carnifex. Call back any demons you have watching Nelson, Nelson's house, Nelson's family, Karen, my house, or otherwise keeping tabs on us. You summon them all back, and let me check with Nelson to see that he and his family are all right. Do that and I'll tell you the name."

Scratch blinked in amusement, then said, "Carnifex."

The demon's ribbon form whipped into the air before us and twisted into its indigo serpentine humanoid shape. It rasped a hiss at me in a way that I had begun to think of as its personal greeting to me.

"And the others," I said, keeping my voice as firm as possible. My head was reeling through possibilities, trying to think of warnings and admonitions I'd read in those old books.

"Demons," said Scratch in a warm tone, "unlike humans, rarely need 'backup.'"

"Then state formally that you have recalled all demons watching Nelson and his or me and mine."

Even though the dead eye never moved, I still felt as though Scratch met my eyes as he said, "I swear that I have done so, and may great Lucifuge Rofocale himself torture me for lies if I have not."

I felt the air pulse with heat when Scratch said those words. Both Xiom and Carnifex made sounds of acknowledgment as though witnessing the oath. Even more, I recognized that name as one of demonkind's heavy hitters.

If I could ever trust Scratch about anything, this was probably it. I pulled out my phone and speed-dialed Nelson.

"You all right?" I blurted out as soon as I heard him pick up.

"What the hell did you do, Roland? Carnifex came to my house. *My house!*"

"I got him called off, you prick. Is anyone hurt?"

"No, no thanks to—"

"Meet me at the dinner spot in half an hour. Our lives just got complicated." I hung up and turned to Scratch. "I swear to you. If you try to screw me out of our deal I will make you pay. No demon will protect you. No spell will shelter you. No hell will hide you. I will come for you and make you sorry for every evil thing you've done in your long, unnatural life."

"The name."

"The name the Texan gave us ... was Colin McReedy." I turned to leave, but Xiom barred my path.

"Relation of yours?" asked Scratch.

"Not that I know of. Can I leave now? I have a lot of work to do."

There was a pause, and I swear I felt that dead eye poking at the back of my skull. "The name sounds ... too western. Too Irish. But I believe the Texan gave it to you. Carnifex?"

"I taste truth in his words. Truth and fear. I believe the Texan gave him that name."

"Well," said Scratch almost to himself, "the Texan hasn't always been called the Texan either. But it's unlikely that a McReedy could have been so far east eight hundred years ago."

"Then maybe the Texan was wrong." I refused to turn around, even though it meant I had to watch the succubus pose. Of course, the sight might have been more appealing if I didn't know what it was. "Or maybe it's been stolen since then. Either way, that's what the Texan said. Colin McReedy."

"Very well, you may leave."

I started forward, but the succubus fluttered its eyelids, refusing to budge from my path.

"If you are lying to me," said Scratch, "then I swear to you, Roland McReedy, that after Carnifex finishes with your body, Xiom shall feast on your soul. And Karen Falk's."

Xiom blew me a kiss, then stepped aside. It bowed me out again, low to show maximum cleavage.

A valiant effort on the demon's part, but I had eyes only for my car and escape. I didn't know how long Scratch would need to find out about my deception, but the clock was ticking.

———

OUT THE FRONT DOOR AND INTO THE GATHERING NIGHT. COLD, STILL air hit me and I realized that the house had been growing slowly warmer as we spoke.

No time to worry about that.

I trotted across the thick grass toward my car, trusting my feet to carry me through the dimness. I fired off a text message to Nelson as I went: "My place instead."

I jumped into the front seat, then made myself pause for three deep breaths. I had to keep my adrenaline in check. Too much money here on the border of Atherton to risk the delay of a speeding ticket.

I gripped the steering wheel with white-knuckled intensity and struggled to stay within five miles per hour of the speed limit until I hit 101. Then I could let cruise control keep me on track as I cut over 85 and finally down 280 to my exit.

I pulled into my parking space to find Nelson waiting. Or at least something that looked like Nelson, wearing an eyepatch.

I narrowed my eyes at what might have been Nelson and said, "What did you say when—"

"You son of a bitch!" Nelson swung a right cross at my chin.

I tried to dodge, stumbled backward in my haste. I sprawled against my driver's side door, off-balance.

Had to be Nelson. A fake would have acted like a friend.

"What?" I rolled to my left, struck a fighting crouch out of reach. "What'd I do?"

"Your fault!" He pulled his billy club and knife. Bent his knees to lower his center of gravity. "That thing was in my house!"

"Shut the fuck up out there!" yelled a neighbor.

"So this is it then." I felt sick to my stomach. My shoulders wanted to sag. So much between us, and a misunderstanding ended the trust. I pulled out my Ka-Bar and billy club. "I guess it's better that I kill you than the Rajah."

Nelson and I faced off. Circled on the asphalt. Maybe ten feet between parked cars. Tight space for a fight. No maneuverability. That would work to his advantage.

Still we circled. Watched. Waited for the other to make the first move.

I tightened my grip, compensating. Nelson had one eye. In two quick steps I could close on his literal blind side. But he would be ready for that. Expect it. I needed an opening.

Nelson began to twirl his knife and club. Probably wanted to add momentum, so if I blocked a blow my missing fingers might work against me. Might let through a strike I could have stopped a couple of days ago.

We knew each other's moves too well to take the initiative. We looked for a lapse. A distraction. Anything.

Then we heard the distinctive click of the hammer being pulled back on a revolver.

As one Nelson and I turned our heads enough to see what looked like Karen. She held her thirty-eight with both hands, her stance wide and balanced.

"I'm pretty confident that Roland could take you, Nelson," she said in a casual voice. "But I think my detective special here removes all doubt about the odds.

"So. Instead of us killing you and wasting the night disposing of your body and lying to the police, what say you put your toys back in your trunk and we all go inside and drink coffee like civilized human beings."

Nelson lowered his weapons, transferred both to one hand. With slow movements, he pulled out the key fob for his Taurus and popped the trunk. He put the club and his Ka-Bar in a small cargo net, closed the trunk, and raised his hands in surrender. What-could-only-be-Karen and I put up our weapons.

"Right," I said, pausing to kiss Karen on the cheek, "shall we see about that coffee?"

———

ONCE WE WERE SAFE BEHIND DOUBLE-LOCKED DOORS — AND thankfully not wards — Karen got coffee together for us while Nelson and I sat at the kitchen table under the soft yellow glow of the overhead light.

I turned to Nelson. "First things first. How did you get your nerve back so fast? I thought it would take all night."

"I don't know. Tish picked me up, saw my eye and freaked out."

"And that didn't make you run and hide?"

"That's just it." A look of wonder came over him. "She was crying and hugging me and asking questions, and I started to feel better."

"Outpouring of love?" I almost hated myself for saying something so hokey, but powerful emotions do have a kind of magic. "Helped the healing?"

Nelson shrugged helplessly. "Then she got me home, and I crossed the threshold and I felt even better."

"Your place, your sense of self," I speculated aloud.

"Whatever. By the time the kids saw me and had their own little freak-out, I felt like myself again. We had an early dinner and ... celebrated that the 'accident' didn't kill me."

"What did you tell them?" This was from Karen.

"Doesn't matter. A lie."

"It matters," she insisted from the counter where she arranged everything on a tray. "They need to know the truth."

"Mind your own fucking business."

"Ease back down in your seat, motherfucker," I said. "And apologize."

"Fuck that," he said, but he did sit down again, the cheap wooden chair complaining under his weight. "The less they know the safer they are." Then he glared at me, at least as much glare as he could manage with one eye remaining. "Or were, until you got a demon sent after me!"

"That was not my fault."

"I was on the john, and that snake bastard just ribboned out of the shower drain in front of me."

"Caught with his pants down," I said to Karen with a smirk, as she set out our cups alongside milk, fresh cream, and real and fake sugar. She poured coffee for us each, and the rich smell smoothed through my system, felt like home. Like Karen. She even put an extra saucer on the tray.

I turned back to Nelson's cyclopean glare. Apparently the coffee smell did not affect him the same way. I said, "Let me guess, it wanted the name."

"Why did you have to tell him about the name?"

"What did you want me to tell him?" I paused to splash the first sip of black coffee onto the spare saucer and Karen smiled. "That we didn't learn anything?"

"Yes! And it's your fault we even have to make these reports."

"The reports keep that thing from spending all day with us, every day until we succeed or fail. And if I told it that we learned nothing, it would have reported that we're still not making progress."

I paused for a sip. I thought I saw understanding flash through Nelson's eye as he dumped too much cream and a cane's worth of sugar into his coffee. I decided not to chance it. "If the demon reports that we're failing, its master may interfere."

"I'd call a demon in my john a pretty big interference."

"I wasn't happy about seeing one wear my panties, either," said Karen, who always took her coffee with a half-teaspoon of fake sugar and a dollop of real cream. "But it least it hadn't come to kill us."

She turned to me. "No taking 'bonuses' on this job, by the way. Cheating's cheating, even with a demon."

"I wouldn't touch that thing to get your soul back." I hesitated. "Well, maybe for that..."

"I'd rather lose my soul," she said firmly. Our eyes met, and we shared one of those 'couple' moments.

"If you two are finished." Nelson waited until Karen and I were done smiling at each other, then continued, "All right. Maybe you had to tell him about the name. But do you have to mouth off to every creature we meet every goddamn second?"

"You've known him six months," said Karen. "What do you think?"

"I didn't 'mouth off' to the Texan."

Nelson shivered when I said that name, and he had to steady his cup with both hands to take his next sip. "Just shows you have at least some survival instinct."

"Come on, Nelson. Most of these things are bullies, just like the Sons of Morning. Give them an inch and they'll take the rest of your life." He started to retort and I spoke over him. "Look. It doesn't matter. We've wasted enough time as it is. I lied about the name."

"You idiot—"

"I told him the name of that F.B.I. agent the Texan mentioned, so it was a real name that the Texan really gave us. It just wasn't the one Scratch wanted."

"I thought you said you didn't play by their rules," said Nelson. "A misleading truth is what your faeries are famous for."

"Good Folk. Maybe that's what Ridges was trying to tell me. Play by their rules, if that's what it takes to survive."

"Exactly," said Karen, and in a flash I knew she didn't mean games of half-truths.

"No—"

"I make my own decisions, Roland," said Karen. "And I want us to get out of this alive too."

"Alive *and intact*," I insisted. "Magic will chip away at you."

"You're working magic?" said Nelson, eyebrows high.

"She's cast one spell, but she needs to stop there."

"I'll cast as many as I need to."

Karen and I glared at each other. Nelson cleared his throat.

"I don't think we have time for this."

"You're right," I said. "I don't know how long it'll take Scratch to work out that I gave him the wrong name. I figure we've got hours to find the real culprit before his pet snake comes calling."

"Half of the supernatural community has to be hunting for this guy. What chance do we have to find him first? Drive around and hope you pick up the scent?"

"Nope. People who rely on magic develop blind spots to the other ways of working." I pulled out my phone. "We've got a name, and we know he can't hide it. There are only so many places in the Bay Area where a guy accustomed to posh living would consent to rest his head."

Even Nelson smiled at that.

15

Actually, there were more than you'd think. Probably because of all the business travelers that come through the Bay Area. Nelson, Karen and I sat for hours at our kitchen table, cell phones in our hands, calling hotel after hotel between south San Jose and Marin, and between Berkeley and Half Moon Bay. We called everyplace that had a fancy ad in the phone book or a decent Internet review.

We must have gone through three pots of coffee and a half-dozen peanut butter and jelly sandwiches as we worked. Under the open phone books, the kitchen table was a wreck of plates, crumbs, and the remains of a bag of off-brand chocolate chip cookies I liked.

Once upon a time, research probably smelled like musty tomes and dusty rooms. For me it smelled like chocolate chips and peanut butter. And coffee, but I was willing to bet that old school researchers leaned on the bean as heavily as we did.

Anyway, it was closing in on midnight when a desk clerk said to me, "I'll transfer your call."

I jabbed the end button before the clerk could make the connection. "Found him! Vivaldi E.P.A."

"Lazy bastard," said Nelson, rubbing his face. "We should've thought to try there first."

"Lazy?" asked Karen.

"He found a victim on the Stanford campus and murdered him at Stanford," I said, picking up my coffee cup to slam down the last few drops. "And he was staying in a hotel just down University Avenue."

"Let's go," said Nelson, rising to his feet.

"What can I do?" asked Karen.

"If you're going to finish that research project, sooner is better." With that, I kissed Karen, and Nelson and I hotfooted it to my car.

"My weapons!" cried Nelson, detouring to his Taurus.

I started the car and pulled out of the parking spot, then backed down the alley to pick up Nelson at his car. Karen came running, and by the time I saw her I barely got the window down before she reached us.

"Take my gun," she said, pushing the thirty-eight at me. "Just in case."

"I've never fired one of these things." It was heavy and cold in my hand, and smelled faintly of oil. All that lethal power held in check by a little trigger...

"How hard can it be?" said Nelson. "You point and click, like a camera."

"Save it for close range then," said Karen, shaking her head with a grimace for Nelson. "Think ten feet or less and you should be okay. Don't get fancy. Aim for the center of mass."

She leaned in and kissed me. The world faded. Love. Fear. The future. All that and more came through in her kiss.

I hated my job. Monsters wanted to eat me. Nelson might make me kill him before this was over. But as long as I had Karen I had to be doing something right.

And we were on a real trail now. I almost felt like the end was in sight. And her kiss made me imagine survival was possible. We might really get to enjoy our money, travel and play, then finally settle down with a house, rugrats, soccer games, PTA meetings. An honest-to-God life.

When we parted she took a step back so I could slip the pistol into the door pocket. I closed the window and hit the gas.

THE VIVALDI IN EAST PALO ALTO WAS RIGHT OFF OF 101 AT UNIVERSITY Avenue. In fact, it was barely inside the E.P.A. border, which probably meant it got a tax break. But I was sure that was why most people called it the "Silicon Valley" Vivaldi. E.P.A. had come a long way in the last ten or twenty years, but its checkered history was probably too recent for a fancy hotel chain. Still, they didn't hold back in their design. The building was intimidatingly big, and lit up the night like its partner-in-size across the freeway: Ikea.

The parking lot was crowded, nearly full. I had to cruise around for almost ten minutes before I found an open, uncovered spot near the exit, a mere three football fields or so from the entrance. No pedestrians near us. Everyone probably safely inside for the night, although I wouldn't have been surprised to see security drive past in a golf cart.

We were here. All we had to do was sneak inside, find Abrahamson, and steal the Djinn's Tear. Easy, right?

"Think they'll have good security?" asked Nelson, holding up his billy club.

"Yeah," I said with a sigh, sliding my own back under the seat. "Better not risk those."

Plenty of practice and cool October air meant that Nelson and I had gotten good at concealing our Ka-Bars. But the billy clubs were just too obviously billy clubs. Some places we could get away with them, places where we either didn't mind people knowing we were armed or where people didn't look too closely at what we carried. But in a fancy hotel full of bright lights and security cameras? No chance. Nothing short of a trench coat would hide those babies well, and trench coats would have sent up a warning flag to every security-type around: *We think we're badasses! Keep an eye on us!*

"Why are you picking up the Colt?"

"Well," I said, "it might be easier to fire if I have it at hand." I slid the pistol into an inside pocket of my jacket.

"Do you have a concealed carry permit?"

"I'm not even sure the gun is registered."

"Put that thing in the trunk."

"Won't do us much good—"

"If it gets us arrested? Or shot? No. It won't." Nelson slapped his hand on the dashboard to get my attention. "Do you think that thing hangs like a wallet in your jacket? No. It hangs like a goddamn firearm."

"Fine," I said, pulling the detective special back out of my jacket. I had to admit, there was something comforting about the weight of it, the feel of it in my hand. I did like the idea of being able to kill some kind of nasty without letting it in arm's reach.

"I'll tuck it in the back of my ... pants ... just as soon as I find..." I looked at it from every angle I could think of. "Where the hell's the safety on this thing?"

"Don't you watch cop shows?" Nelson snorted with a smirk. "No safety on that gun."

"They give cops a gun without a safety?"

"Not anymore they don't."

"Fine." I popped the trunk and opened my door. "The pistol stays here. But if not having it gets me killed, I'll haunt you *and* your descendants."

"TELL ME YOU HAVE A PLAN," SAID NELSON AS WE APPROACHED THE curved, glass-and-steel edifice. He made a show of looking slowly all the way up. "I don't want to go door-to-door in this place. It'd take a week."

Apart from a middle section that looked like a top-down view of a wide letter 'w' and included some stonework, the front looked entirely made of windows, even if not all of them were transparent from where we were.

I double-checked my Ka-Bar before we reached the entrance. "The Texan said Abrahamson won't have it on him. But lazy as he is, he'll have it nearby. So we search."

We entered a world of wide spaces and tasteful décor. Marble and wood set the stage for expensive-looking art and discreet sitting areas with comfortable, but empty, chairs and couches. The place smelled … clean. Nothing I could put my finger on, except maybe a suggestion of flowers. Not even a specific flower smell, just vaguely floral.

Guests did mill about, though: checking in, or heading for the elevators or the bar. Two separate bellmen tried to help us find the front desk — not that it was concealed — but I sent them away with claims that we were meeting a friend.

Maybe I felt underdressed compared to the suits and chichi outfits around me, but I swear the bellmen looked relieved that Nelson and I weren't guests. Made me want to check in here sometime with Karen and wander around in shorts, sandals with socks, and Hawaiian shirts. Probably give someone a heart attack.

"So if it isn't 'on him,' then it probably isn't in his room," said Nelson. "You're thinking the hotel safe?"

"Would you trust the hotel safe with an … heirloom like that?" Had to check myself from calling it an artifact. Never knew who might have been listening. I puffed out a breath and focused on my awareness, letting my voice grow more distant as I continued. "I'm hoping that if we poke around in here I'll pick up the trail."

Nothing through the lobby. Nothing past the front desk or back near the service elevators. Nothing near the conference rooms, bar, restaurant — how big was this place?

Finally, over by a bank of elevators, I felt my face contort as I picked up a whiff of the foul reek I recognized. "Got it. It was carried on this elevator."

"How long ago?"

"What am I, a bloodhound?" I pointed. "It was carried on that elevator."

"Can you pick up the path it followed out? Or up?"

"I didn't get a hint of it until just now. Maybe they take it in and out by different routes, but always using this elevator."

Nelson pushed the button. I cocked an eyebrow and he shrugged. The door opened after only a matter of seconds. We boarded the elevator, but both groaned a sigh when we looked at the panel. The top two floors required special keys. I reached out and pushed the button for the top floor that nobodies like us could reach. It whisked us up in quick silence.

"Still smell it?"

"Yeah, but just a hint, hanging around the back of the mouth." I glanced at Nelson sideways. "So, do you have a plan?"

"Nope. You?"

"I figured that maybe Abrahamson stays in one room, the biggest and best they can give him, and rents a second room on another floor where he's concealed the Tear. Leaves instructions for no maid service, and no one has a reason to go in there."

"That ... actually sounds plausible."

"Yeah," I said with a snort. "So obviously it's not the case. But it can't hurt to check, right?"

My shoulders seized backwards as though I'd felt a dozen tarantulas crawling up my spine. Something behind us. Something big. Smelled like horse sweat. But I noticed it too late.

"Actually," said a voice that was so deep we felt it more than heard it, "that was close to the truth."

Nelson and I tried to spin around, both of us reaching for our knives. But we were too slow, too late.

Huge, thick hand. Bigger than my face. Horse sweat smell stronger. Vise grip on my head. Hot. Blinding.

My skull. Nelson's skull. Thunderclap.

Explosive pain. Then nothing.

I woke to the sensation of someone gently slapping my face with an old, worn baseball glove. And by gentle, I mean hard enough to rock my head, but nothing compared to the earthquake damage my skull screamed about from the spot that had bashed against Nelson's head.

The smells came to me next: sweat and livestock right in front of me, citrus air freshener underlying everything else, but around the edges I could pick up the foul residue of the Djinn's Tear.

My butt was planted on a wooden chair that might have been comfortable under other circumstances, the kind with a shaped seat and a rounded back that curved into arms. My elbows and wrists had been tied to those arms, and my ankles to the legs.

My limbs tried to scrabble for freedom anyway, because whatever smelled like sweat and livestock was powerfully unnatural and disturbingly close. The combination made every inch of my skin crawl to the point that my testicles were seriously considering retracting up into my body.

Against every instinct, I opened my eyes. In front of me, peering at my face in assessment, was a humanoid head big enough for a rhinoceros, with greasy black hair, beady black eyes, and two tusks protruding from the lower part of its mouth past its wide, flat nose. It wasn't carrying a baseball glove, so that rough leather must have been its hand.

My first impression had been right. That hand *was* larger than my head. In fact, if this thing stood upright it had to have been nine or ten feet tall. But it seemed most comfortable with its knees and back bent, bringing it down to almost human height, even though its bulk spread easily twice as broad at the shoulders and hips as Nelson's widest point.

The word 'ogre' came to mind, but more from childhood fairy tales than any research I'd done.

"Awake and alive," it rumbled. Its voice was so deep I worried it would disturb the nearest fault line. "Told you I only knocked them out."

"You might have given them concussions," said a tired male voice. I heard the trace of an accent, but I couldn't place it.

I let my eyes dart around the room, trying to get a quick feel for the situation. The room was bright, but the light didn't hurt me, which I knew was a good sign. The chair I was strapped to turned out to be a bar stool. Next to me sat Nelson, unconscious and similarly strapped down by what looked like white nylon cord.

Our barstools were at a bar at one end of ... a suite? Bar, refrigerator and kitchenette were closest, near a large, unlit stone fireplace. Opposite the fireplace was a window wall, with a dining/meeting table in front of it.

A step down from us led to a sitting area with large, comfortable couches done in blue and red above a tan carpet and a low, wide coffee table. Our combat knives and their sheaths sat on the table.

I could see four doors from my position and guessed them to be: hallway (had checkout time sheet on the back), coat closet (near the hall door), bathroom (half-open into darkness) and ... bedroom? I was not sure about the last one because the little bit I could see looked like lit hallway.

The man with the tired voice lounged on a blue couch, a bottle of Teufelsbrau beer in his scarred hand. The ogre — or maybe it was a troll — had its back to me. It was still speaking.

"You have me to handle your violence. Trust me to do my job."

"You are quite right. My apologies." He toasted what I decided had to be an ogre, then turned to me. His eyes were so startlingly blue that they almost glowed, even from some fifteen feet away. Something unnatural about him ached behind my eyes, but that might have been my massive headache. "Roland McReedy, I presume?"

"I might be," I said as I watched the ogre stalk to the hallway door and hunch, facing the room. I got a chill from the silence of its movement, not fair from a thing so massive. "And you, I presume, work for Enoch Abrahamson?"

The man chuckled. "Don't look like an Israelite, do I? Funny thing about the Djinn's Tear are the little details that no one tells you. Whatever name you first claim aloud after acquiring it becomes the name you're stuck with for life, even if it was a lie told to an innkeeper who turned away Christians."

"But..." This did not match what Snigdha had told us. "The Mongols and the Tartars..."

"Yes, they warred over it. And I fought too. Stranded after Louis IX's famous disaster of a crusade. I continued my mercenary ways until I saw my opportunity." He sipped his beer. "But the past is the past. What matters is the future. I presume you and Mr. Milner are here to try to steal my Djinn's Tear?"

A low growl came from the direction of the hallway door. I clenched to dissuade my bladder from its natural reaction and held my gaze on the man in front of me. He raised a droll eyebrow.

"Oh, do be quiet, Stig. These two are not in a position to harm us. In fact, they might be useful. But we must establish a few things first. So, my question?"

"Yes, we came to steal the Tear."

"For yourselves?"

"I can't say who we work for."

"You'd be surprised what you would say to stop the pain," said Stig.

"I will handle this," said Abrahamson. He turned back to me. "Then let me tell you. Of those prominent members of the Bay Area occult underworld who would be interested in the Djinn's Tear, only two have failed to bid: Nicholas Scratch and the Rajah." He pointed, first at Nelson and then at me. "The Rajah is known to employ two humans who acquire things for him. And you have just told me you are working for someone. Ergo, you work for the Rajah."

I kept my mouth shut, then snorted at the realization that Nelson was unconscious and missed me passing on a sarcastic remark. I couldn't even enjoy it because my head kept trying to split with pain.

"That leaves Mr. Scratch as the wild card. Unless..." He looked at me, narrowed his eyes, then said to Stig, "Awaken Mr. Milner. Gently please."

The ogre's huge, hairy bare feet failed to make so much as a creak in the floorboards as it came over to smack Nelson's face gently with one garbage-lid hand. Nelson rocked his head back and forth, groaning as he came to.

Nelson blinked awake and grimaced against his headache. Only then did his eyes widen and his back stiffen in fear of what crouched before him. But he didn't let go of his bladder this time. That almost made me sigh in relief. Nelson had his nerve back, which meant we were as close to full strength as we ever got.

Not that being at full strength meant much with us tied to barstools.

———

"Are we here to talk or die?" asked Nelson, testing the cords that bound him to his barstool. They looked as tight as mine.

"That remains to be seen," said Stig, who returned to his place of menace over by the hallway door. "I know what my choice would be."

Abrahamson introduced himself to Nelson, and Nelson looked as surprised as I'd felt at the blond man's identity. "Mr. Milner, how much is Mr. Scratch paying you to steal my Tear?"

"Don't answer!" I snapped at the same moment as Nelson said, "He isn't."

Abrahamson looked back and forth at us, then settled on me. "He must be blackmailing you then. Otherwise you wouldn't have been so worried about what Mr. Milner might say."

"Anytime you're finished playing detective," said Stig.

"Now, now," said Abrahamson, coming to his feet. He moved as lithely as a dancer. "We can't talk properly until we understand each other."

Abrahamson walked around the couches until he could lean against the back of the one closest to us, no more than two steps away. He finished his beer and tossed the empty to Stig, who ate it in one bite. Abrahamson clapped his hands together once.

"So you are in rather a bind, are you not? The Rajah demands that you steal the Djinn's Tear for him, and Nicholas Scratch would force you to steal it for *him*. What to do, what to do?"

Abrahamson tapped his chin with one finger as though pondering the question, but his eyes were steady. He already had his answer in mind.

"Tell you what. I have heard tell of the resourcefulness of the Rajah's agents, and that you have tracked me down proves to me that your reputations are deserved. Very impressive for humans. You remind me of some men I knew back in my mercenary days.

"So I will offer you a way out. Swear that you shall not seek to rob or harm me or mine, and I will free you from your obligations to all supernatural beings. You will be as unfettered as newborn babes, save for any human ties you have."

"We accept!" said Nelson.

I held my silence, expecting Abrahamson to have more to say, but he merely looked at me and waited.

"No," I said. "I won't let you murder for me."

"Come on," said Nelson. "One death to save us both? To save Karen?"

"Karen wasn't included."

"I'll expand the offer to your loved ones," said Abrahamson with a wave of his hand. "Believe me, there's no one better at wishing than I am."

"Yes," said Nelson. "We agree. Let's do this."

Now I was tempted. All I had to do was agree and I would free Karen from her debt to Scratch. Yes, my own freedom was part of the offer, but I could get sweet Karen her soul back.

I just had to murder an innocent person. A virgin yet.

"No."

"Damn it, Roland!" Nelson turned back to Abrahamson. "Fine. Then I'll take the deal."

"I'm afraid you have to both agree," said Abrahamson, "or the deal's off."

"This is our way out, Roland." Nelson implored me with wild eyes. "Free and clear and alive! Go live in luxury with Karen."

"I thought my deal with the Rajah would leave me free and clear. So did you."

"Not the same thing. We both knew we'd owe him."

"That's just it, Nelson. We knew there was a price, but not how steep it really was."

"*This time we know the price!*"

"Yes. We have to murder a virgin. Snuff out the life of some poor kid who has done nothing wrong, who hasn't even really started living yet."

"You won't have to do anything," said Abrahamson. "Just bring me the virgin and I'll handle the rest. You never even have to see it happen."

I shook my head. Nelson screamed in frustration.

"Too bad," said Abrahamson. "But I can't let you live if you—"

"Wait!"

Abrahamson turned to me, his pale eyebrows arched high.

"No one can offer you absolution. Not as a price. You could go to a priest—"

"I was excommunicated centuries ago. Not an option."

"Well, even if someone could offer absolution in trade, the Djinn's Tear can't be sold. It can only be taken by force or stolen, the same way you acquired it yourself."

Abrahamson furrowed his brow as he thought. Had I given him an angle he hadn't considered? I tried to think of a way to press my advantage, but he spoke first.

"Even assuming that's true, what difference does it make to whether you live or die?"

Hard to talk fast with my pounding head distracting me. If I came out of this alive, Karen and I might use some of her lottery money to invest in ibuprofen.

"Look. You want absolution? You're never going to get it. Not while you sacrifice virgins to make your dreams come true. But..." I had to hurry this along because I could see his interest fading. "But what if someone manages to *steal* the Tear?"

I paused for effect, hoping my words would kick-start some connection in his head, give him an ah-ha moment. But if Abrahamson had one, I saw no sign. Still, I had his attention again. I just needed to sell him on my plan.

"You can't give it away either. It has to be stolen." I chose to ignore the taken-by-force option with that ogre mere feet away. "Then you don't have the temptation anymore. Then you can face your loss and have a what-have-I-done moment, with or without the church's blessing. Then you can review your past with remorse or regret or whatever and devote the rest of your life and wealth to … I don't know … trying to atone."

"It's a wonder he didn't become a priest," mumbled Nelson.

"We know you don't have it here," I said, hoping that what I saw in Abrahamson's expression — one eyebrow raised and the other drawn down — meant he was considering my words. "So maybe you could just let us go. Maybe we steal it and you're free to pursue what you really want. Maybe we fail and your life goes on.

"Either way, Nelson and I are no threat to you. You could crush us without trying, so why bother? Our deaths wouldn't even bring you a good parking space, much less a wish."

"True," said Abrahamson. "But you would give Stig the best meal he's had in a while. And maybe that's enough."

16

***

"Find me when you're finished," said Abrahamson on his way to the hallway door. "And this time, try to contain the noise and mess. I'd prefer not to change hotels just yet."

Stig might have smiled, but its tusks made the expression come out more snarl and grimace. Still, those beady eyes gleamed with pleasure, anticipation. The ogre began to approach, its considerable weight swinging forward with each quiet step.

The cords pulled at my skin as I writhed, trying to loosen them. My eyes cast about for help, anything I could use.

Nothing.

I could see Nelson struggling with his own bonds, rocking his barstool hard enough that he might tip it over. The way our luck was running, he'd knock himself out and I would have to face this thing without him.

Bound to a chair while some kind of ogre or troll thing came slowly closer, without even the decency to make noise.

Wait. Quiet steps. And how could a thing that massive ride an elevator? Much less appear in an elevator without Nelson or me noticing? And I knew this was the same big bad beastie who gave Nelson and me our Friday Night Fights headaches. I could tell by the desperate way the skin on my neck begged to be sheltered inside my body.

The characteristics of this thing sounded familiar, but I couldn't place them.

"Hope you don't mind," said Stig in a casual rumble as it hefted the closest couch, "but I like to play with my food. Improves the flavor."

Nelson screamed, a throat-tearing bellow of rage and frustration and fear that knifed pain into my aching skull. The look in his eye told me that his purpose was not mere expression. He hoped that someone would hear.

Also, at least half of his rage and frustration appeared to be aimed at me.

"Good one!" said Stig as it moved a second couch. The maybe-ogre was clearing the center of the room as though to give us space to fight. A fight that would be short unless I could remember what looked like an ogre but moved with the stealth of a goblin.

Stig set down the couch and raised his fists, encouraging. "Do it again!"

Nelson panted, glaring hatred at me.

"No? Pity." Stig lowered his fists. "I love that sound. That's why we have two floors to ourselves."

Stig picked up our knives in one hand, and with the other tossed the table to land upside down on the couches, which were now gathered over by the open door to the lit hallway that might have led to a bedroom. The non-ogre then closed the bathroom door and turned to face us.

"Now, mighty warriors. I return your weapons."

Stig threw our knives one at a time. Both flew laser straight and cut the cords binding our right arms at the wrist and elbow. I expected blood to flow, but my skin remained uncut. At least for the time being.

"Cut yourselves free, then, please, escape if you can."

Those throws. Such precision. And "Abrahamson" with his blond hair and pale skin. Northern European origin. Northern Europe ... Vikings...

The vikings had throwing contests, didn't they? But they didn't have ogres, per se. They had etins and alfs and svartalfs and giants and jötuns and trolls and ... dwarves. Dwarves? Something about dwarves...

I searched through my memory as I cut myself free. Nelson did the same (at least the cutting part). We jumped off the stools and fell into fighting stances. We instinctively covered each other as we had for the past six months. As though we hadn't argued over murdering innocents.

I didn't kid myself though. We were only allies in the face of a greater threat.

Stig smiled even broader. Drool dripped down from the corners of its mouth in long strands. It reached wide its arms...

I had no idea what I was facing. No time to figure it out. I had only one alternative, and I prayed it would work.

"Mithrandir I name myself, and proclaim by air and sea that I am matchless in my wisdom unless my match you prove to be."

"What the hell are you doing?" muttered Nelson out of the side of his mouth.

"Shut up and trust me," I whispered back.

My skull throbbed. My heart pounded a counterpoint in my chest. I had phrased the challenge as well as I could. I'd given a name that was not my own and cobbled together something approaching rhythm and rhyme with at least a little alliteration. Was it enough to begin the contest of wisdom out of Norse myth?

Stig tapped a tusk with one long, dirty nail. Its eyes narrowed.

If I was right about Stig's origins, if not the creature's exact nature, it might not be able to refuse the challenge.

Stig's shoulders slumped. Its head tilted in what I thought was consternation. It sighed a breath that blew back my hair and filled my nostrils with foul evidence of its poor dental hygiene. Finally, it spoke.

"Stig my clan have named me, and by earth and rock I swear that all our heads shall be the wager for your wisdom I will dare. But first I think a toast is meet to celebrate this time, so drink we first to Vafthruthnir. I shall fetch the wine."

Damn! I had an advantage because I was able to give a false name, but by accepting the host duties and offering the proper drink, wine, Stig had pulled even.

Stig looked longingly at the space it had cleared for our fight, then sighed again and stepped behind the bar. I could hear it rummage around, but was too busy to worry about what kind of wine it would find.

I raced my mind through everything I could remember of the Eddas. As guest I would have to answer first.

Stig poured two glasses of a deep red pinot noir and offered me one. Nelson looked put out at not being offered any, but I had no attention for him.

Stig raised a glass and toasted Vafthruthnir, a giant famed for wisdom. I toasted Odin, who bested Vafthruthnir at the contest of wisdom.

Stig stepped back to hunch an arm's length from me. Well an arm's length for the non-ogre, which meant about six feet from me. I sat back down on my barstool, collected my thoughts, and waited.

"Speak now, Mithrandir, and tell me all that you do know. What came before what came before? How far back does your wisdom go?"

"Before even the beginning the Ginnungagap was all, with only frozen nothing there within its gaping maw."

That was an easy one, but they always start easy. Even the Norse had stories of the void before creation. But Stig gave me no time to congratulate myself.

"Speak now, Mithrandir, and tell me all that you do know. How came something out of nothing? How did our something grow?"

"All began when fire met ice and out grew sacred Audhumbla. First in flesh, and life, and blood, we all go back to her."

I stumbled a little over that one, but the essence was there. Hard to remember the details about some freaky primal cow birthing giants. I must have answered well enough, because Stig continued.

"Speak now, Mithrandir, and tell me all that you do know. What formed the world, and sky above, how came it all to—"

The question gurgled into silence. Nelson, completely ignored by both Stig and me, had snuck up behind the possible-ogre and shoved his Ka-Bar hilt-deep up through the thing's neck and into its skull, twisting as he thrust.

Blood should have gushed all over Nelson, but not a drop. His knife came out dusty.

"That was a good distraction," said Nelson as he cleaned his blade on the thing's back. "We should search the place anyway. Maybe the Tear isn't here, but we may find a clue to its whereabouts. Roland!" He snapped his fingers at me. "You with me there?"

"I ... you..."

"Yeah, you were playing magic games with it and I just fucking killed it. Hell if I'm going to let you bet my life on some supernatural game of trivial pursuit."

I shook myself, head and shoulders, but still felt off. That was not how a contest of wisdom was supposed to end.

"I never agreed to that crap anyway," Nelson continued, coming around the bar to grab a beer. "Want one? Roland! Come on, man, we have work to do."

I managed to get to my feet, but something still felt wrong. I couldn't put my finger on it. My stomach roiled like I was on a roller coaster, unsettled and constantly changing direction. I looked at Nelson, and I could feel my puzzled expression: open mouth, crinkled eyes, sheathed Ka-Bar loose in one hand. I took the beer with the other.

"You were going to murder—"

"Look." Nelson set down his knife and held up his beer. "You and me, we don't exactly have clean slates. Not with life, not with each other. Hell, there are probably times when you want to kill me too. But never forget our goal, Roland. I want out, and so do you."

Nelson jerked his thumb to point over his shoulder. "Abrahamson offered us a ticket out and you pissed on it. Now our only chance is to get that fucking Tear. Are you going to stand there and whine or are you going to man up, have a beer with me, and get this shit done?"

"I could have taken him, you know. I know my Norse stuff pretty well."

"Prove it on your own time. Right now we're on the clock."

I took a deep breath, felt my head begin to clear from the aborted magic of the contest, and clinked my beer against his. We drank.

———

WE TURNED THAT SUITE OVER LIKE COPS LOOKING FOR DRUGS. THE mattress, the couch cushions, everything that could be picked up got sifted and tossed. Everything else we went over with a fine tooth comb.

But we came up with nothing. Not even any cash worth pocketing. Of course, we were a bit rushed, knowing that Abrahamson might come back at any time. Plus, Nelson was slowed by his reduced peripheral vision. Abrahamson might not have had the Djinn's Tear on him, but we couldn't risk what his other handy resources might be.

We did find a room safe in the bedroom closet, but it was unlocked and empty. Nelson and I stared at it.

"I'm starting to think this guy lives a pretty clean life, all things considered," said Nelson. I began to respond, but he cut me off, "I don't mean morally. I mean he hasn't gotten caught up in anything else. I don't know about you, but I expected this guy to live like Scratch, but look."

He took in the room with a sweep of his hand. "He's got a few changes of clothes, but no extensive wardrobe and nothing *too* expensive. The sheets don't smell like sex, so while he's probably not going without, he isn't overindulging either. No sign of drugs. No excessive alcohol. Even the beers in the bar came from a store, not the mini bar. It's not like he can't afford room service prices."

"Wait. Store?"

"Yeah, you think the hotel carries, what's it called, Teufelsbrau?"

"No. No, I bet it doesn't." I turned and dodged detritus as I ran through the bedroom and back down the short hall into the main room of the suite. Nelson followed, asking about my idea, but it wasn't an idea really. Just a hope, and I worried that speaking it aloud would evaporate it.

I got to the coat closet door and ripped it open. Two jackets and an overcoat. *Where was it? Think, Roland!* I started rifling the pockets. Nelson shrugged and helped, but I found my target first: a crumpled receipt from a liquor store, complete with a street address.

Excitement sang through my veins. We were close now. I could almost taste that sour reek.

What a thing to look forward to.

"Come on," I said to Nelson and pulled open the suite door, all my weight on the balls of my feet. "We need to go."

"To the liquor store? If you want another beer, he has plenty."

I stopped and turned to my partner. I used a deep breath to try to push down my excitement and keep my frustration from showing. "What do we know about this guy?"

"He likes strong beer and avoids complications."

"No. He's lazy." I held up the receipt and tried not to notice my missing finger. "But he's been here."

Realization dawned on Nelson's face. The liquor store had to be near someplace Abrahamson went frequently. We were a good step closer to our goal.

We ran together to the elevator.

We held a quick pace, but not quite a run, through the lobby. Hotel security was grateful enough not to tackle us. In fact, I think they were happy to see us go. One of them gave me a look that distinctly said, 'good riddance.' I couldn't imagine why.

Well, actually I could. We were not-quite-running through their expensive lobby after one-thirty in the morning. Plus, if you added together the cost of everything Nelson and I were wearing, including our watches and combat knives, and the total was still less than what some of these guests paid for a tie.

On the other hand, that might have been my self-consciousness. Even without the eye patch and missing fingers, Nelson and I probably would have earned security's suspicion by looking like guys who just got beat up, killed someone, and tore up one of their suites.

Although, to be fair, Stig wasn't really a someone so much as a some*thing*. Heck, Nelson was lucky that death by combat was a big deal to the old Norse. Big enough that pretty much all their nasties could be killed by the judicious application of sharpened (or blunt) metal. If he had tried that on the few Japanese spirits I knew of, they would have eaten his face. Or worse.

We loped to the car because it was too far away for a sprint. Lord this place was big. Finally, though, our sweaty bodies were strapped into the cloth seats with the Camry's engine raring.

Once again I had to fight not to speed. If I managed to come through this assignment in one piece, I wanted a car I could drive fast, something I could take on a beautiful freeway like 280, with the top down, Karen beside me (probably with her top up, but you never knew), and just open it up and fly.

But right now I would have been a fool to risk tickets or police-related delays. We had lost time to unconsciousness and I had no idea how much longer we had before Scratch put Carnifex back on our tail. So I eased up University Avenue to Middlefield Road and hooked a right. A block later, somewhere around two in the morning by the Camry's clock, I pulled into the parking lot of a small, unloved strip mall.

No pedestrians. No parked cars. From left to right we saw only a sandwich joint (closed), a liquor store (open), two empty units and a store whose sign declared it a dry cleaners, but that looked as open and empty as the two places next to it.

I felt a catch in the back of my mouth, something strong and unnatural nearby. I did a quick-breath relaxation and opened as wide as I could. I could smell it at last, the Djinn's Tear, foul as ever and strong enough to make me gag. Which did not do good things for my lingering headache.

"Tell me that's good news."

"No. I'm just ... retching. Come on."

We crossed the parking lot. Nelson pulled his lock picks out before I could. I stood there and feigned bored amusement as Nelson picked the padlock while trying to portray, with his body language, that he was having trouble with his key.

If anyone watched our pantomime, I didn't see them.

Finally he got the door open. We drew our knives and went in.

The old dry cleaner's front counter was still there, and its door to the employee area, but the big rotating clothes rack was gone, as was all the dry cleaning equipment. The whole place smelled like chemicals, lending a disgusting counterpoint to the odor of the Djinn's Tear. But still, the prize was here somewhere for the taking.

All I had to do was keep myself from puking up D.N.A. evidence all over the scene of our little Unlawful Entry crime.

I had to lead now, past the battlefield casualties of discarded hangers and plastic covers. I started deeper in, flicking on a key ring L.E.D. flashlight as we left the streetlights behind. Nelson pulled his own light to maximize our view of fossil outlines of old equipment and curious spots on the floor. No way the last tenant got their security deposit back.

My nerves were screaming *danger* nonstop, but I had to hope that was the Djinn's Tear. This close to it I had no prayer of noticing any other supernatural thing. The foul reek overrode my senses and kept my skin crawling. Not a good combination in a darkened room, with a small flashlight and a nervous partner.

Nelson panted for breath, though whether from excitement or our distance running I couldn't say. His flashlight hand trembled.

Not that I was much better. My flashlight hand shook, making the shadows move, and I kept darting the light around at anyplace that looked big enough to hide some dangerous guardian.

"Take a breath, would you?" said Nelson. "I'm getting carsick over here."

"Breathing just ... makes it worse..." I dove to the floor at a pile of plastic suit covers and puked out my dinner. Nelson sighed and stood guard over me until I finished.

"You get to carry that out, you know."

"Hey, I'm only puking because I had to open myself up to this stuff so we could do our job."

"Speaking of which..."

I pushed back to my feet. My head throbbed, but otherwise I felt better. The stink of the Djinn's Tear still assailed my nose, but it made me less nauseated. I even managed to keep my flashlight hand steady. Now I could see a closed door at the end of the room. Right in the middle of one of those old machine outlines.

"Is it me," I said, "or does that whole wall look new?"

Nelson ran his light along the wall. "Not even a coat of primer."

"Of course," I said relaxing enough to stand straight. I might still have some nasty guardian waiting for me, but at least no one was likely to call the cops. "Abrahamson."

"You think he bought the place?"

"Bought ... rented ... what's the difference?"

"Hey," Nelson said, jostling my shoulder. "This means you probably don't have to worry about the vomit."

We lost a few minutes scouring the wall and door with our flashlights, but found no trace of runes, symbols, etchings, or anything else to indicate protective wards. But that made sense to me. If the Djinn's Tear could not be hidden by supernatural means, perhaps it couldn't be guarded by supernatural means.

The door was thick, of course, possibly reinforced, and locked in at least three places. Nelson and I looked at each other and shook our heads. All that work on the door, and only bare sheetrock for the walls. Nelson and I pulled out our billy clubs and began to hammer holes in the wall next to the door, just about the height of the handle.

"Hotel safe would have been more secure than this," said Nelson while we worked.

"Nah," I said. "Too many ways to fool the hotel staff with magic."

"Safe deposit box then. No one said the key couldn't be hidden by magic."

"Now you're thinking."

We punched through the last hole. Nelson turned his back and mule-kicked through the perforated wall. He paused and turned to me. "Why didn't he think of a safe deposit box?"

"Limitations of the supernatural. They underestimate human resourcefulness."

"But this guy is no demon or ghul. He's human."

"Hardly," I scoffed. "Humans don't live eight hundred years. I don't know what he is now."

Nelson shrugged and we cleared out more of the hole. I reached through and unlocked the door. We swung it open.

The back room was twenty feet wide by ten feet long. The air hung with tension, like a low-grade hum in our ears, except that there was no sound. Plug in deodorizers tried in vain to cover the smell of death — blood and shit — with a suggestion of a sea breeze.

To our right was a big, thick teak dining room table covered in telltale rust-colored stains, as was the thin beige carpet around it. To our left was a small office refrigerator, two executive style roller desk chairs, and a small, round coffee table. On the table sat a more than a dozen gold and platinum rings and bracelets — some plain, some ornately carved, and others jewel encrusted — and in the center, sitting a velvet pillow, a sapphire the size of my fist, shaped like a teardrop.

"I presume we're taking them all," said Nelson, sounding like he hoped to walk away from this with a fortune of his own.

"That would be a mistake," I said slowly. "Some of these things might be cursed."

"What is this, *Indiana Jones and the Last Crusade*? Someone's going to tell us to choose wisely?"

"Give me a second." Despite the powerfully unnatural presence before me, I tried to open my senses wider. I slowed my breathing, let it grow shallow, shallower, still. Then a single deep breath as I forced my skin to relax and make my whole being just ... perceive.

My head tried to split open, my stomach revolted, and I dropped to all fours and vomited all over the thin carpet until I didn't have even any more bile to bring up and I could only manage dry heaves. Tremors wracked my limbs and sweat plastered my hair to my head and my shirt to my torso. My stomach continued to churn with the need to vacate.

I fought to close back down. I focused on the smell of my vomit. Disgusting though it was, it was human, basic, and, well, mine. Sure, it kept me trying to spit up more, but it filled my attention well enough to ground me firmly back in normal human perceptions.

I struggled back up to my knees, slowly. "Too close ... I can't ..." I managed. "I don't..."

Nelson stared at me for a moment, and for the first time in days I saw compassion in his eyes. "Shut it down, Roland. We're here. You done good. We don't need to worry about the other jewelry when the correct choice is obvious..."

Nelson reached for the giant sapphire teardrop.

"No," I screamed. I tried to dive for him, but my legs were weak and I only barely managed to get my arms around his feet enough to trip him up, not tackle him.

In a single movement, Nelson stepped free of my grip and spun to face me, Ka-Bar and tiny flashlight raised to a fight. Then his shoulders slumped and he relaxed.

"Of course not." He sighed. "I hate to ask you to open up again, but we need to know which."

"I know ... stands out plain." I got back to my feet and stepped up beside Nelson as we ran our flashlights over the sparkling collection. I wiped sweat out of my eyes and with a shaky hand picked up a platinum slave bracelet that bore a single, small sapphire.

I don't know what I expected when I picked it up. Voices in my head maybe, whispering of the power at my command. Seductive or encouraging voices, downplaying that little virgin-sacrifice detail while extolling the possibilities of my newfound power. Or maybe a sense of euphoria surging through my veins. Something like that.

But I got nothing. It was just like picking up any other piece of jewelry. If I hadn't already smelled its foul reek, I would not have known what it was. But I did know.

"This ... is the Djinn's Tear."

Carnifex reached between us, snatched the bracelet from my hand, and rasped, "Thank you. I'll take it from here."

Nelson and I stabbed at the demon, but it twisted into its ribbon shape and vanished.

Worse, we heard a scrabbling sound from the main room, like claws over wood.

17

———

"Shouldn't this place have a back door?" I asked, waving my flashlight like a lunatic and lamenting that we had left an open door between us and whatever was coming when we could have locked it behind us.

"There!" Nelson pointed with his flashlight to the far corner of the room, past the table-cum-altar. Fifteen, maybe twenty feet away from us. A simple white door with multiple locks.

From the main room we could hear fleet steps and wet growling.

"No time," I said. I kicked over the coffee table, scattering thousands of dollars worth of gems and jewels. Maybe millions. I pulled a roller chair close, in case I thought of a use for it. Nelson and I took up positions behind the table like a shield, our flashlights trained on the doorway.

But the thing did not run in. Whatever it was, it knew that doorway represented possible danger. I muttered, "Wish I'd grabbed the gun."

It came through the doorway low, crouched, but I recognized it in an instant. That ghul we hunted the other night. And following behind it came a second ghul, just as large and just as ugly. Neither one of them made the least attempt to look human, with their gray skin stretched over their thin limbs, and their stringy hair dangling.

They spotted us immediately. Stepped wide to give each other room to maneuver. Our old friend targeted me. The other focused on Nelson.

Nelson abandoned our table-shield. Probably afraid of getting cornered. He stepped out to meet his ghul, crouched low and Ka-bar high. Flashlight spearing the ghul's gray chest.

Me, I waited right where I was. Ka-Bar held in front of my face. My flashlight trained on my ghul's eyes. Not that it seemed to notice.

"Come on, come on come on," I encouraged just above a whisper. My foot in position and ready on a roller chair. The ghul took slow steps toward me.

As one, the two ghuls screamed like the howl of a sandstorm. They leapt. Ugly purple claws spread wide. Jaws slavering.

I kicked out, propelled my roller chair into my ghul's midsection. Not to hurt it, though I had hopes. Not even to halt it. Just to buy myself a second. Just to fold the ghul over the chair like a limp towel.

That part worked. My turn to pounce.

I dropped my flashlight. Grabbed the ghul's stringy hair. Forced its head forward. Aimed for that sweet spot, where the top of the spine meets the neck.

I stabbed down. My blade bit through muscle and tendon. Black blood sprayed me. Hot. Rank, like rancid beef.

My steel caught on bone, separated linking tissue. I twisted. The blade refused to come free. Still, my ghul had to be down. No way it was going to walk away from that.

I turned to check on Nelson, but could only see his ducking, swiping ghul in the spotlight of Nelson's flashlight. At least I could hear his moving bulk and litany of soft complaints as he fought.

But then my knife pulled against me.

Claws clamped my wrists tight. My vague night vision showed me the outline of my ghul rising, throat misshapen where my Ka-Bar remained.

My panicked limbs reacted before my mind could adjust to the horror. I fell backward away from the unyielding grip, my leverage aided by the ghul's position: half-folded over a roller chair.

As I fell, my legs came up into the back of the chair and shoved. Ghul and chair flew over me, our locked arms forcing all of the momentum into a tight arc.

Ghul slammed into floor. Chair slammed into ghul. I got yanked feet over head. I managed to tuck my legs in mid-air, so I landed knee-first on the padded back of the chair. Wrenched my ankles but made me the top of the pile and crushed the ghul beneath me.

The gripping claws slackened and fell limp to the carpet. I scrabbled off for my flashlight, whirled around and saw my ghul, dead. The fall had finished what my stab started, with the chair and my weight ensuring the deed.

I spun my light to see Nelson pinning his ghul to the wall. His knife stabbed over and over into its back and side, beneath what would have been a rib cage on a human. The ghul's arms were limp. Its back was a bloody black mess.

"I think it's dead, Nelson."

He must have heard me because he stopped stabbing. He pulled its head back by its hair and slit its throat from ear to ear, just to be sure. He let go of the corpse and bent to pick up his own dropped flashlight.

"No," mocked Nelson. "The ghul won't want revenge. It'll avoid us. 'Cause we beat it."

"You think we just happened into the path of the ghul we milked? And it had a friend?" I put my feet on my ghul's shoulders and grabbed the handle of my Ka-Bar. Getting a firm hold took me three tries. Without my little fingers, my grip felt ... unfinished, all the way up my arms.

Once I came as close as I was going to get to a grip I liked, I yanked my combat knife free. This severed the ghul's neck completely and made its head roll to my left.

I looked back at Nelson. "Someone set these things on us."

Nelson stared at me, red lines gouged on his cheek and throat by ghul talons, his blade still smeared with ghul blood and worse.

Combined with the missing eye the wounds gave him a grizzled, medieval look. "So, Scratch has the Tear."

"So, Scratch *stole* the Tear. From us." I cleaned my knife and hands on the carpet. "I say we go get the cheating bastard, and force him to give back the Tear and relinquish Karen's soul in the process."

"Now that," said Nelson with a smile, "is a plan I can work with."

I DROVE WHILE NELSON DID HIS BEST TO CLEAN HIS WOUNDS USING THE car's vanity mirror and the first aid kit from my trunk. I'd already snagged a couple of the wet naps to wipe down my own face and hands. I practically bought those things by pallet. They helped reduce the immediate squick factor of my job until I could get home to a scalding shower.

They also made me vaguely presentable, at least from a distance. They didn't do nearly enough for the stench, which included my lingering vomit as well as the rotted-meat smell of ghul blood. But at least my face and hands wouldn't be visibly covered in blood. And the border between Menlo Park and Atherton was not a place I wanted to drive while covered in ghul blood.

Well, I couldn't think of anyplace I *would* want to drive while covered in ghul blood. But why risk some rich neighbor calling in a S.W.A.T. team because she thinks she sees a serial killer or something?

Of course, if I did get pulled over, the blood on Nelson's and my clothes would have meant a trip downtown anyway. Then again, perhaps not. Ghul blood came out black, not red, and was thicker. Wet naps have their limits, but perhaps Nelson and I would look as though we were covered in chocolate syrup. If not for the smell.

Yeah, I didn't buy it either.

In other words, I once more paid scrupulous attention to the speed limit as we cruised up Middlefield Road through Palo Alto. Quiet, this time of night. Only the occasional odd car around us on the four-lane road. We passed houses, apartments and small businesses, but mostly bushy trees and green lawns.

Once we were in Menlo Park I had to slow further as I turned onto side streets to cover the rest of the way, until finally we reached the high wall and sheltering trees of Scratch's house.

The wall didn't open when we pulled into Scratch's driveway.

"Fuck," said Nelson.

"You didn't honestly expect him to just let us in, did you?"

"The blood won't stanch." Nelson pressed a cotton pad to his throat, then pulled it away. A trickle of dark red blood oozed out. At least the wound was on the side he could still see. "The scrapes are shallow. They should have stopped bleeding by now. Are ghul claws infected?"

"Probably. No time for a hospital now though."

"Screw the hospital. The Rajah will take care of it when we bring him the Tear."

Nelson dropped the cotton pad to join its predecessors and his used wipes on the floor of the front passenger seat. I chose to believe he was distracted by his bleeding, and not deliberately making a mess.

We got out of the car, and I retrieved the pistol from my trunk. I tucked it into my jacket pocket.

"Just what we want the neighbors to see," said Nelson.

"How many people are awake and watching the street at two-thirty in the morning?" I closed the trunk. Quietly. "Besides, look where we are. What we're about to do. Cops are the least of our problems."

"Good point," he said as we surveyed the high, twelve-foot stone wall and the two rows of sequoias. "How do we get in?"

"The same way we retrieved lost balls and Frisbees when we were kids." I started to shinny up a tree.

Sequoias would not have been my first choice to climb, but these were young enough that I could get my arms around them, with grooves deep enough to grip with my hands and shoes.

"I never climbed trees when I was a kid," said Nelson, below me. "I liked riding my bike."

I glanced over my shoulder and saw that Nelson stood firm, clearly unwilling or unable to follow me up that tree.

"Crap," I said as I reached the lowest, reasonably thick branch I could find, about eight feet up. I stared at Nelson. He shook his head. I fished my key fob out of my pocket and popped open the trunk. "Grab a moving blanket and toss it up to me. We'll use it as a rope."

"You don't carry rope?"

"I'm not the one who needs it to climb a tree."

Nelson grumbled something disrespectful about rookies but came back with the moving blanket. He stepped around to where the trees shielded him from public view and tossed me the blanket. I braced myself on the branch and began to lower the blanket, then stopped myself with a smack on the forehead. I yanked the blanket up and started to crawl across the branch toward the wall.

"What about spells?" asked Nelson in a worried voice.

"Oh he's got them all right," I said as I crawled. "Like a low-level background hum from the wall. But I don't think his wards will stop us. The ones I saw last time set up a normalcy field, keeping outsiders from caring what happens here.

"Plus, he can't risk frying a burglar when a neighbor might see, or depleting the local population of birds and squirrels through attrition."

The branch thinned before I could reach the wall, so I had to back up a little to a spot thick enough that it might hold my weight if I stood. I held the blanket with one hand, the branch with the other, and worked my feet under me to a crouch.

Teetering back and forth, I pulled the corner of the blanket up and gripped it with my teeth, trying not to think about how much time and how many uses of the blanket had passed since it was last washed. I held my tongue in the back of my mouth and refused to close my lips.

Maybe the germs couldn't get in if I didn't taste them?

In a single movement I let go of the branch and leapt at the wall, slamming my chest into the stone, whuffing the air out of my lungs, and jarring loose the blanket from my teeth. But my arms clasped the top of the wall, and my body pressed the blanket flat against the stone. I craned my head forward and bit down on the cloth again. I hooked into the stone as best I could with my fingers and clambered up to the top of the wall. I swung one leg over, took the blanket out of my mouth with one hand, and panted until I caught my breath.

Once I recovered a bit I lowered the blanket. Nelson grabbed the end and we twisted it into a reasonable facsimile of a rope. He put his first foot on the wall, tested his grip, and used the blanket to walk up the side of the wall. As soon as I felt his weight pull against me, I dropped over the wall's inside edge rather than risk getting yanked to the ground a la Humpty Dumpty. I didn't like the odds of help from the king's horses and men.

My choice did mean that I had an easy route down to the ground, counterbalanced by Nelson's weight. Nelson, on the other hand, reached the top and almost tipped over. But I could only do so much for the guy.

Besides, my ankles still weren't thrilled with my landing on that chair during the ghul fight. At least my headache seemed to be gone. That surprise attack in the elevator felt like a lifetime ago.

Nelson hung down the inside wall by his fingertips then dropped the rest of the way, cushioning with his knees, ankles and waist as best he could, but it wasn't enough. He bounced back up, swearing, and hopped around on his right foot, left foot held high.

"Sprained or broken?" I asked. I had my billy club out and my other hand on the pistol as I swept my eyes over the well-maintained grass and gardens of the grounds. Eerily silent under starlight alone. The glow from the street lamps was cut off by the walls and trees, and if the house or garage were lit, those lights stopped at the windows.

The place looked still as a tomb, which was not an image I really wanted in my head. Especially if Nelson was down.

"Can you walk?"

"Probably." He wasted another moment grunting and swearing before taking a few ginger steps. "Fuck it," he finally pronounced.

"It'll hold my weight. Mostly." He drew his weapons and looked around. "Spooky. Where do you think they are?"

"In the house. Long as Scratch has been at this, he'll have a special ritual room."

"Ritual?"

"You telling me you don't think he has a virgin ready for sacrifice?"

"Crap."

We hustled across the lawn as fast as Nelson could move, which wasn't very. But either his injury wasn't as bad as we feared or adrenaline had kicked in for him, because he looked steady enough. We reached the front door and after a foiled, half-hearted hope that it would be unlocked, Nelson stood guard while I picked the lock and deadbolt. They were simple locks, the kind that were probably installed with the house back in the Sixties, and I had them unlocked in short order.

I pushed the door open on smooth, oiled hinges, but felt the skin of my hand crawl when I tried to push through the doorway. The front door stood open, but I physically could not cross the threshold.

All this work, and we were stopped by an open doorway. One single ward.

Behind us, along the driveway, the stone wall began to move.

Nelson and I dove for cover, but there wasn't any. Scratch didn't keep bushes, shrubs or trees near his front door. Not even a flower bed within diving range to conceal us. We had to settle for flattening against the well-trimmed grass along the edge of the house and hoping that the dim starlight would conceal us.

Yeah, I didn't like our chances either.

Before the wall finished opening, truck high beams ruined my night vision, made me cover my eyes. I heard the roar of a gunned engine.

By the time I could look again, a huge Lexus SUV came blazing across the lawn to skid to a halt in front of the door, tearing up the lawn. Engine and lights still on.

Three doors flew open. Three fresh-faced triplets in honest-to-God chain mail leapt out of the driver and passenger doors up front. Servitors from the Sons of Morning, in full armor, complete with hoods that had holes for their faces, and skirts that covered most of their legs. They carried huge, two-handed swords that might have been taller than they were.

And those swords looked sharp.

A moment behind them, jumping out of the back, came their mistress, Sapphira. She wore something that looked like a black combat gi, if it were designed by Marc Jacobs: sexy and deadly all at once. She carried a freaking katana in a lacquered, rune and sigil covered scabbard that had to double as some sort of wizard staff. Between the gi and the sword, the magic coming off of this woman made my stomach turn flip-flops.

I felt a fleeting moment of gratitude that I had long since emptied my stomach of anything to regurgitate.

"Mistress—" said one of the triplets, pointing at me.

"We'll deal with them later. Scratch first." And with that she took a low, balanced combat stance, one hand on the hilt of her sheathed katana, the other on its scabbard. She snapped the blade free and into a forward cut at the ward on the open doorway.

Static roared in my ears, made me wince. Nelson must have heard it too, because he shook his head hard.

Sapphira's back foot slid forward until she stood straight, shoulders squared. She sheathed her sword and strode through the doorway without looking back. After a moment of shuffling, she was followed by her ... knights? Nah. Knights are supposed to be noble. Those things were just servitors.

Nelson and I shared a few seconds of stunned disbelief before we forced ourselves to our feet and charged in after them.

WE GOT THREE STEPS INSIDE SCRATCH'S HOUSE BEFORE SCREECHING TO a halt on the thick, plush carpeting. Well, Nelson hobbled to a halt, really, but I screeched. The door to the left, where we had met with Scratch before, was closed. The doorway to the right looked just as dark as every other time I'd seen it.

Sapphira and her flunkies might have gone there.

"Where would Scratch keep a ritual room?" asked Nelson.

"I don't know. Probably low or high."

"No stairs."

"Yeah... I know..."

I kept glancing around, expecting to see Scratch's pet succubus. Even though I knew he would want her fighting Sapphira's minions. But something nagged at my head, made me keep checking for her. And not Carnifex either. Just the sex demon.

Then I realized what I was hearing, and it clicked. All around us, the foyer groaned with activity. Literally. The orgy scenes in every painting were alive and in full swing, complete with soundtrack. Downright creepy, considering the number of nonhuman participants.

Even creepier, the foyer *smelled* like sex. As though the paintings were more than just paintings. That was just wrong.

Nelson pointed to the open doorway on our right and took three steps that way, but something else bothered me. Made me think I'd overlooked an important detail. Not even the magic in the room, although I felt enough of that itching at my skin.

It was the huge wardrobe in the corner. One of the doors hung open. Just a little, but that wardrobe had always been closed.

I cleared my throat enough to get Nelson's attention, and pointed at the wardrobe with Karen's detective special. Nelson cocked his head with a frown that said he was more curious about why I cared than about the wardrobe.

I creaked open the wardrobe, and inside was a passage that smelled like rich, oiled wood.

"If this opens into Narnia," whispered Nelson, "I'm going to run home for Tish and the kids."

"I doubt it would be the Narnia you're looking for." I gestured to the paintings. "Not in this place."

The passage looked long and dark. I had to put away my billy club to turn on my keychain flashlight.

Into the darkness we went.

THE PASSAGE CURVED AROUND AND DOWN AT A STEEP ANGLE. IT STILL smelled like rich, oiled wood, making me wonder if Scratch made his minions oil the whole passageway.

Nah. Even Scratch wouldn't oil the bottom of a steep wooden passageway. Not one he had to use too.

My neck tried to duck with every step, as though my body didn't trust the passage not to collapse on us. The air was still, as though it should have been stale and dusty, however fresh it tasted on my tongue. I wanted it to move though, to drift across my skin like a breeze instead of hanging there as though the air itself was dead.

Or maybe it was just that I felt hemmed in. This would have been a hell of a place to fight a skirmish. No room to maneuver.

On the other hand, having the high ground at this angle could be a strong advantage.

I tried to listen for sounds of a fight — or at least a ritual — but I could only hear Nelson swearing behind me. No doubt his ankle wasn't up to this. My own weren't much better. Still, I didn't want to risk him slipping and taking himself out of action.

"Hold the light," I said, "and lean on me."

"Don't be stupid. If something comes up, we'd be dead before we could raise a weapon."

I shrugged. He had a point.

So we each struggled with our steps down the sloping wooden passage — the same expensive material as the wardrobe had been — around its tight left hand curves to reach a door.

The stillness in the air now bothered the hell out of me. Air moves. That's its nature. Air that doesn't move...

Magic was probably a factor, but there were so many spells and entities running around this place that my skin crawled constantly. I couldn't differentiate.

Nelson and I took up positions next to the door. Each of us had a Ka-Bar in one hand, and a billy club and keychain flashlight in the other.

"Think there'll be light on the other side?" asked Nelson.

"Yep. As soon as we get this door open, drop your light."

"Ready."

"Here we go," I said, and kicked open the door.

18

———

When I kicked open the door two things happened at once. The first was that my ankle screamed about my idiocy all the way up to my hip. The second was that a wave of warm, moist air hit us. Sure, it smelled like old stone and damp earth, but that air belonged in some tropical jungle, not an underground ... arena?

On the other side of the door was an immense stone chamber. The whole thing was shaped like a dome hewn from solid granite. Had to have reached at least twenty feet high and sixty feet across. In the center of the room was engraved a giant pentagram surrounding a six-foot stone altar, complete with beautiful blond co-ed on top, naked, bound, gagged, and writhing against her chains.

Near the altar stood Scratch, dressed in a ritual robe of blood red with black symbols etched along every edge and the Djinn's Tear worn on his left arm. He held a black-handled dagger in his right hand and a silver chalice in his left. But he faced his opponent instead of his sacrifice.

Sapphira stood three paces from him, her sheathed katana held in both hands, like a staff between them. Both chanted in swift sure voices.

Off to our left, Carnifex fought two of the triplets, using claws, tail, and darting teeth to keep them at bay while evading every swing of their two-handed swords.

Across the chamber, Xiom the Succubus darted out of the third triplet's sword reach thanks to her bat wings. I wondered whether her ... influence would work on a servitor, but she answered the question by alighting the servitor's back and tearing its head off with a snapping twist.

All this magic. All these creatures. And yet I hadn't fallen to my knees with the need to purge their unnaturalness from my system. That worried me, but I shoved it to the back of my head. No time.

The succubus presented a decent target as she swooped to aid her master. I raised my pistol, then stopped. "Nelson? Think we can let them kill each other and take on the victor?"

"No. Now shoot something!" He gritted his teeth and hustled for the fallen sword.

I raised the pistol, but hesitated. If I shot the succubus, all the nasties would turn to me as the next threat. Plus, the bullet might not even harm her.

If I shot the remaining servitors, they would probably collapse. The trauma would probably ruin their structural integrity and unmake them. But then again, one gunshot might not do it. And I might need the servitors to hold off the demons for now. The demons were wild cards.

No, the only two targets that might have been human enough to die by gunfire were Scratch and Sapphira.

But which to shoot first?

While I hesitated Carnifex caught one of the remaining triplets between steps, momentarily off-balance, and ripped its throat out with a quick claw. But the odds between bad guy groups evened again when Sapphira merely poked the tip of her katana-staff at the succubus and made her vanish.

The distraction cost her. Scratch tapped the chalice with his dagger, and blood bubbled up and overflowed its rim, spilling onto the floor. Sapphira swayed, unsteady and paling noticeably. But she held her grip on her katana-staff.

Nelson picked the headless triplet's sword. It looked heavy and awkward in his hands, but he raised it above his head and limped a charge at our two main foes.

I had to choose a target. Sapphira had sent a spectral hound to kill me. Scratch had kept Carnifex on my ass for days *and* held the deed to Karen's soul.

I raised my gun and fired at the warlock. In the confined chamber the report hit my eardrums like a punch. My shot missed. Chips of stone flew from the altar. The co-ed shrieked.

Idiot! What did Karen tell you? Less than ten feet!

All the bad things turned to face me.

That was a lot of supernatural attention. More than I had ever dealt with all at once. And all of it had bad intention.

I froze.

I wanted to run closer and shoot again. I wanted to drop the gun and flee. I tried to do both and did nothing. And nothing was all I could do. Not a single muscle would respond. My eyes refused to even blink. I felt caught, suspended, while all the monsters stared at me, like they couldn't believe a fool like me dared to interrupt their little war.

Nelson kept his hobbling charge, but if they saw him they paid him no mind. Not that he moved a whole step during my frozen moment, so it couldn't have actually lasted more than a fraction of a second.

But it felt like eternity.

SUDDENLY, TIME BEGAN AGAIN.

Carnifex took advantage of the distraction to tear out the remaining servitor's throat with its teeth. Tore right through the chain mail like wax on a piece of cheese.

In a single motion Sapphira drew her sword and swung a one-handed attack at Scratch. He raised his dagger to block. I heard the buzz of a Jacob's ladder as the blades jerked to a halt six inches from each other. The air between them dripped purple sparks.

Their eyes locked and they continued chanting nonstop. But sweat poured down Sapphira's face, and her arm shook.

I finally got my feet moving, but Carnifex tackled me to the ground. Cracked at least two of my ribs in the process. The detective special spun out of my grip and bounced over near the altar.

The demon pinned me down. I felt as though I had gotten trapped under a semi. Not only could I not move my limbs, the weight and strength of the demon began to grind my bones into the stone beneath me, even through my flesh. I had trouble getting enough air for a single breath. What little air I could draw tasted of blood and old death.

Sick pleasure in its eyes, Carnifex flared its hood to full width and hissed at me, its breath a moist cloud of foul smells. "Give me another order, mortal," it jeered, inches from my face. I could barely discern its sibilant words through the ringing in my ears from the gunshot. "Tell me to fuck off. Banish me from your mighty presence."

The stench grew so thick I gagged on what little air I could manage. I glanced about, wild for some kind of weapon, some kind of help. But nothing was at hand, and even Nelson focused his attention on Scratch, sneaking up on Scratch's dead-eye side and drawing back his borrowed sword to stab at the warlock.

"No help for you." The demon rasped a laugh, and I was sad to realize my ears were clearing. Now I would have to listen to its taunts. "Xiom is gone. Not even oblivion for you. Only misery for your body and soul until the end of time."

Its tongue slithered out and traced the edge of my chin. Pain surged through my system, as though white phosphorous burned each nerve ending in turn. I couldn't even pass out. The pain kept me conscious.

A scream ripped its way out of my throat. I must have had some wind left, despite the demon's crushing weight. I have no idea how long that scream went on. It felt to me like years, but I could not have had that much air. I do know that it ended abruptly.

So did the pain. And the crushing weight.

Through the bliss of vanished suffering I realized that Carnifex was gone. But that wasn't all. Scratch had fallen to the floor, screaming and holding his dead eye. The tip of Nelson's sword was covered in some sticky, yellowish-greenish ichor. Sapphira drew back in surprise, then crowed in triumph.

I tried to force my limbs to move. I needed that gun, but my body begged me to stay still. Even breathing that moist, hot air hurt. I settled for flopping into a vague sideways roll toward the pistol.

Bad idea.

Pain seared out from my cracked ribs, flared through my body. But at least the movement got me steadily closer to my goal.

Nelson swung his long, heavy sword at Sapphira, a slow, awkward sweep. But her blade was no lucky found weapon. She knew what she was doing. She slapped her lacquered scabbard against the flat of Nelson's blade, turning aside his strike. She carried the momentum of her movement into a spin and slashed Nelson across the chest, from shoulder to hip.

Nelson dropped his sword with a dull clatter, and collapsed to his knees.

I managed to swing the gun around the side of the altar. From no more than five feet away I emptied the barrel at the evil bitch.

My first bullet took her in the calf and knocked her leg out from under her. The second missed as she hit the ground, trying to swing her sword and scabbard to interpose. My third, fourth and fifth shots took her in the torso, then the gun clicked empty for four more pulls.

I needed to move.

I couldn't waste time just lying there. Nelson needed my help. The clock was ticking, and I didn't know how bad his wounds were. He might have died already.

Nevertheless, I lost time sprawled on the stone floor, shaking with what I'd just done. I reassured myself that magic had made Sapphira part ways with humanity long ago, but deep down I knew she wasn't as far gone as Scratch. Not yet. Even though she had wanted to be. Even though she would have killed me without hesitation, had sent the black dog after me, and probably those ghuls too. Still, I needed time.

As my hearing cleared further, I could make out three different sounds: whimpering and rattling from the co-ed, moans from Scratch, and short, rapid breaths from Nelson. Still alive! I wanted to run to his aid, but my whole body ached with bone-deep bruises and worse. I settled for crawling to his side.

Nelson's hands clutched his chest, literally trying to hold himself together. His skin blanched from blood loss. I could smell his innards, but not the bathroom odor I'd been dreading. Maybe she hadn't opened his bowels.

Maybe Nelson still had a shot.

"The girl," croaked Nelson.

"She's fine," I said, in the most soothing voice I could. "Scared, but I'll—"

"No." He coughed. Spasms wracked his body, forced out more blood. "Djinn's Tear. Use it."

"You can't be—"

"Save my life ... clear debts..."

"I can't—"

"Owe me ... stabbed eye ... no more snake demon..."

"I can't kill an innocent girl."

"Owe...me..."

Nelson passed out, his breaths shallow, blood still flowing from his long, deep cut. I didn't know much about medicine, but it looked like most of the real damage was stopped by his rib cage. My own chest muscles twitched in sympathy, not that they were much better off.

I wasn't sure how long Nelson had, but I'd always heard that gut wounds took a long time to kill you. And I did believe his bowels were intact. That had to help, right?

I needed to staunch his bleeding, but I could hear Scratch moving around behind me. I heard a soft metal clink, and looked down to see the Djinn's Tear next to me.

"Take it," said Scratch, his once-clear voice now a rough grind. He had his hands folded, imploring me from the granite floor. "You win. Just don't kill me."

"Return Karen's soul."

He spat out some harsh sounding syllables and pulled a piece of paper out of the air. I snatched it from his hand and could tell at a glance that this was the contract.

"Swear this is the only copy ... and that you are returning her soul but allowing her to keep her wealth ... and anything she reaps by it with no further obligation ... and no revenge or recriminations ... against me or mine."

I couldn't believe I got that whole sentence out. I wasn't in much better shape than Nelson. Well, apart from his blood loss.

"I ... so swear, and quitclaim all rights to her soul and to all vengeance against you and yours. Now leave in peace."

I shredded the contract, and dropped the pieces where he could watch them fall. Then I grabbed Nelson's fallen sword in both hands, swung it high, and hacked at Scratch's throat until the bastard's head came clean off. Sapphira might have been mostly human, but Scratch was all monster as far as I was concerned.

I tossed the sword aside. That was one less foul thing to run around the world, "buying" souls from the unwary.

"If ... you're ... through..." said Nelson, his voice weaker. "Use it. Save me." He coughed and red foam coated his lips. "Save us both."

I picked up the Djinn's Tear. I looked at the beautiful, terrified woman chained and helpless on the altar. She started writhing, trying to get away, saying, "No," over and over again.

I picked the sword back up.

MY SPENT BODY COULDN'T MANAGE MUCH OF A MIGHTY SWING AT THE sacrifice's thick chains, and the strike telegraphed new waves of pain through my body, wrenching my face into a grimace.

The poor girl began blubbering and crying in what I'd like to think was relief, because even through her terror she must have realized I was trying to free her.

"Asshole..." said Nelson.

"I can't do it, Nelson." I dinged more of the blade's edge with another weak but painful swing. Why did the bastards need two-handed swords anyway?

"No." He coughed. "If ... you won't use the Tear ... find the fucking key."

I dropped the sword and smacked myself in the forehead. Bad idea, as it turned out. Bruised and exhausted as I was, that smack almost knocked me on my ass. It certainly did stagger me back a few steps and ring my bell a little.

I set down the sword and dug through Scratch's robe until I found a small key tucked into his sleeve. I approached the co-ed on the altar, holding up the key in one hand and making a calming gesture with the other.

She had finally stopped crying and held her eyebrows high in what I hoped expressed something positive, but for the life of me I couldn't think of what right then. I unlocked her wrists first and she drew her arms down in a vain attempt at modesty.

I couldn't unsee everything I'd already seen, but I turned my head to give her at least the illusion of privacy and unlocked her ankles next. She rolled off of the altar and hid herself against its thick stone legs.

"It's all right," I said, wincing with every breath and word. "My name ... is Roland McReedy.... My partner here ... is Nelson Milner."

I took a slow, steadying breath, gritting against the sharp pain that sparkled through my rib cage. But at least my voice was steadier when I spoke again.

"We're not part of what they did to you, and we'd like to see you get home safe and sound."

I glared at Nelson, who gave a weak shrug. I grabbed his Ka-Bar and tossed it over the altar where it would land near her, but not too near.

"I figure holding that might help you feel safer. Cut off your gag when you're ready." I started stripping the robe off of Scratch. "I need this robe for Nelson here, but as soon as I've bound his wound," — I glanced over and saw her green eyes watching me from around the altar — "I'll strip the clothes off the dead woman here so you'll have something to wear."

"What about my clothes?" Her voice was high and tight, but together. She might come through this in one piece yet.

"Hate to say it," I said as I ignored Nelson's grunts of protest and wrapped the red robe around his torso, "but they've probably been burnt. Mr. Scratch here never intended to let you leave."

"You killed him."

"I did. And the woman."

"You said you'd let him go."

"No. He asked me to let him go. I never intended to let that son of a bitch live." Was that a lie of omission? Was Nelson right about me spending too much time with the faeries? Was I starting to internalize some of their rules through games with the truth?

I shoved that thought aside for another time.

She was quiet then, while I worked. The only sounds were small grunts of pain from Nelson as I bound his cut as tight as I could with the robe and cord Scratch had worn. Not much, but it would do for now. It would have to.

Odd though. I felt nothing while stripping Scratch of his clothes to help Nelson, but I felt embarrassed to strip Sapphira. I had to look away as I did it.

"Why did you kill her? She wanted to save me."

"No," I said without turning. "She wanted to kill Scratch and sacrifice you herself."

"Why?"

The sheer depth of emotion in that one word hit me like a slap. She sounded as though everything in this poor girl's world hinged on that one question. She teetered on the borderline of sanity, and my answer would decide which way she fell.

I looked into those green eyes as I threw her Sapphira's black top. I wanted to lie to her. Supernatural rules and games be damned, I wanted to comfort this poor woman. I wanted to tell her that the bad people were just insane, hide her from the truth of what evils ran around this world. Let her sleep at night believing that the only monsters in her world were human.

Then I thought of Karen, who sold her soul because she didn't know what things went bump in the night.

I picked up the platinum slave bracelet with its small, single sapphire. "This little trinket is called the Djinn's Tear..."

19

———

I never asked her name, the woman who was almost a virgin sacrifice. I had seen her naked. I had seen mortal terror in her eyes. But somehow asking her name would have felt too personal. She had been through enough. Let her keep whatever privacy she could manage.

I did tell her the truth and she listened, wearing a dead woman's bullet ridden clothes and clutching Nelson's Ka-Bar like a security blanket. I told her who Scratch was, and Sapphira. I disavowed her of the notion that Nelson and I might be saviors or heroes.

Then again maybe she'd heard what Nelson wanted me to do with her, because she didn't look at us like heroes or saviors. She looked at us like we were fellow victims, which I guess was what we were, in a way.

I did tell her that we were just two dumb bastards who got stuck working for a monster because it looked like the easy way out of our messed up lives. Which was what we definitely were.

And I didn't hold anything back about the Djinn's Tear. I told her what it was, and why Scratch and Sapphira needed her. She didn't ask any questions as I talked, but when I finished she did ask one: "What are you going to do with it?"

That was the big question, and I didn't have an immediate answer. But that was all right. I had plenty to deal with in the meantime. My makeshift bandaging had staunched Nelson's blood loss, but he was pale and weak, plus he probably had a sprained ankle. My ankles weren't in great shape either, plus I had cracked ribs and more bruises and sore muscles than I could count.

Getting Nelson out of this hell hole would not be easy, but I couldn't just leave him there either. Heck, we had resolved the Scratch issue without further endangering Nelson's family. Even if he weren't near death, he might have been willing to put our little differences behind us.

Well, even if he wasn't ready to do that, I was. And if saving his life didn't send that message, I didn't know what would.

I put Karen's empty pistol back in one pocket, and the Djinn's Tear in another. I pulled out my flashlight for the long trek, and grabbed Nelson by the shoulders, once more ready to drag him from a bad scene.

Every step was torture. Pain lanced through my body, grinding my teeth. Nelson lost consciousness by the third step. Without a word, the girl took one shoulder and helped pull. The way went easier after that, by which I mean it succeeded, even though I lamented that no amount of ibuprofen was going to handle my pain.

Together, slowly, we got Nelson up that long passage and out onto the lawn, about halfway across the grass to the wall. Letting go and easing him down onto the grass felt like obscene bliss after all that pain.

The almost-sacrifice stared at the Lexus with its lights still on and its engine still running, but didn't say anything. She could probably tell I was the kind of working-class stiff who wouldn't own a Lexus, even if I could now afford one.

But I didn't care about the SUV. I glanced to reassure myself that the driveway 'gate' had remained open from Sapphira's entrance, then turned and went back inside.

"What ... no! What..." The girl grabbed my arm with one hand, her other still holding the knife, albeit down at her side.

"This place is evil. It needs to burn."

She blinked at me, then nodded and came inside to help.

THE VIRGIN WASN'T MUCH HELP, I'M AFRAID. SHE GOT TWO STEPS inside, saw the obscene art (stationary again), and huddled on the floor, shaking her head and holding the knife in both hands. I lost a moment wondering what the hell Scratch had done to the poor thing while 'preparing' her for the ritual, but shook it off and got back to my search. I just had to hope that some good therapist would help her.

At least the bastard needed her to be a virgin. And magic did not permit technicalities. Scratch might have scarred her psyche, but I knew that neither he nor anybody or anything acting on his behalf had touched her body. Not that way, at least.

It wasn't much. But it was something. I just hoped it would be enough.

I found plenty of smoking supplies and very hard alcohol in Scratch's too big lounge. It kept that size, even after his death. I might have been impressed, if I weren't strung out and in pain, both mentally and physically.

As it was, I tried not to think about the room's size. But just like during the fight, I recognized that it was wrong but didn't feel sick. Then again, maybe I just couldn't get far past the pain in my ribs. Lugging Nelson's fat ass, even with help, had not done me any good.

I sprinkled plenty of booze around, then lit wood, furniture and paintings. I got a bit of a blaze going then called nine-one-one from a landline I found in the hallway. I pushed my voice up into a falsetto, trying to sound old and quavery. "There's a fire, and one of my guests is hurt."

I dropped the phone, and the woman and I got out of there. I hated abandoning Nelson, but I wasn't strong enough to carry him farther. I had to hope the EMT's got there in time.

ONCE MORE I FOUND MYSELF DEEP IN THE STANFORD CAMPUS, BUT driving this time. And no fiery letters in the sky. Just moderately lit narrow streets, plenty of greenery, and the occasional pedestrian and bicyclist despite the hour.

Mind you, being here was not my choice. I wanted to drop the woman off at the Stanford Emergency Room where she could get immediate care. But she insisted on a spot near the dorms: well-lit, but not near enough any of the buildings to tell me which one was hers.

I couldn't bring myself to deny her this. Not if I could give her some comfort through familiar surroundings. Still…

"I'd really feel a lot better," I said as I pulled to a stop at the intersection she had chosen, "if I could see you safely reach someone you know."

"I'll be fine," she said, despite the tremors shaking her arms and legs. She still clutched Nelson's knife in one hand, but with the other she kept combing through her hair, the same couple of locks over and over. She stared out the window. Tried to smile, but couldn't quite manage it. "Don't worry about me."

"I just want to know you're coming out of tonight in one piece." I felt my eyes tear up and tried not to show it. "Somebody should get to have a happy ending out of this mess."

"I'm alive and … intact. That's more … more than I expected." She looked at me, meeting my eyes for the first time since she'd put clothes on. "Thank you for … thank you."

I tried to say something, but she opened the door and ran flat out for the dorms. Unsteady on her bare feet, but her steps urgent.

I reached over and pulled the door closed, deliberately not seeing which building she ran to. That was the last bit of privacy I could spare for her.

I spun the wheel around and headed for home.

If Nelson lived, I'd have to tell him that I owed him a Ka-Bar.

20

For the life of me, I don't remember the drive home from campus. I don't remember parking, or even unlocking my own front door, though I had to have done all of these things.

I do remember the hug Karen gave me when I came in the front door, and not just because it made me squeak with pain.

I was just so happy to see her that everything looked brighter. My ribs even seemed to ache less.

I was home.

"Strip," she ordered, and even though the stern look in her eye promised checking me for injuries rather than lascivious assault, I still gave her a stupid grin and enjoyed how good she looked in faded jeans and a worn tee-shirt.

I snapped my hand in the air in a got-your-nose movement and said, "Got your soul."

I then promptly passed out.

I woke up shivering, cool relief spreading into several of my most painful spots. I blinked awake on the saggy cushions of our couch, stark naked with towel-wrapped bags of ice on my ribs, ankles, left shoulder, and head.

The living room lights were off, but I could see. Then I realized the hall lights behind me were on, which kept the living room lit, but dim. Comfortable. I smelled coffee and grilled cheese, but my stomach complained when my eyes failed to see these wonders.

I did see Lancelot, asleep in his terrarium. *Good old Lancelot. It'll take more than demons and warlocks to end you, won't it?*

Was his tail always so long and serpentine?

Karen came into the room carrying a black and white striped blanket I'd never seen before. She draped it over me with tender care: wool so soft it had to be older than both of us. It smelled older than us too, with hints of mothball and old lady.

Karen finished arranging the blanket, tucking it in closer here and there, then stoked my cheek with a gentle smile and sat on the coffee table.

"Did you really get my soul back?"

I nodded.

"This may sound weird, but I think I felt it come back. A sudden shiver of comfort while I was reading." Her eyes widened in hope. "And we get to keep the money?"

I nodded again.

She let out a sigh with a half-smile that numbed my aches better than any icepack. She leaned in, whispered, "Thank you," and kissed me, soft and sweet. When she sat back she held up the Djinn's Tear. "Then this is a present?"

I had to clear my throat a couple of times before words would come out.

"Nope. That's the Djinn's Tear."

"It should be ugly."

"What do they say about books and covers?"

"That you can tell the genre." She waved the platinum band to make her point. "It may be beautiful, but this is still a slave bracelet."

"Either way, it goes to the Rajah."

"The hell it does."

"Karen—"

"No." She swept one hand through her bangs, even though they weren't in her eyes. "Look, I get that you had to work for him. He got us out of a bad spot. But he didn't do anything we couldn't have done ourselves for the cost of a couple of tanks of gas. We were involved with minor players, not organized crime. If we had moved to Kansas or something, no one would have followed us."

"Yeah, but then we would have lived in Kansas."

"Chicago, New York, whatever. The point stands. You've paid that thing back, with interest. This" — she waved the bracelet again — "amounts to serious overpayment. Not to mention *your fingers*. And Nelson's *eye*."

"Maybe worse for Nelson." I told Karen everything that had happened since we saw her last: Abrahamson, Stig, the aborted Contest of Wisdom, finding the bracelet, its theft by Carnifex, facing the ghuls, the race to Menlo Park, Sapphira's assault, the stone chamber, the virgin sacrifice, the battle, Nelson's injury, and the fire. I finished by telling her about the nine-one-one call and how I prayed they got Nelson to a hospital in time.

"Why didn't you take him yourself?"

"I wasn't sure I could do it without hurting him further. Besides, they'd have made me stay."

"True." She cocked a sculpted eyebrow at me. "Though you probably should be in a hospital. Those ribs are at least cracked, maybe broken."

"I'm conscious. I might have had to answer questions for the police." An exhausted sigh made me pause. "Then again, maybe not. No reason to connect us with the fire..."

"Except for the dead bodies."

That woke me up. "Scratch and Sapphira? They must have burned up in the fire. I made sure to douse part of the wardrobe passage."

"Honey, unless you left out the part where you dragged them up into the house, their bodies are in a solid stone chamber." She met my eyes and nodded at the dawning realization she saw. "Yep. They will find those bodies. And you probably left a trail of blood when you dragged Nelson all the way up that passage and out onto the lawn. The fire most likely got part of the trail, but—"

"But it will be obvious that Nelson was there, and that he was cut by the sword, and that..." I sat up, dropping towel-wrapped bags of ice and sparking pain up and down my body. Pain and exertion had made me sloppy. "Oh, God! Shell casings from your gun! And my fingerprints were on that sword handle!"

"I've already wiped the pistol and tossed it down a sewer grate. We have some time because you called for a fire, not a homicide. They'll have to find the bodies, call it in, get a forensics team out there and go over the crime scene." Karen sighed. "I bought us tickets for an eight a.m. flight to Brazil, but I don't think you're up to flying."

"I'll fly."

"You're going to sit in an airplane seat for what, eight? Twelve hours? In your condition?"

"Better than a jail cell. It'll take the cops time to sort everything out and ID me. They probably won't have an APB out on me until at least ten, maybe noon. That sees us at least two hours in the air."

"Assuming they managed to pull a good print off of that sword, which is no guarantee. We have money now, Rollie. We can afford a good lawyer. Maybe we don't run for a change."

"Maybe it is too late to run," growled a voice from the doorway.

Karen and I turned our heads slowly, but I already knew that voice. The Rajah had come to collect.

"I'll take the Djinn's Tear now," said the Rajah, one hand extended. It wore a blousy purple shirt with rich blue pants, and stood just inside the living room, its purple slippers on the edge of the carpet. I could smell the cardamom from its tea, and a hint of cinnamon.

"You and your partner have done well, Roland McReedy. Enjoy a week off, with pay, before reporting for your next assignment."

Karen's eyes rounded wide with shock, her jaw slack. Me, I had no surprise left. I never heard the door open or close. I had no idea the Rajah was there until it spoke. And yet I just couldn't muster any surprise.

Or so I thought. But then someone knocked on the door, and I discovered that even fatigue, injury and two pounds of ice could not numb me entirely. My head snapped around as fast as everyone else's. Four o'clock in the freaking morning and someone was knocking on my door, simple and polite as though it were four in the afternoon.

For a moment, none of us moved. Even the Rajah seemed taken off guard. Its eyes narrowed, and the near-subsonic growl of a huge cat rumbled out of its throat.

"Tryin' ta be polite out here," said a loud voice on my front porch, "but my patience does have its limits."

I recognized the drawl of the Texan and had to fight the urge to pull the blanket over my head and hope this was all a bad dream.

I knew better.

I was wide awake in the middle of the night and all the monsters knew where I lived.

I should have run into that fucking jail cell. I would have been safer. At least the nasties in a jail house were all human.

The Texan continued, "I suggest ya'll invite us in, so we can do this neighborly like. 'Cause if I have to take this door down, there won't be nearly as much talkin'."

Karen, the Rajah, and I all looked at each other. "Come in," called Karen, and I winced. That might have been a bluff. The Texan might not have been able to enter uninvited.

The Texan opened the door and moseyed on in, huge smile on its face. One step behind the Texan followed Enoch Abrahamson. Abrahamson's eyes lit on the Djinn's Tear, still in Karen's hand. "Ah, there it is. I told you McReedy stole it."

"No," I said, very aware that I was naked under my blanket, but forcing my wretched body to stay sitting up anyway. "I *tried* to steal it from you. Scratch's demon stole it first. I tracked it to Scratch's place and took it by force from Scratch and Sapphira."

"By force you say," said the Texan.

"Roland McReedy was working for me..." began the Rajah, but Karen interrupted.

"And I took it from Roland," she said, plucking some kind of Asian-looking ritual dagger off the coffee table. It had a blade like a sharpened trowel and an evil-looking head on the pommel.

I wanted to know what it was. Hell, I wanted to know where she got it. But this was not the time to ask.

Karen held up the Djinn's Tear and said in a challenging tone, "So it's mine."

The Texan's smile widened, and more rows of teeth began to show. It shook out its wrists and too-long fingers, and a waterfall series of cracks and pops echoed a warning through the room. My stomach curdled, a feeling that had nothing to do with the supernatural nature of all the things around me and everything to do with a basic need to flee for my life.

Karen paled, but stood strong, determination narrowing her eyes. She held the Djinn's Tear a little higher, shook it to make her point. "What am I bid?" she said.

Everyone else blinked. Including me.

"Karen..." I began, but she cut me off.

"I know. Snigdha told you it can't be sold, only stolen or taken by force."

"The events of this week seem to confirm that," said Abrahamson.

I didn't like the way he looked at Karen, like a John who hasn't seen a woman in years.

"Maybe that's because it's always gone to people who want to use it. Me, I want to break this thing in half, smash it with a sledgehammer, melt it down, and junk the debris. So maybe it'll let me sell it, out of a sense of self-preservation."

The Texan laughed, a sound that crept up my back like a spider under my skin. The shiver that followed made me my teeth clack in pain.

The Texan said, "Little lady, I'd pay good money to see you do just what you said. But money ain't the coin of this here realm. So I'll bid three favors, and you're boy there can give you some idea what my favors might be worth."

The Texan winked at me and my empty stomach soured. Suddenly coffee and grilled cheese sounded much less appealing.

"Any other bids?" asked Karen.

The Rajah screamed like a mountain lion and surged forward. Abrahamson pulled a freaking claymore out of his pants like some reject from *Highlander* and whirled a wide swing at the Rajah. Karen crouched low and stabbed out with the ritual dagger. The Texan hung back and watched.

I tried to jump up and help Karen, but all my body managed was to roll off the couch and onto the floor. I landed in a crumpled, painful heap on carpet and wet towels, not even the wool blanket to cover what remained of my modesty.

I heard blades meet flesh. Karen screamed. By the time I got my head above the coffee table enough to see, the fight looked over. Karen's shirt was torn half off and her left arm dangled at a painful angle, dislocated at the shoulder.

The Rajah lay dead at her feet, its body twice as broad as I'd ever seen it, apish in shape and hairiness, but its detached head resembled a Bengal tiger.

The Texan only laughed, deep and full.

Karen's dagger and Abrahamson's sword were coated in thick gray blood. The Djinn's Tear lay on the carpet where Karen must have dropped it when her arm got wrenched. Pain made her breathing ragged, and little whimpers escaped her even though she held a ready pose. Abrahamson held his sword point-down, as though he considered the battle over.

"That should have required a divine weapon," said Abrahamson. "Or at least a blessed weapon."

"Money talks," said Karen.

"That may be," said the Texan, "but I'd say you're not getting your security deposit back."

"We might be covered," panted Karen, "against acts of rakshasa... Have to check the rental agreement."

"Seems I've helped free you from your bondage," said Abrahamson. "So I think we're done here. I'll just take this off your hands."

Abrahamson bent forward to pick up the Djinn's Tear. Karen screamed and jammed the dagger into the soft spot at the back of his head, driving the blade up into Abrahamson's brain, and twisting as she went. I don't know if he died instantly, but it was close enough not to matter.

Rusty dust like dried blood poured out when Karen removed the dagger.

The Texan chuckled again, and I realized it had one extended arm holding Abrahamson's neck in position. I also realized I had never seen it move. The Texan gave Karen a fond look. "You've got to tell me where you found her, McReedy. I've just got to get me one."

"He didn't," said Karen, pivoting to point her dust-covered dagger at the Texan. "I found him. Now..."

Karen must have seen the rows of teeth in the Texan's smile and the extended arm still holding Abrahamson, because she started shaking from knees to knife hand. Her breaths came fast and pain made them sound almost wet.

"...Are ... are you smart enough to leave, or do we find out if blessed weapons can kill you too?"

The Texan retracted its arm and tucked its thumbs into its belt. It tilted its head to look at Karen sideways, but its hat never looked to be in danger of falling off.

"Ma'am, I bet you would be all kinds of tasty. The kind of tasty I'd just love to savor for a long time. And I think McReedy here knows I'm lookin' forward to takin' a bite or two out of him as well.

"But..." It paused to raise its hands slowly in the universal gesture of surrender. "...you two get a pass from me tonight. That snake sumbitch Carnifex is gone, and I'm bettin' your boy here is responsible for that. Aintcha?"

"Basically."

"I'd love to hear how that fight went, but I think that's a tale for another time. Point is, I'd like to show a little appreciation for that. So I'll leave here in peace, and I'll ... dispose of Abrahamson's body for ya. Don't worry 'bout the Rajah there. His remains'll vanish, come dawn."

"Cops'll be here before then, with all the noise we've been making."

"Not too quick, are you boy?" The Texan frowned at me. "Shame. I expected better. Tell me. How do you think I hunt in areas that get crowded without ever drawing John Law's attention?"

"You drew F.B.I. down around El Paso."

"That's better," said the Texan with a smile. "Now then, I ain't talkin' about the feebees. Lotsa ways to make them disappear. I'm talkin' about the local boys. Can't start killin' them without a major ruckus."

"You cloak the area around you?"

"That's a boy. You might keep that in mind." The Texan turned back to Karen. "Now if you'll just take a neighborly step back, I'll grab the crusader's body and let ya'll start lickin' your wounds."

I couldn't see Karen's face, but I'd have bet that her eyes narrowed at the same time mine did.

"Rollie? Can we trust him?"

"No," I said, which earned me an aw-shucks grin from the Texan that almost made me start crying. I just didn't have anything left in my tank. "But if the Texan wanted to kill us right now, I'm not sure we could stop it."

"Bet on it, McReedy. Even if you were both fit to fight."

Karen hooked the Djinn's Tear on the tip of the ritual dagger, eliciting yet another chuckle from the Texan. It struck me that the Texan was letting us live as much for our amusement value as for any vendetta with Carnifex. Once Karen had the bracelet, she backed off two steps. The Texan grabbed Abrahamson by his belt and hoisted the corpse over its shoulder.

"You two stay safe now," said the Texan as it headed for the doorway. "I want you nice and healthy for the next time we meet. And McReedy?" It gave me its widest smile yet, showing far too much mouth and far too many teeth, even for a shark. For the first time in hours, the sheer unnaturalness of something shivered along my arms. "There will be a next time. Bye now."

"Texan?" I said, which earned me a puzzled look copied letter-perfect from some human. My neck tried to crawl into my shoulders, but I pushed the question out anyway. "Could you have come in if we hadn't invited you?"

The Texan gave me a wink, tipped his hat, then turned and left.

21

———

WE MISSED OUR FLIGHT. IT COULDN'T HAVE BEEN HELPED. I MANAGED
to pop Karen's shoulder back in its socket — a process nearly as
painful for me, I think, as for her — but then all we could manage to
do was swallow about half a bottle of ibuprofen each and collapse
together into bed.

We woke sometime in the afternoon — I might have known the
time had Karen not demolished my alarm clock — starving and in
pain. Between us we successfully gathered and ate food in the
kitchen.

The Texan was right about the Rajah's body. It didn't even leave a
trace on the dagger. Of course, Abrahamson's dusty blood was all
over the floor, Karen's clothes and her dagger. It looked like rust that
wasn't confined to metal. Smelled about like rust too.

But speaking of the Rajah, I had a question for Karen, once we
had settled down onto the living room couch with cold cut sandwiches and glasses of filtered water.

"How did you know the Rajah was a rakshasa?"

"Made sense." Karen shrugged with one shoulder. "Illusions,
Indian appearance, ate humans, tiger themed decorating, loved indo-
lence and opulence."

She took a bite of her sandwich and reached for the TV remote, but I wasn't ready to let the topic go just yet.

"But some rakshasas in the Mahabharata were said to be good. And it might have been disguising—"

She held up the hand with the remote, asking for a pause until she swallowed.

"Was I right?"

"Yes. I mean, that corpse sure looked—"

"Then you might have figured it out months ago if you hadn't overcomplicated the question." Karen quirked a half-smile at me. "Or maybe I'm just smarter than you are."

"That's how I'd bet," I said, and kissed her. I wanted to stop with the questions, but one in particular gnawed at me, even more than hunger did. I glanced at my uneaten sandwich before asking, "Where the hell did you get a ritual dagger anyway?"

"Oh, that old thing? I've had that for years—"

"Karen..."

"All right," she said with a laugh that made me smile. "Snigdha got it for me."

"You went to see—"

"Yes I did." Fierce independence gleamed in her eye. "You said no magic. Well, I didn't cast anything. But once I figured out that the Rajah was a rakshasa, it just seemed ... appropriate to ask a naga to help me kill it."

"Well that proves it." I kissed her again. "You're smarter than I am."

"Duh, Rollie," she teased. "Now let's check the news."

"Do we have to?"

I knew checking the news was important. I knew we had to know what the police had figured out, when they might be coming for me. But still, my stomach had spoken, and at that moment all I cared about was the taste of my turkey and swiss on whole wheat. And news, well, I worried about what it would do to my appetite. I didn't even want to turn on one of my talk shows.

Maybe Karen saw all that in my face. I don't know. But I do know that she didn't ask any questions. Just set down the remote.

"Either the police are coming or they aren't," I said. "I'd like at least a couple of hours to try to relax."

I started eating, and tried not to imagine a S.W.A.T. team knocking down our front door.

I had better luck at eating.

WHEN THE COPS FAILED TO SHOW UP IN THE FIRST HALF-HOUR, I actually fell asleep. I guess my body wanted a break from the stress. When I woke up, the television was off and Karen was reading a chess book. Lancelot snacked on a grasshopper, which meant that we were getting on to late afternoon.

I checked my watch. A couple of minutes before five, when at least one of the local channels was guaranteed to be running the news.

Karen set down her book and looked pointedly at the remote. I sighed and turned on the five o'clock news. I came into the middle of a story that had made national news and had, by the look of it, been on every channel for hours.

Apparently a nine-one-one call about a fire led police to the Atherton home of a serial killer. They found the remains of hundreds of bodies on site, and one person not quite dead: Nelson Milner, badly wounded and barely alive on the front lawn. He had yet to regain consciousness as of the latest reports, but the police looked forward to interviewing him.

He was reported to be out of danger and in stable condition, a fact that made me sigh with relief, however much the pain of my chest expanding made me regret it.

It seemed that the early news reports had been unclear about whether Nelson was a victim or an assailant, but less than five minutes after the initial mention of Nelson on the air, an actual victim showed up at the Atherton police station. Her name was kept private, but she gave details about her kidnapping, torture and near murder — including details tying her experience to other recent unsolved murders in the Bay Area, details that the police had withheld from the press — and more importantly to me, how she was rescued by Mr. Milner and his unnamed partner.

Police had questions for this unnamed partner as well, and urged him to come forward.

Yeah. I was sure they had questions. And fingerprints on at least one murder weapon. And probably a nice comfy cell with a roommate considerably less personable and appealing than Karen.

Me show up at a police station? Of my own free will?

That was not happening.

THE NEXT SEVERAL DAYS WERE ALL ABOUT ICE PACKS, IBUPROFEN, AND delivered food of every stripe once we ran out of cold cuts.

And, of course, watching the news.

The story grew old as information stopped flowing in. It sparked again two days later when word broke that Nelson was awake and talking. He gave interviews for every local news station, plus at least one national network. I heard they also had him set up to do the rounds on late night talk shows, once the doctors let him go, and maybe even a book deal or a movie of his story.

Nelson, bless him, kept my name out of it. He admitted to having a partner, but refused to name that partner. He said that if his partner didn't want to come forward, he wouldn't make me.

Under other circumstances, the authorities might have threatened Nelson with jail for interfering with police procedure. But Nelson was a national hero now. No way any politician would let him go to jail.

I didn't care. He could have all the fame. I just didn't want the police coming after me. I kept expecting them. The almost-sacrifice might have given them a description. Plus they probably had my freaking fingerprints. There might even have been a witness to my car sitting parked outside Scratch's house.

But no cops came.

By the third day I started to worry, jumping at every shadow, which hurt less than it had the day before. I tried to find solace in feeding Lancelot, but even watching my gecko eat couldn't soothe me. I kept thinking about his tail. It started reminding me of Carnifex.

I felt that trouble was coming, no matter how Karen told me to relax, assured me that the cops probably knew who I was but didn't care. "Some cops don't like asking too many questions when the bad people die," she said.

'When the bad people die.' Weird for me to think that, for once, that category didn't include me. Oh, who was I kidding? I didn't go after Scratch for any altruistic purpose. Saving that girl was a side benefit. The media could think what it wanted. I wasn't a hero.

Karen and I were flopped on the couch, discussing dinner about an hour before dusk, when someone knocked, three quick raps. I managed to get to my feet first and took gentle steps to the doorway.

I opened it with my billy club in one hand, hidden behind the door.

"Why are you still here, boyo?" asked Ridges, his two-foot height on my doorstep with hat in one hand and cane in the other. "Dear old Ridges keeps telling you and telling you to flee this mad place, but, oh, no, you won't be so smart as all that—"

"I'm hurt too bad to fly." That brought his eyebrows up into his hairline. It helped that those eyebrows already had a high arch to them. "I need to give my ribs a few weeks."

"And the trains have stopped runnin', then, is that right? And the gas stations all stopped selling fuel, have they?"

"Well—"

"Listen, me lad, and pray, listen well this time, for even dear old Ridges, who travels the world rightin' wrongs and talkin' sense to the senseless like yourself at every turn, even he gets tired of the sound of his own voice when his words plainly fall over and over again on deaf ears that ought to know better, especially when their fathers' fathers can trace their name back to the Old Country..."

"Is someone there, Rollie?"

"Just a second." Could Karen not hear him?

"...but foolish as you are you have the sense at least to keep some of the old ways and to cleave tight to that girl of yours as though your very life depends on it. Which it might. So listen good, you great sleeveen, because I'm only going to say this part the once and I think it best if you point your ears the right way for a change: take your girl and leave. Cross the country. Cross the world, if you like. But leave. Because me and mine have been keepin' a few things from lookin' your way, and the time isn't long before those things find you here anyway. What with you sitting still in this bog of an apartment of yours, the first place where every living thing would think to look for you if it weren't for me and mine keeping their eyes elsewhere."

"But if I leave..."

"Once you're gone they won't find you, try as they might. Mountains, rivers and such like do still have their voices, and in this land they speak very loudly. Loud enough, I'm thinkin', to drown out even the noise a gobdaw like yourself tends to make."

"I..." The objection died on my lips. "We'll leave in the morning."

"'s all I wanted to hear."

I was staring right at Ridges when he vanished, but I still didn't see it happen. Somehow he just wasn't there, and it took me a few moments to realize it.

"Who were you talking to, Rollie?" asked Karen from over my shoulder. "Police?"

"No. We need to leave, babe. As in tomorrow morning."

"Are you sure you're up to it?"

"I have to be. We can drive until I'm fit enough to fly. Maybe even get me checked out in a hospital, once we're across the state line. Maybe past some mountains..."

"Where do you want to go?"

"Right now it doesn't matter. Away." I smiled at Karen. Ridges kept riding my Irish heritage, but my mom's family came from somewhere else, someplace most people wouldn't think to look for me. "But once I can fly, let's go to Pakistan. I think it's time to trace my mom's roots."

EPILOGUE

A Nevada doctor told me that I most likely cracked about three ribs, and bruised at least three others, but the x-ray didn't look bad: nothing was broken enough to be out of alignment. Karen's Internet-found treatment of ice and ibuprofen — no wrapping the ribs — was about the best we could have done. He did give me prescription strength ibuprofen though. He also recommended bed rest, but we needed to keep moving.

We did make two more stops in Nevada: a pawn shop for rings, and then a little hole-in-the-wall wedding chapel. Karen thought about hyphenating her last name, but decided that Falk-McReedy sounded too much like Fuck McReedy, so she dropped the Falk.

Took us about six days to reach New York, where Karen had a cousin living out in the Bronx: married, no kids but trying. That was not a happy reunion. They ran out of things to say to each other in less than five minutes, and before a half hour had passed we all four gave it up as a bad idea.

They did take Lance off our hands, for which I was grateful, swearing to give him a good home. I felt like I was abandoning the poor little guy, but he had started reminding me of Carnifex. Besides, I could not have taken him overseas anyway.

Karen and I spent two weeks in Manhattan, mostly resting, but shopping a little. We had abandoned almost everything we owned when we left: one suitcase each, filled more with possessions we refused to abandon than anything else.

We caught a couple of plays on Broadway, ate in a few fancy restaurants, and settled into the fact that somewhere in there we really did win the lottery. We might have been on the supernatural lam, but at least we got to live like we were on our honeymoon.

About two weeks after we reached New York we boarded a flight bound for Madrid, our first stop on our way to Benazir Bhutto International Airport, Pakistan. Apparently I had cousins just outside Islamabad. They were expecting us. Mom called ahead.

Karen developed a permasmile the minute we got married. I think some part of her unclenched, maybe even finally accepted that I wasn't going to run out on her. Me, I kept waiting for the other shoe to drop. I expected the Texan to show up around every corner, or maybe another black dog, courtesy of the remaining Sons of Morning.

But at last we boarded our plane. First class seats of course, even if the flight did leave at five a.m.

Once we were over the Atlantic I managed to relax. I had mountains, rivers, lakes and a whole lot of land between me and the things that wanted me dead. Now I was crossing an ocean too. I was about as safe as I would get.

I hoped Nelson followed through on his plan, moved to Boston or something. Made a shitload of money on his book or movie deal. Poor bastard deserved at least that much. Then again, even if the public forgot him overnight and he never made a dime, the Rajah was dead. Nelson, like me, was free. And what's more, Tish and the kids got to hear the whole nation call him 'hero.'

No one called me hero, but I didn't need that. It would have felt like a farce anyway. But I had Karen, and I had money that didn't come from other people's suffering, for a change.

As the sun rose over the sea, I smiled at the beautiful panorama of reds and yellows above the deep blue water.

Sometimes, being human rocks.

SIGN UP FOR STEFON'S NEWSLETTER

Stefon loves to keep in touch with his readers, and loves to keep you reading. The best way for him to do both is for you to sign up for his newsletter.

Sign up at http://www.stefonmears.com/join

If you sign up for Stefon's newsletter, you get...

- Monthly updates about his publishing and travel schedules
- His latest news, in brief, and answers to reader questions
- A free short story for signing up
- List-only offers and occasional specials
- Plus a free short story every month!

ABOUT THE AUTHOR

Stefon Mears tries not to bargain with rakshasas. Stefon has more than thirty books to his credit, and he never stops writing. He earned his M.F.A. in Creative Writing from N.I.L.A., and his B.A. in Religious Studies (double emphasis in Ritual and Mythology) from U.C. Berkeley. He's a lifelong gamer and fantasy fan. Stefon lives in Portland, Oregon, with his wife and three cats.

Look for Stefon online:
www.stefonmears.com
himself@stefonmears.com